Two Steps Forward

ALSO BY GRAEME SIMSION

The Best of Adam Sharp

The Rosie Effect

The Rosie Project

Two Steps Forward

A Novel

Graeme Simsion & Anne Buist

HARPER LUXE

An Imprint of HarperCollinsPublishers

TWO STEPS FORWARD. Copyright © 2018 by Graeme Simsion and Anne Buist. All rights reserved. Printed in the United States of America. No part of this book may be used or reproduced in any manner whatsoever without written permission except in the case of brief quotations embodied in critical articles and reviews. For information address HarperCollins Publishers, 195 Broadway, New York, NY 10007.

HarperCollins books may be purchased for educational, business, or sales promotional use. For information please e-mail the Special Markets Department at SPsales@harpercollins.com.

FIRST HARPERLUXE EDITION

ISBN: 978-0-06-284582-5

HarperLuxe™ is a trademark of HarperCollins Publishers.

Library of Congress Cataloging-in-Publication Data is available upon request.

18 19 20 21 22   ID/LSC   10 9 8 7 6 5 4 3 2 1

This book was inspired by the people who walked with us, who welcomed us, and who mark and care for the Way. We hope it will inspire others to undertake their own journeys.

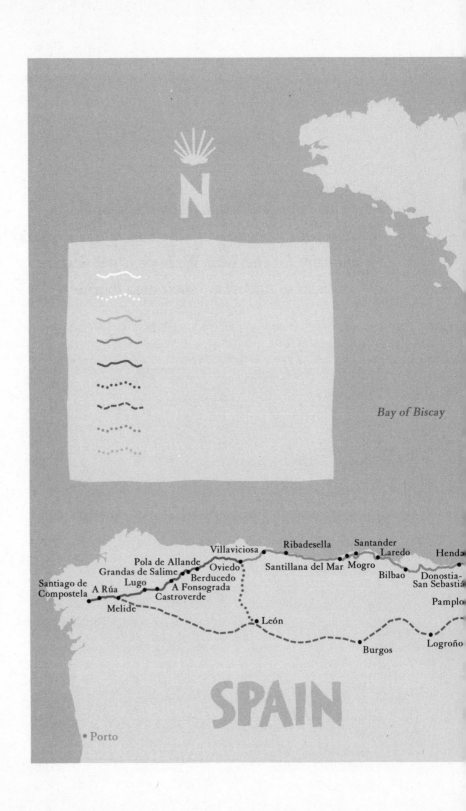

N

Bay of Biscay

Santiago de
Compostela
A Rúa
Melide
Lugo
Castroverde
A Fonsograda
Grandas de Salime
Pola de Allande
Berducedo
Oviedo
Villaviciosa
Ribadesella
Santander
Laredo
Henda
Santillana del Mar
Mogro
Bilbao
Donostia-
San Sebastiá
Pamplo

León

Burgos
Logroño

SPAIN

• Porto

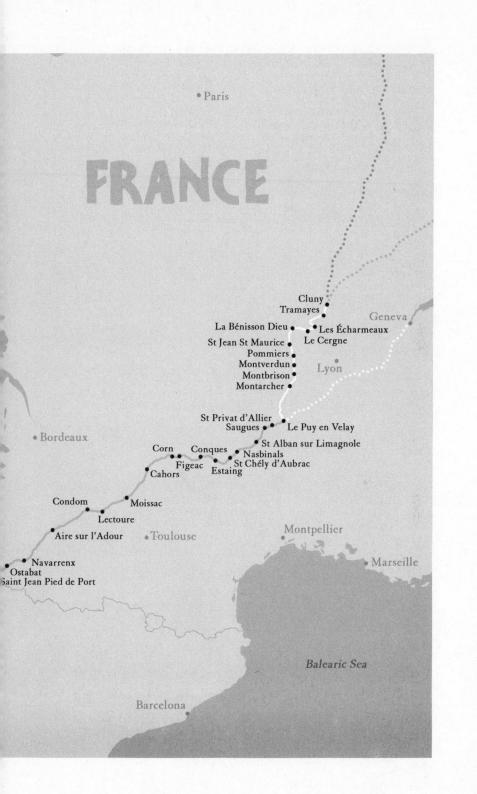

There is a time for departure,
even when there is no certain place to go.
      —TENNESSEE WILLIAMS

Midlife is when you reach the top of the ladder
and find that it was against the wrong wall.
      —JOSEPH CAMPBELL

Two Steps Forward

1
Zoe

Fate took the form of a silver scallop shell in the window of an antique store in the medieval French town of Cluny. It was laying on its back as if waiting for Botticelli's Venus, luring her with a cluster of coloured stones at one end of a white enamel edge. For some reason, I was drawn to it.

Maybe the universe was sending me a message; it was hard to know with my head being in another time zone. I had been travelling for twenty-four hours since I walked out of my home in Los Angeles for the last time, feeling nothing. I guess I was still in shock.

LAX: 'Just the one bag?' Yes, and in it everything I owned, besides three boxes of papers and mementos I'd left for my daughters.

Charles de Gaulle Airport: obnoxious male official, trying to give me priority over a woman in a burqa. He didn't understand my protests, which was lucky, because he was directing her to the European Union passport line. It moved way faster than the foreigners line he sent me to.

Immigration officer: young man, perfect English. 'Holiday?' Then, when I gave him my passport: 'Vacation?'

'*Oui.*' As good an answer as any.

'Where are you staying?'

'*Avec une amie à Cluny.*' Camille, who I hadn't seen for a quarter of a century. The vacation she had been pushing me to take since we were at college in St Louis, and that Keith had cancelled three times.

The officer half-smiled at my schoolgirl French. 'Your visa is for ninety days in Continental Europe. It expires May 13. It is an offence to remain after that.' I wasn't planning to. My return flight was in a month. I'd be lucky if my money held out until then.

Riding the train to downtown Paris: *Paris*. In spite of everything that had happened, I felt a thrill at the thought of studying a Monet at the Musée d'Orsay, immersing myself in an exhibition at the Pompidou Centre and sitting in a Montmartre café sketching an elegant Frenchwoman.

Cluny–La Sorbonne subway station, right in the Latin Quarter: 'This is not the Cluny you are looking for. The address is in Burgundy. Not far. Less than two hours on the TGV—the fast train to Mâcon.'

Gare de Lyon: 'One hundred and forty-seven euros.' You're kidding me. 'It is more cheap on the slow train. But not from this station.'

Paris–Bercy station: 'Four hours and nineteen minutes, then you will take the *autobus*. One hundred and thirty-five euros. For the train, only.'

By the time I reached Cluny—the one southeast of Paris, halfway to Italy—the winter sun was setting and the streetlights were creating halos in the light drizzle. I had only made it thanks to strangers who passed me from railroad platforms to ticket counters to bus stops like a baton in a relay race. They'd earned some good karma.

I followed the signs to Centre Ville, dragging my suitcase. One of the wheels had developed a death rattle and I hoped that Camille's complicated instructions would translate into a short journey. I had cancelled my cell phone at the same time as the electricity and water.

I found myself in the central square, bounded on one side by a majestic abbey and on the other by its ruined ramparts.

A bunch of young men—and one woman—burst

out of a bar. They were wearing long grey coats decorated with hand-painted designs. The woman's got my attention: the artist had done a fine job of rendering the colours and swirls of Japanese anime.

I managed *excusez-moi* before my French deserted me. 'Art students?'

'Engineering,' she said, in English.

I showed them my directions to Camille's. She had written, in French, 'go directly out of the square', but hadn't said which way.

'We do not know Cluny well,' said the student. 'It is better to ask at a shop.'

So I found myself outside the antique store, which I had at first mistaken for a butcher because of the black metal goose that stretched out from the door. I have always felt a connection with geese. They co-operate, look out for one another and mate for life. The goose is also the symbol of a quest—like finding my flaky college friend.

The pull of the jewelled scallop shell in the window was strong, even a little unsettling. Recent life events had left me wondering if I was attuned to the universe at all, so when I got a clear signal it seemed wise to pay attention. I bumped my suitcase up the steps into the store.

A trim man of about fifty with a narrow moustache smiled tightly. '*Bonjour, madame.*'

'*Bonjour, monsieur.* Ah . . . this.' I pointed. '*S'il vous plaît.*'

'*Madame* is American?'

'Yes.' Was it that obvious? He handed me the charm, and as I held it I had the feeling again, the one I had relied on to make major decisions throughout my life: *this is meant to be.*

'*Madame* is walking the Chemin?'

'I'm sorry . . .'

'The Camino de Santiago. The Way.'

I was vaguely aware of the Camino, the pilgrims' path in Spain, from skimming Shirley MacLaine's memoir. I could not see the connection with a scallop-shell charm in central France.

The antique dealer must have taken my nod of understanding as confirmation that I was planning to follow, literally, in Ms MacLaine's footsteps.

'This St Jacques will take *madame* to Santiago in safety.'

'I wasn't planning . . . Why a scallop shell?'

'The scallop, the St Jacques, is the symbol of the pilgrimage. St James. Santiago.'

'Okay . . .'

'Scallops floated the boat that was bringing St Jacques to Spain.'

Not in any Bible I'd read. I turned the shell over in my hand, eyes closed as I let myself disappear for a moment into thoughts and feelings I had been too busy to deal with, until the antique dealer coughed.

'How much?' I asked.

'Two hundred and fifteen euros.'

Dollars and euros: about the same. I'd never spent more than a hundred dollars on a piece of jewellery.

'It is from the late nineteenth century,' he said. 'Gilded silver and enamel. Possibly it belonged to royalty of the Austro-Hungarian Empire.'

'I'm sure it's worth it.' Well, not that sure. 'But I can't afford it.' It would be like Jack spending all his money on the beans.

'The walk is not expensive. Much is given free to the pilgrim.'

'No . . . *merci*,' I said, putting down the shell.

Madame was not planning to walk any further than Camille's. The antique dealer looked disappointed but gave me directions in a mixture of English and French.

I pulled my case up the hill, hoping I hadn't mixed up *à droite* and *tout droit*—right and straight ahead. I couldn't get the scallop-shell charm out of my thoughts. *Destiny speaks to those who choose to hear.*

As I left the old part of town, I looked up. At the top of the hill there was a cemetery and, silhouetted against the darkening sky, a huge elm tree. Beneath it, a tall man was pulling what looked like a small horse buggy. It was a strange sight but his single wheel was doing better than mine, which chose that moment to break in two.

2
Martin

My final trial of the cart, up to the cemetery and back, marked the end of a project that had begun six months earlier, when Cluny was sunny and crowded with tourists and I was enjoying my morning coffee at the Café du Centre.

Some might have said I was fortunate to have been sitting at an outside table at the exact moment that the Dutchman staggered down the street. There's a certain kind of person who focuses on the random, rather than your preparation and what you do with it.

'Staggered' was an exaggeration. He was doing remarkably well, considering he was probably in his late fifties, a little overweight and carrying a golf trolley on his back. Two large wheels protruded and, as he passed, the reason for his not making use of them became obvious: one was buckled. I sprung up and caught him.

'*Excusez-moi*,' I said. '*Vous avez un problème de la roue?*'—You have a problem with the wheel?

He shook his head, unaccountably denying the obvious. My first impression of how he was doing had been the right one. He was out of breath and sweating, though the August day had yet to heat up.

'You are English?' he said—not the most tactful response, as I had been working on my accent.

I extended my hand. 'Martin.'

'Martin,' he repeated. It looked as though switching languages was not going to improve communication.

'You?' I asked.

'I am from Holland. There is no problem with the street. It is my cart that is the problem.'

He must have heard *roue*, wheel, as *rue*, street. We continued in English and established that his name was Maarten. He was not a golfer but a hiker, and the cart held his clothes and equipment. He had spent the night in his tent on the outskirts of town, and was now hoping to find somewhere to have the wheel repaired.

I didn't fancy his chances. He would have no problems finding chocolates, overpriced Burgundy or souvenirs of the abbey, but I was unaware of anything resembling a repair shop. There might be something in the Zone Industrielle, but he could expect a frustrating time finding it, and some regulation or strike or employee absence that would leave him cooling his heels until the repairer was disposed to assist.

'I should be able to fix it for you,' I said.

It took all day, minus time out for a lecture. I had only been working at the ENSAM—the School of Arts and Engineering—for a few weeks, but knew my way about.

The wheel was damaged beyond repair and had been flimsy in the first place. Our problem attracted a few students, and soon we had an impromptu design workshop underway. In the interests of education and community engagement, we cannibalised a hand truck with inflatable tyres and welded the assembly to Maarten's trolley. The rubber handle grip had perished, and we fashioned a grooved metal replacement. The result was a definite improvement. He and the construction team, in their painted coats, were duly photographed for the school website.

In the course of our work, I asked Maarten the obvious question. 'Where are you headed?'

'Santiago de Compostela. I'm walking the Camino.'

'From here?'

One of my English colleagues had 'done' the Camino and was more than a little proud of it. But my recollection was that the walk started at the French–Spanish border.

Maarten set me straight. 'Obviously, all the pilgrims did not come from this one town. In the tenth century, they could not get on a plane or train and meet at some tourist hotel in St Jean Pied de Port. They walked out of the doors of their homes as I did.' Cop that, Emma. Try walking from Sheffield next time.

There were feeder routes all over Europe, including the Chemin de Cluny, which Maarten had now joined. Most converged at St Jean Pied de Port on the Spanish border for the final eight-hundred-kilometre leg—the Camino Francés, or French Way, that Emma had walked. Maarten had already covered 790 kilometres, from Maastricht.

'Why the cart?' I asked.

He tapped his knees. 'Most walkers are carrying a backpack, but it is hard for the knees and back. Many walkers are not young.'

I could relate to that. The aftermath of my middle-aged attempt at the London Marathon had been a knee reconstruction, and advice to avoid further wear, tear and trauma.

'Where did you get it?' I asked.

'It was invented by an American.'

'And you're happy with it? Besides the wheels?'

'It's a piece of crap,' he said.

It was 8 p.m. by the time we finished, and I offered Maarten a spot on the floor of my flat.

'I'll buy you dinner,' I said, 'but I want to know all about your cart.'

'You have seen it. It is very simple.'

'No, the practicalities. What it's like to use, what the problems are, what changes you'd ask for.'

An idea had been growing. I was sure I could come up with a better design. There were a lot of questions to answer before I could put pencil to paper, but the important thing was to understand the requirements. And, as I tell my students, you don't get requirements by sitting on your bum writing a wish list. You get out in the environment, ideally with a prototype, and find out what's really needed. Maarten had done this for five hundred miles with the product I would be competing with.

We established that the cart was hard work on rough ground, and awkward to manoeuvre along narrow tracks, where the handle twisted constantly in the palm. Maarten had been forced to follow the bicycle routes, which included some unpleasant stretches on main roads.

Over cheese, I asked him about the pilgrimage. I am not a religious person, but I was curious about the logistics. Maarten was not religious either. He had been retrenched from a civil-service position and did not expect to work again. His reasons for undertaking such a long journey were vague, but his choice of route made sense.

'Good signposting, water, hostels for a shower and a meal. If you break a leg or have a heart attack, you will be found by another pilgrim.'

My flat was a short walk from the town centre. I had organised it through Jim Hanna, an expat from New York who had come to Cluny to marry a Frenchwoman he'd met in the States. The marriage had failed, but not before producing a daughter, who tied him to France for the foreseeable future.

Jim had found me a pair of old armchairs, and Maarten and I sat in them, drinking *eau de vie de prune*. The liquor had been my first purchase in Cluny but I'd gone easy on it after one night of drowning sorrows.

'No family?' I asked.

He shook his head. 'My partner died. You?'

'A daughter in Sheffield. She's seventeen.'

Sarah and I texted each other sporadically. She would

rather I had stayed, but she would inevitably have been drawn into Julia's and my recriminations, until she was spending half her life worrying about what she shared, who she stayed with and whose side she appeared to be taking. I knew all about the damage that estranged parents could inflict on a teenager.

'What are you going to do when you're finished?' I asked.

'That is why I am walking. To consider this matter.'

'And so far, no ideas?'

'There is plenty of time. If I do not have a solution by Santiago, I can consider it further on the walk home.'

In the morning, I watched as Maarten dragged his trolley from the ENSAM to rejoin the Chemin. It barely handled the cobblestones, and I was already envisaging the suspension for a version that would be pulled along the Pennine Way, the Appalachian Trail and by a thousand pilgrims on their way to Santiago.

Designing a better cart was easy. Just strengthening the wheels would make a difference, and upgrading the suspension would improve the off-road capabilities. But I was looking for a more dramatic step forward.

The breakthrough came from applying the techniques that I was paid to teach.

'So,' I said to the four students who had stayed back

after class, 'we're stuck. How can we encourage innovative thinking?'

'Beer.'

'Sometimes. Don't tell your parents you heard it from me. What else?'

Pascale, in her anime-decorated coat, raised her hand. 'Dr Eden, we can push the limits; extend parameters to their boundary values.'

'Go on. What parameters do we have to play with?'

'The wheelbase?'

'And the extreme values are?'

'Infinity and zero. Both wheels pushed together. To make a single wheel. But—'

'What did she say?'

'A single wheel.'

'No, after that.'

'*But.*' Laughter.

'Our job now is not to find reasons to reject Pascale's idea, but ways to make it work.'

'If stability is the problem, we add another handle. Simple.'

The final design owed more to rickshaws and sulkies than golf trolleys, but was far more manoeuvrable than Maarten's version. The single wheel allowed for a sophisticated suspension system, which was impressive to see in action as the wheel rose, fell and twisted to accommodate the terrain.

A hip belt with clips reinforced the impression of man-as-horse, but freed both hands, allowing the use of sticks—*bâtons*—which were favoured by many walkers. Maarten had noted the difficulty of negotiating rivers and fences, and I added straps to allow the cart to be lifted onto the back for short distances.

From the beginning, I had been looking for an investor. After many emails, I attracted some interest from a Chinese manufacturer and two outdoor-equipment distributors, one German and one French. They would all be at a trade fair in Paris in May, but they would not be satisfied with an inspection of my prototype. They wanted evidence that it could survive a long-distance walk. The French required proof that it could cope with their country's conditions, which were, of course, unique. I was in no position to pay for such an extended trial.

I turned the problem over in my mind for a week or so, but kept coming back to the same answer. My teaching contract ended in mid-February. It was time to move on, to do something more substantial towards rebuilding my finances. The cart represented my best chance of doing that. And the person best equipped to test it, make running repairs and improvements, and communicate the results to prospective investors was me.

I would walk the Camino from Cluny, pulling the cart nineteen hundred kilometres over French and Spanish terrain, taking photos and video, and blogging to build interest. I needed to reach Santiago by 11 May, allowing two days to get back to France for the trade fair. If I started as soon as my teaching duties were over and covered twenty-five kilometres per day, I would make it with a week to spare.

Winter was not the ideal time to start. The hostels on the two-week section between Cluny and Le Puy would likely be closed and the trail across the top of the Central Massif snowbound, forcing me to take the road.

My savings allowed for around a hundred euros a day, enough for basic accommodation and food. I did not dwell on the fact that by the time I got to Paris I would be penniless again.

I was sorry to be leaving. The students and faculty had made me welcome, despite not having met me at the best time of my life.

I reached the cemetery at the top of the hill. I had read that, under French law, cemeteries were required to provide drinking water. Sure enough, just inside the gate was a tap labelled *eau potable* which splashed ice-cold water over my bare legs when I tried it.

The cemetery had the best view in town, and I spent a few minutes surveying the fields, trying to make out the walking track through the drizzle and fading light.

3
Zoe

The rain had set in by the time I arrived at Camille's address on the town fringe, dragging my broken case. A compact minivan turned into the driveway and a woman jumped out, slamming the door behind her. She was wearing bright-blue eyeshadow and matching nail polish. With her tight jeans, midriff showing despite the cold, and high-heeled boots, it was obviously Camille—but a Camille even younger than when I had met her. It had to be her daughter, Océane. The impression of maturity disappeared when she opened her mouth, shouting back at the man standing half-in-half-out of the vehicle.

I didn't understand a word, but didn't need to. Océane spun around, then stormed up the path to the door.

The man looked at me and shrugged. Her father? I couldn't remember his name. Before he could get back in the van, an older version of Océane flew down the path toward him, screaming more abuse. This one was my age, thin in the pinched way French women sometimes are in movies, urchin-style black hair, cigarette in hand, feet in moccasins. Camille. She banged on the hood as he reversed out, then turned with the same precision as her daughter and stormed past me. A second later, she stopped dead, turned, mouth open and hand on hip.

'Camille. It's Zoe,' I said.

She looked at me like I was an alien. I guess I was. And I was soaked. Maybe I should have called.

'Oh my God! You are not arriving tomorrow? You must come in the house.'

Camille kissed and hugged me, then linked her arm in mine and led me and my case inside.

The television was up loud. A golden retriever loped into the hallway and started barking as Camille pulled me into the kitchen. 'I can't believe you are here finally! We have so much to talk about! So much time and so much happened.'

She was right about that. I had told myself I needed to see her face to face, that what had happened was too big for written words. But maybe I was afraid that if I saw my new life on paper, it would become real to me.

Camille started unloading food from the refrigerator. The kitchen was a mess, catalogues and magazines on every surface. Her son—Bastien, eight—was on the floor in the corner, engrossed in a video game which was emitting sounds of gunfire.

'You are alone?' said Camille over her shoulder.

'Yes, I guess I—'

'I mean, in life. This is why you are here, *non*?' She had grabbed the telephone. When she hung up she was looking smug. 'Jim. He was coming tomorrow but he will come tonight. He is American. Divorced. A real-estate man from New York.' Camille rubbed her finger and thumb together. 'What is your plan?' She didn't wait for a reply.

'Tomorrow you will come to lunch with us, yes? You will see the famous abbey, then Monday we will shop in Lyon.'

Océane joined us and started an argument with Camille, maybe the same one she'd been having with her father. I could identify with this. I'd had every imaginable argument with teenage girls.

Camille threw open the door of the refrigerator and grabbed a bottle of white wine.

'Océane wanted her boyfriend to stay the night at her father's. Of course this is not possible; she is only fourteen years. But she told him she was taking the contraceptive pill and now he is complaining to me.'

Maybe I hadn't had this conversation. My girls had gone to college before it had been an issue.

Camille poured two big glasses of wine and gave one to me. 'Her father is a *poule mouillée.*'

A wet chicken? There had been another before him. After the *crétin* in St Louis.

'You still have a very . . . busy life.'

Camille waved her arm. 'No, no, all that it is over. I am a wife and mother. Cluny is not Paris. But you are soaking in water. Océane, show Zoe her room. *Your* room.'

By dinnertime I had showered and changed, and was more spaced out than tired.

'You are here on vacation?' asked Gilbert, whom Camille had introduced as her 'current husband'.

'Not exactly . . .'

We were interrupted by the doorbell. Jim was maybe five years older than me, wearing black chinos and an expensive-looking blazer. He looked a bit like George Clooney. He kissed Camille's cheeks, greeted Gilbert in what sounded like perfect French and looked at me. I hoped he wasn't a Republican. The last thing I needed was an argument about politics.

We did introductions, then sat for dinner.

'*Lapin*,' Camille announced, putting a platter on the table. 'I remember you do not eat red meat, and I have two bunny rabbits in the freezer.' Camille knew the story about my father and brothers killing a deer when I was eight. I would have become a vegetarian anyway, just not so soon. Camille had never understood.

'So, what brings you to Cluny?' Jim asked.

The table had gone silent for the first time. Under the gaze of five sets of eyes, everything that had been impossible to write was now impossible to say.

'Camille has been inviting me for twenty-five years.'

Jim smiled. 'You'll be here for a while? We should get together.'

When he turned to Gilbert for more wine I frantically signalled Camille: *no way.*

'There is an insect bothering you?' asked Gilbert.

'I could give you the unofficial guided tour,' said Jim.

'*Lapin?*' Camille, passing the plate back to me again.

When she disappeared to the kitchen and Gilbert went to fetch another bottle, Jim asked, 'First time in France?'

'Yes. I've travelled a lot. But not outside of America.'

He smiled; had I wanted someone to show me around, I could have done a lot worse.

'*Fromage* of the region,' Camille announced. For the last week, I had been following a vegan diet, thinking about making a permanent change, but after a meal of bread and endives I was ravenous. And the cheese was amazing. Three kinds, all soft, one from goat milk, one blue.

Jim got up to leave and kissed me on both cheeks.

'So, Wednesday? Lunch?'

'Um . . .' But he had taken the answer as given. Looking like George Clooney would do that.

'I can't,' I said to Camille as soon as the door closed.

'But he is so . . . perfect.'

'I'm not ready.'

'One must always be ready,' said Camille.

Finally, I said what I had been trying to say all night. But it came out muted, like a half-story, without the heart and soul, the fact without the substance.

'Keith died.'

'*Mon Dieu!* You didn't tell me,' said Camille, wrapping her thin arms around me. 'Men. Their hearts, yes? Unpredictable.'

Gilbert frowned. 'This is very sad. When?'

At last, someone was listening.

'Three weeks ago.'

I fell onto Océane's bed. I thought I would sleep for ten hours but after two I was wide awake.

Camille was . . . exactly as I should have expected. I had helped her at a time of need back in college and knew she would do the same for me, but matching me up with the local bachelors was not the kind of help I needed. What I needed was headspace: time out to lick my wounds, make sense of my unsettled feelings and balance my chakras. None of my new life felt real; it was like all my emotions had been thrown into a box and someone had put a padlock on the lid.

Thoughts of the scallop shell kept me awake for a long time. What was it trying to tell me? By morning it had given me an answer. The goose had been right: a quest of sorts, a new beginning. Over breakfast I told Camille that I was going to take a walk to clear my head. A long walk.

4
Martin

I had planned to depart the following day, Sunday, but discovered too late that my *credencial*—a document I needed to produce at hostels to secure accommodation—was not available from the tourist office. The woman rebuked me for walking at the wrong time of year, when they could not possibly be expected to have information available, then grudgingly phoned the local representative of the Association des Amis de St Jacques and made an appointment for the Sunday afternoon. 'I am sorry but that is when he is available. *Monsieur.*'

I had to collect a map for my British Army GPS. It needed to be signed for, so I'd had it sent to the local outdoors shop. The logistics team in London confirmed that it had been delivered, but by the time I finished up and settled my rent with Jim the shop had closed.

Jim also contributed to Sunday not turning out as planned. He fetched up at my door and offered to buy me a late breakfast. He may have felt that he was losing his only friend. He spoke passable French, but there is a social barrier that outsiders struggle to break through.

We had coffee and croissants, and talked for a long time about nothing much, beyond the fact that the married Frenchwoman who had been pursuing him earlier in the year had introduced him to a Californian named Zoe. Jim had charmed her into a date.

I arrived at the outdoors shop fifteen minutes before the lunch break. The proprietor was not there, and I was served by a hawk-nosed older woman who pointed me to a stand of paper maps.

'*Un USB*,' I explained. '*Une livraison.*' A delivery.

She feigned incomprehension and, when I repeated my request in slow, precise French, shook her head. How could she be expected to know about personal arrangements with the proprietor?

Our impasse was broken by the arrival of a woman of about forty. She was dressed conventionally, in jeans, long woollen top and trainers, but there was something about her that made me think, at first, that she might be from the Christian commune in nearby Taizé. She was surveying the hunting gear with undisguised distaste.

'*Bonjour, excusez-moi*,' she said, addressing *madame* in an accent that not only made mine sound like that of the president of the Académie, but pinpointed her origins—America, and, I'd have been willing to bet, California. At a time of year when tourists were thin on the ground, she had to be Jim's new flame. She was his type: attractive—blue eyes, shoulder-length auburn hair, easy smile—Anglophone, and bound to leave him high and dry when her holiday was over.

She continued, '*Je ne parle français très bien.*' I don't speak French very well. No argument there.

She mimed hoisting a rucksack onto her shoulders. '*Une* backpack.'

Before I could step in and interpret, *madame* replied, in perfectly adequate English, 'Of course. What size do you require?'

Zoe—it was surely her—made a sizeable box with her hands and *madame* headed out the back, giving me a chance to duck behind the counter to look for my package. I was rifling through envelopes and small boxes when I looked up to see Zoe watching me with crossed arms. When *madame* returned, Zoe pulled her aside and had a word in her ear. *Madame* directed a dirty look towards me, though I was now innocently browsing the maps.

The backpack she had brought out was at least seventy litres, which was about the size Zoe had indicated. Perfect, if she was planning to fill it with designer clothes and carry it no further than the distance between the taxi and the baggage check-in at Charles de Gaulle. As *madame* turned towards me again, Zoe sneaked a glance at the tag. I could have told her it was unlikely to have a price on it.

'How much?' she asked.

'One hundred and eighty-five euros.'

'Oh. Do you have something cheaper? Like last year's model?' She laughed and, to my surprise, *madame* joined in. After a short *sotto voce* conversation, *madame* disappeared out the back again. Zoe remained in place, patently to keep an eye on me.

I was about to introduce myself—'I believe we may have a friend in common'—when I caught the oh-so-serious look of disapproval on her face.

Instead, I picked a compass off its display stand and went through the motions of slipping it into my pocket. I watched Zoe vacillating between calling me out or calling *madame*, then, just as she was about to do the latter, I put the compass, now in my other hand, back in its place.

It took her a moment to realise that I was taking the piss with the sort of trick you'd perform for a seven-year-old. The trick I *had* performed—more than once—for seven-year-old Sarah, ten years ago.

She shook her head slowly, pointed to where *madame* had gone, and mimed lining me up with a pistol, two-handed, in American-cop fashion. The message was clear: *what sort of idiot tries to steal from a gun shop?* Except the idea of *madame* returning with a .45 in her hand was so unlikely as to be ludicrous. I grinned and Zoe grinned back, then covered her mouth with her hand to stop herself laughing.

I thought, I hope Jim introduces us at some point, then remembered: tomorrow I'd be on the road to Santiago with only myself for company. I felt a sudden twinge. It had been a long time since I'd had a playful moment like this—a hint of a connection, even—with a woman. I'd probably only allowed it because of her link to Jim.

Madame emerged, shaking the dust off a smaller pack. 'You can have this as a gift,' she said. The reason for the pack being stored out of sight was immediately apparent, though probably not to an American. It was an *édition spéciale* for the 2010 World Cup, featuring images of the French captain and coach. The froggies had disgraced themselves and imploded in a storm of public bickering that had led to a parliamentary inquiry, and much mirth where I came from.

Zoe left with her bargain, but not before sending a final smile in my direction. *Madame* waved a bunch of keys at me. '*Fermé.*'

'*Attendez*'—wait—I said, but there was no point arguing. With luck, the proprietor would be back after lunch. As I left, I checked the hours. Closed Sunday afternoon. And all day Monday.

5

Zoe

At the tourist office, a slim young woman was turning the sign to *Fermé*.

'Can you wait a minute?' I said. 'I need information about the Camino—the Chemin. *S'il vous plaît.*'

She beckoned me in. 'It is okay. There are five minutes.'

It took a bit longer. She had brochures, but more on the history and sights than the practicalities. The French seemed to speak English and were happy to talk. The guy at the antique store had spent fifteen minutes giving me a history lesson and reassuring me that most walkers were on a spiritual journey rather than a religious one before selling me the scallop shell.

'Do you have a guidebook?' I asked.

'The guide comes out in February.'

Right. I had left LA on February 13.

'Where is your destination?' she said. 'You are going to Santiago, or you will stop at the Spanish border?'

'How far is it? To the border?'

'A thousand and one hundred kilometres. Approximately. Seven hundred miles.'

For a moment, I was overwhelmed. It was a familiar feeling, and I knew how to deal with it—but on this occasion the mantra was so right that I nearly laughed. *One day at a time.*

My flight home was March 16 . . . thirty days. Two days to get back to Paris. So, twenty-eight days. Seven hundred miles . . .

'Do you have a calculator?' I asked, miming punching the keys.

She passed me one from under the counter.

Twenty-five miles a day, exactly. How fast did I walk? Four miles an hour? Just over six hours a day. If I started early, I could be done by lunchtime with the afternoon free to find a place to stay and see the sights. I could budget around twenty euros a day, with some left over to get me back to Paris. If the antique-store guy was right, and things along the way were cheap or free, it would be enough.

I gave the calculator back. 'The Spanish border, I guess.'

'Excellent. The French section is more difficult, but smaller numbers, better scenery, superior food and wine.' She didn't have to say 'superior people'. 'Spain is an *autoroute* of pilgrims; every day you are running to find a hostel, and also you have the . . .' She mimed sleep, then scratching herself frantically. Bedbugs.

'Is there a map?' I asked.

'The map is in the guidebook.'

Right.

'It is not necessary. You follow the scallop shells. Signs. On the trees and lampposts you will find St Jacques pointing the way.'

A peaceful walk in the French countryside following an ancient route. Simple living with time for mindfulness and renewal. Maybe it was already happening. I had surprised myself in the hunting store, laughing for maybe the first time since Keith had died. But joking about guns?

'You are leaving when?' she said.

'Today.' The answer came without thinking, but I knew instantly it was the right one. *If not now, when? If not you, who?* I needed to look after myself, deal with Keith's death in my own space, before I could think about shopping with Camille, who didn't deserve to have someone from the distant past laying their pain on her. Océane could have her room back.

'But it is winter.'

'I grew up in Minnesota.' *That* was cold. Here it was about forty degrees outside. Walking would warm me up. 'And Spain is south, right?'

She wrote down the name of a café. 'Monsieur Chevalier is meeting another *pèlerin*—pilgrim. At fourteen o'clock.' She rolled her eyes, maybe because someone else was stupid enough to walk in winter. 'For a small price, you get your passport for the hostels from him. Also, advice.'

I had lunch at Camille's. It was more relaxed than dinner had been. Gilbert was out with friends, Bastien ate in front of his video game and if Océane was there I didn't see her.

'You must stay!' Camille said. 'How will there be enough clothes? Cream for the face?'

'I'll have to leave stuff here, if that's okay?'

'There will be too much time to think.'

She stuffed my pack with food, gave me a long hug and her phone number for when I realised this was all a crazy mistake and, finally, wished me luck and *courage*.

The café was at the far end of town. The bartender pointed me to a corner table, where a man of maybe sixty, with a kind face, glasses and a cross of medical tape on his balding head, was sitting. Skin cancer, I figured. All that walking in the sun.

'*Bonjour*,' I said. 'Monsieur Chevalier?'

The Frenchman looked over his glasses at me with brown eyes framed by long lashes and dimpled cheeks.

'*Oui*. And your name is?' He spoke English with an accent that reminded me of his namesake—I half expected him to start singing.

'Zoe Witt.' I explained the tourist office had sent me and put out my hand. Monsieur Chevalier took it but leaned in and planted a kiss on each side of my face.

'You will have coffee?'

My look must have given me away. 'It is paid for,' he said, and held up three fingers, not to the bartender but to a tallish man in a familiar checked jacket waiting at the bar. The shoplifter from the hunting store.

Monsieur Chevalier pulled out a passport-sized folder, which concertinaed to reveal squares for stamping, like a girl-scout badge book. He stamped the first square *Cluny* with a graphic of a scallop shell and what looked like a lamb. I'd earned my lamb stamp just for starting.

'How much?' I asked.

'There is no charge.'

'But the tourist office . . .'

'This is your first lesson of the Chemin. Take what is offered. You will have chances to help others and you will take those chances also.'

The shoplifter came to the table with three coffees: two little black ones and a larger one for me with a jug of cream and two sachets of sugar. '*Merci.*' Another thing to pay forward. The shoplifter said something to Monsieur Chevalier in rapid French. From his body language, I figured he was making a light-hearted complaint about picking up the tab.

He extended his hand to me and, as I shook it, his eyes dropped to my chest. French men were no better than Americans. But I sensed something between us changing, and not in a good way. He sat down without introducing himself.

I got it. Before he'd started playing games, I had actually caught him trying to steal something. Awkward.

He looked a bit older than me but was in good shape. Six foot, or a little over; brown hair, neat; and now, cautious, unrevealing eyes. A hunter, for sure. Charming when he wanted to be.

Monsieur Chevalier continued with me. He had made the journey from Cluny to Santiago five times, including one return trip.

'Why are you walking?' he asked.

'It's hard to explain. I feel I've lost touch with the universe . . .'

He didn't push it. Instead, he shared some of his own wisdom. My sneakers were not perfect but they would do to begin with. I should change my socks every day and not wear them wet in the evenings; blisters—ampoules—were inevitable but could be treated by running a needle and thread through them, and leaving the thread in place. I needed safety pins to hang clothes, which could dry on my pack during the day.

'Only two things are certain on the Chemin,' Monsieur Chevalier concluded. 'The first is ampoules. The second is that when you arrive at the Santiago cathedral, you will cry.'

As I wasn't intending to go beyond the Spanish border, the crying was not going to happen then, though I knew I needed to do it sometime.

Monsieur Chevalier noticed my scallop shell and became quiet for a few moments, channelling something.

'Zoe,' he said, his accent making my own name sound exotic to my ears, 'this shell will go to Santiago. And when you finish your journey, you will find . . . what it is you have lost.'

He looked a little longer at it, maybe sensing its

emanations as I had. 'I have the intention to walk the Spanish section in April. Perhaps I will see you.' And finally: 'The Chemin will change you.'

I finished my coffee, picked up my pack and walked toward Spain.

6
Martin

By the time Zoe departed, with only a curt nod to me, I was feeling less than favourably disposed towards both her and Monsieur Chevalier. The balding version of Gerard Depardieu, with his contrived gravitas and a hint of the fanatic, was predictably attentive to the younger woman. I was more surprised that Zoe was about to stand Jim up to walk the Camino for hazy spiritual reasons. And that her finances, supposedly insufficient for a rucksack or a cup of coffee, had run to 275 euros for a souvenir.

The scallop-shell charm that I'd spotted hanging around her neck as we shook hands had been in the window of the bric-a-brac shop for some time. A month ago, I had enquired about it, with an idea that Sarah might like it as a memento of my walk. Late nineteenth century, possibly Viennese, possibly Russian, said the shopkeeper, watching my reaction to see which I would prefer. I would have preferred affordable.

I had listened in silence as Monsieur Chevalier waxed lyrical about the Camino: he did seem to know what he was talking about, and was likely being more generous with his advice than if he had been giving it to me alone.

With Zoe gone, he reverted to French. 'I need to see your boots.'

'I don't have them with me. I've used them before. I'm an experienced walker.'

That was stretching it a little, but I'd done a few days in the Lake District with my friend Jonathan, a British Army brigadier, only a year earlier.

'The Chemin is not a conventional walk.'

'They're good strong boots. I'm very happy with them.'

'For ninety days, you require light boots. Heavy boots are a grave error. Blisters will be guaranteed. Also, problems of the knees.'

If anything was going to scare me into taking his advice, it was the risk of knee injuries. But I would be pulling a heavy cart, and would need all the ankle support and grip that I could get.

'You will carry your own backpack?'

Putting aside the technicality that I would be hauling rather than carrying, I did not think there was much option. Sherpas were likely to be a bit thin on the ground in rural France.

'Is there an alternative?' I asked.

'It is possible to have the pack *portaged*, by taxi.' This was news to me. I knew there were services on the Camino Francés in Spain, but my research had not turned up anything in France. 'If you are incapacitated, this is understandable. But otherwise . . . You will be staying in the hostels?'

'I'm planning on hotels and *chambres d'hôte*. I thought I should get the *credencial* just in case.'

'You should stay in the hostels. At this time of year, they make little money. It is generous of them to open at all.'

Monsieur Chevalier produced my *credencial*. Like every official in France, he found it necessary to demonstrate that his job involved a high degree of personal discretion.

'I will give you this, but you must stay in the hostels.' The words *petty* and *bureaucrat* both come from the French.

He stamped the first square with some ceremony and added the date. 'Forty euros.'

Half a day's budget. I handed over a fifty-euro

note, which *monsieur* inspected before passing me the change. He must have caught my reaction.

'Less than fifty euro cents a day. Along the way, you will see how much volunteers have done to make your journey safe and comfortable. It is right to return even a little.'

Fair enough. But he could have spared me the lecture.

Then he looked intently at me and delivered the benediction he had given Zoe. 'The Chemin will change you. It changes everyone.'

He doubtless thought that would be a good thing.

7

Zoe

The sky was cloudless, and there was some warmth in the winter sun. The blue and yellow scallop-shell markers—stickers about two inches square—were easy to find on lamp and fence posts, trees, gates and buildings. The road rose steeply out of town, then flattened out, taking me into my first forest.

It was a paler version of home, with soft, muted colours. One of my happier childhood memories was of kicking up the darkened leaves of fall that were strewn thick on the ground, as they were here. The trees were barren, and occasional conifers reminded me of Christmases in upstate California and Colorado.

In the dappled sunlight, I saw a deer in the distance and watched her for a while, conscious of the silence.

Eventually, she turned and in one bound leapt over a log and disappeared into the dark.

The trail took me in and out of the woods and through farmland. The small paddocks were marked with tracks in the mud and divided by rock fences. A large white cow roused itself from its bed in the mud to watch my progress and I was conscious of how peaceful this journey was going to be. Alone in the natural world, I would have time to think and feel and remember. My hand went to my pendant. The scallop shell provided a nest for the small heart charm that Keith had given me. We had been different, Keith and I, but we had come to understand each other and work within those differences.

Right now, there were more urgent things to think about. The ancient pilgrims had hospitals and monasteries that provided food and a place to sleep. Many were still standing and some offered beds, according to the brochure in the tourist office. But where were they?

After two hours, with the sun beginning to set, the track led me into a small village. *Sainte Cécile*, said the sign. The auto-repair shop and café looked long abandoned, and through the window of the bakery I saw paint tins and drop sheets. The public bathrooms were closed. There was just a church and a restaurant—and a teenage boy sitting on the sidewalk. The music coming from his cell phone was loud and strange in the silence, and he didn't acknowledge me. One of the cows in the shed behind him lifted its head briefly.

A small, grey-haired woman answered my knock at the restaurant: '*Fermé.*'

'Would it be okay to use the restroom?' I asked.

She shook her head and it took me a moment to realise that she wasn't saying no—she just hadn't understood my English.

'*Toilette?*' It was a good word to have remembered. I didn't want to mime it.

That worked, and I used the time to figure out my next question.

'*Un hostel? Un motel? Un trailer?*' I asked, tipping my head and resting it on my hands.

She pointed down the road and held up ten fingers. Ten miles—no, kilometres. Whichever, I wouldn't make it before dark.

'*Pelèrine?*' she said, pointing to my backpack. It took me a moment to recognise the feminine form of the word for pilgrim. '*Chemin de St Jacques?*'

I nodded and she continued in French, none of which I understood, but I could see that she related to what I was doing and wanted to help. She gave me a glass of water. I think she figured I was going to walk on.

The cows didn't look like they wanted company, which left only one place to stay: appropriately enough for a pilgrimage, the church. Open and empty, no signs prohibiting it. There were some cushions, and I lined them up along a pew.

I was brought up in a God-fearing family, though it was my father we feared more, but when I went to college I left the church behind. Camille's Catholic guilt during our year together hadn't encouraged a return to the fold. The final severing was my mother's doing. When I told her about the help I had given Camille, she disowned me. In return, I disowned religion. In the twenty years since, I had only set foot in a church twice. The first time was for my mother's funeral. She had died of cancer and I hadn't seen her in the three years since we had our final showdown. She had never met her two granddaughters.

The second time had been three weeks ago, for Keith.

Now I was in a small, dark, cold French church for my first night on the Camino. On the positive side, I had not spent a cent since leaving Cluny. With all my clothes on I was warm enough—just. Madonna and child smiled down on me from the pulpit, and maybe Sainte Cécile was lurking somewhere. The hard reality of the wooden bench and a coat that was not meant to be a winter blanket taught me my first lesson of the Camino. My scallop shell might get me to Spain, but if I wanted to travel in comfort I'd need to do some planning.

8

Martin

In lieu of carrying a magic scallop shell, I had made thorough plans, which now had to be shifted back a further day. I organised accommodation for my first night at a bed and breakfast run by an Englishman in Tramayes, nineteen kilometres down the track. For the second night, I booked a private room at the hostel in Grosbois. My investment in the *credencial* would pay its first dividend.

Jim had extended my lease in exchange for beer and company. I broke the news about Zoe and he took it in his stride, but was surprised by my take on her.

'I didn't pick her for a hard-ass. I'd guess she said yes to lunch because she didn't want to hurt my feelings. Hope I didn't drive her out of town.'

On reflection, I had probably been unreasonable in

my judgment. She was entitled to have second thoughts about a date that had been set up by her friend. It's hardly a grand deception to say 'I can't afford it' in the hope of getting a better price on a rucksack—especially in France, where shopkeepers refuse to budge an inch outside government-approved sale periods. And it wasn't her fault that I hadn't bought the scallop shell for Sarah when I had the chance.

My kit was laid out on the floor for a final check.

Walking clothes: boots, three pairs of socks; Gore-Tex jacket with hood; walking pants, waterproof over-pants; two sets of thermal underwear, fleece, four specialised walking shirts; convertible woollen hat/balaclava/scarf; gloves; glasses; sunglasses; watch. For evenings, a spare pair of walking pants, shoes that could double as emergency walking boots and a cashmere vest.

Camping equipment: tent, sleeping bag, sleeping mat; microfibre towel; tiny gas stove, aluminium pot, cutlery.

Toilet bag and medical kit. I had kept it minimal: every village in France seems to have a pharmacy.

Electronics: lightweight PC; power adaptor; phone doubling as camera; miniature tripod; rechargeable batteries for GPS; charger; earphones; memory sticks. I could have used the phone as my GPS but Jonathan had mailed me a military-spec unit and a cheque for two hundred pounds drawn on the army in exchange for a report at the end of the walk: 'You don't want to be trying to keep a phone dry in the pouring rain, just when you need it most.' The maps were still on a memory stick at the outdoors shop.

Thermos; water bottle; torch; compass; Swiss Army knife; last year's guide for the Chemin between Cluny and Le Puy—an orange booklet listing accommodation and services; passport; wallet with credit card, cash and photo of Sarah; business cards; *credencial.*

I had decided to walk with *bâtons.* If any part of my body was likely to let me down, it was my knees. One had been rebuilt; both needed to be treated with care. The carbon-fibre, shock-absorber-equipped sticks would take some weight off.

Harmonica. In my twenties I had messed around with music but had not played for years. Maybe I could use some of the free time on the track to revisit my artistic side.

A selection of spares and tools, including tyre pump.

'*That* fits into *that?*' said Jim, pointing first to the array of equipment on the floor and then to the three detachable bags that were the cart's storage units.

'Room to spare. And the suspension can take eighty kilos.'

'Then pack something else.'

'Such as?'

'Something that'll look good in the photos. It's like vacation rentals. You know what the houses are like around here, pretty shabby a lot of them. But for a few euros, you buy some nice wine glasses, a coffee machine, couple prints on the wall . . .'

'Brilliant. I'll carry a painting to brighten up the hostels.'

'Listen to me. Take a glass or two, folding chair, a little coffee machine for that burner. Then you've got a photo of yourself by the track, drinking a coffee, looking like—'

'Like a right wanker.'

'Who's gonna buy this cart? People with bad backs. Boomers. Trust me, I know my market.'

'You know the market for people who sit on their bums drinking wine and coffee.'

'Same people. They like their little luxuries. I'd forget the cart and start a shuttle service to carry the packs.'

'They already exist. But no respectable pilgrim would use them unless they had a disability.'

'Or nobody was watching. Anyway, I brought you a farewell present.'

Jim gave me a three-pack of condoms and I laughed.

'I doubt I'll have much use for these in France. Probably no one else walking this time of year.' As soon as I said it, I realised the awkwardness.

Jim smiled. 'Say hi to Zoe if you see her. And think about the coffee machine.'

9

Zoe

When I woke up in the church, all I could think about was coffee. I would have traded my whole bag of cosmetics for a cappuccino. A woman coming in to pray looked surprised to see me. Or maybe she was shocked at how I looked. I shrugged. 'The village could use a hostel,' I said.

The restaurant wasn't open but the employee who had helped me the previous evening was there. She didn't have soy or almond milk—and didn't understand 'fair trade'—but the espresso was hot and strong. Two euros: my first Camino expense. The extra hot water to make it drinkable was free.

It took me a few minutes to locate the scallop-shell signs again. I ate one of the apples Camille had given me, lightening the pack as well as fuelling myself. Below me were clusters of houses in the crevices, and hamlets at the bottoms of the hills. Some of the houses higher up the hill looked larger. One, hard to see among the trees, might have been a château.

After three hours on the trail, the scallop shells led me past the church into the main street of Tramayes, where there was a stream of people in and out of the supermarket. The other stores were closed. I followed signs to the public bathrooms and they were closed too.

So was the tourist office.

I took off my pack and looked at the notices in the window. I didn't need much French to translate the prices, which started at twenty-five euros, except for what seemed to be a free pilgrims' refuge. Small kitchen, toilet, hot water, shower. Wait, that was *no* hot water, *no* shower. I hadn't showered since Camille's. I wanted to cry.

A couple a few years older than me stopped.

'*Puis-je vous aider?*' said the man—neat, fit-looking, with wiry grey hair. Can I help you?

'*Je ne parle français très bien.*'

'*Je ne parle* pas *français très bien,*' he said, and smiled. 'Need to get that one right.'

'American?' said the slim blonde woman in designer jeans.

They introduced themselves as Richard and Nicole,

Australians. They owned a vacation home in the village.

'You're doing the Camino!' said Nicole.

'Trying to.'

'That's France, I'm afraid,' said Richard. 'Everything's closed on a Monday in this region. Elsewhere it's whatever day of the week you happen to arrive. As we discovered.'

'You walked the Camino?'

'Last year. From here. Just on two thousand kilometres. Eighty-two days. Life-changing.'

If they could walk to Santiago, I could make it to the Spanish border.

'What were you looking for?' said Nicole.

'On the Camino or right now? Somewhere to stay. A map. Actually, anything. I'm a bit unprepared.'

'We used the maps in the guidebooks. But we threw them out when we were finished with them.'

Richard and Nicole exchanged glances.

'You're welcome to stay with us,' said Richard. 'Next town's Grosbois—nineteen kays.'

'Twenty-one, remember?' said Nicole.

'Regardless, you'd be mad to try to do it today.'

Take what was offered, Monsieur Chevalier had said.

We walked to a renovated stone farmhouse on the

outskirts of town. When Nicole discovered I had spent the night in a church she was horrified, and ten minutes later I was soaking in the bath.

Over a lunch of homemade potato-and-leek soup and Camino stories, I learned that Richard was a management consultant—and company director. It was hard not to squirm. I probably did when Nicole said she worked for Australia's largest mining company. As a lawyer.

She may have misread my expression. 'It must be a bit scary doing this alone.'

'I'm okay so far. Taking each day as it comes.' Easy to say on Day Two. After a bath.

'There's a village every ten or so kilometres,' said Nicole. 'Usually less.'

Richard smiled. 'Multiply by five, divide by eight.'

'About six miles,' I said.

'Right. Or you could start thinking in kilometres. It's not a bad system.'

I helped clean up, then found some printer paper and took it with my pencils into the courtyard. I sketched the house—but couldn't resist putting my hosts in the foreground. Keith and the girls had always thought my cartoons were hilarious, but they were family. I'd made Nicole glamorous, yet there was a touch of Joan Collins. Richard was more Al Pacino.

I needn't have worried. 'It's so Richard!' Nicole said.

'So *you*,' said Richard. He turned to me. 'Are you okay if I put it on our website?'

'Sure.'

'I don't suppose you could draw something for our Christmas cards?'

Nicole took me upstairs to see if any of their stuff would be of use and would not take no for an answer. However life-changing the experience had been, Nicole was over it. But she wanted their equipment to be put to good use. Or maybe just disposed of so they couldn't use it again.

'The trick,' said Nicole, 'is to pack light. I carried six kilograms and Richard had ten, including his computer.'

'He took his computer?'

'First lesson of the Camino: everyone does the Camino their own way.'

Nicole pulled out a white ski jacket.

'This is our daughter's. She's never going to wear it again. Don't worry, that stuff around the hood isn't fur. But it won't be waterproof.'

'I can't possibly . . .' But it was already in my hands. Then her daughter's barely used walking shoes—a perfect fit—thermals, a pair of walking pants and a light plastic pair to go over the top when it rained. *Do not walk in jeans.* That would be lesson number . . . ?

She threw in an almost weightless silk sleeping bag, a towel which folded to the size of a large cell phone, and a packet of Compeeds—Band-Aids for blisters. And a two-cup thermos.

Nicole emptied my cosmetic bag and put my toothbrush, toothpaste and tampons to one side. 'Now,' she said, pointing to the rest, 'allow yourself one non-essential item.'

I remembered my thoughts of earlier that day . . . but since when was deodorant non-essential?

'This isn't a hypothetical,' Nicole said with a lawyer's firmness.

I picked out the deodorant stick.

'What about the vitamins? I've been thinking about using the walk to go vegan.'

'Your choice.'

'I need my sketchpad and pens,' I said, adding them to the pack.

Nicole took out the deodorant. 'It's winter,' she said. 'When it gets warm, you'll need sunblock too.'

I left the room feeling like I'd had a full makeover. For the third time in a week, I was leaving stuff behind.

I put Camille's phone number in the plastic packet Nicole had given me, with my passport and *credencial*. In case I was found dead from vitamin deficiency.

When they weighed my loaded pack, minus food,

water and coffee, it was a bit over six kilograms. Thirteen pounds: a quarter of what I had checked in at LAX.

And I needed to ask. 'You're from Sydney, right?'

'I am. Richard's from Adelaide,' said Nicole.

'Is Sydney far from Perth?'

'About the same as New York is from LA. Why?'

'I knew an Australian from Perth, years ago. Shane Willis.' It was a long shot.

She shook her head and gave me a wry smile.

Next morning, Richard walked into the village with me and bought us coffee. He offered to pay for the Christmas-card sketches but didn't insist when I said no.

'Thank you for everything,' I said. 'I didn't expect . . .'

'Private wealth trickling down. See, it does work.' He kept a poker face for a few moments, then laughed. 'Keep an open mind. Go with the flow. The Camino walks *you*.'

I had considered the physical challenge. I had thought of being alone and of the stuff I still needed to sort through. But a challenge to my world view, discovering corporate lawyers and company directors being generous and accepting of liberal vegetarians, had never occurred to me.

10

Martin

On the Tuesday morning, I manoeuvred the cart down the stairs from my empty apartment, clipped the side rails to my hip belt, had breakfast at the Café du Centre and walked to the outdoors shop. The proprietor retrieved my package from behind the counter—exactly where I'd been looking before Zoe had drawn attention to me. Then, unemployed, unattached and free of debt to anyone, I headed down the main street of Cluny, pulling everything I owned towards Santiago de Compostela.

The first kilometre of my journey was on the road, easy going for the cart. I had not yet loaded the maps into the army GPS, so had to rely on the signposts—stylised scallop shells, their radial lines converging to indicate the direction.

As I walked along the left side of the road, facing the traffic, I discovered I was a curiosity. Drivers slowed for a look, and several called out *Bon Chemin* or *Bon courage*. A male driver of about my age pulled over.

'You are walking the Chemin?'

'Yes.'

'To the border?'

'Santiago.'

'*Formidable.* Where did you buy this?'

'I built it.'

'So, it is a French design.' He got out of the car and examined the cart. *Formidable*, again. If he had been a manufacturer of hiking equipment, my journey might have been over.

As a scallop shell pointed me onto a climbing track and the morning fog lifted to reveal a cold, clear day, I had a feeling of self-sufficiency and simplicity that had been missing in my life for a long time. There is a great deal of satisfaction in working with proper equipment. I was wearing a thermal undershirt, buttoned walking shirt, fleece and jacket, cargo pants, ski hat, gloves and sunglasses. It was only a couple of degrees above zero, but there was no wind.

I was walking the Camino for financial reasons, though it would be disingenuous to pretend I did not see it also as a personal challenge. Nineteen hundred kilometres on foot pulling a load was a significant physical undertaking. That said, I had not envisaged any great psychological impact. I had dismissed Monsieur Chevalier's prediction that the journey would change me. But in the first kilometre, it did. I felt good: independent and free.

My situation was well short of the middle-class portfolio of house, car and money in the bank that had once been my lot. But it was an advance on six months earlier, when I had owned precisely nothing, was carrying a bit of lard and was, in retrospect, an emotional mess. I wondered how some of my peers would have fared if they had found themselves jobless and skint at fifty-two. Jonathan, for instance.

We had sat in the living room of his Georgian pile, where I had taken up temporary residence, drinking an eighteen-year-old Macallan, his attempt at an appropriate drink for an occasion that needed marking but not celebrating. He raised his glass and did his best.

'At least she didn't clean you out.'

'Not through lack of trying.'

'Come on, Martin.'

The documents were in my bag, fresh from my final meeting with the solicitor. I had a healthy bank balance, partial compensation for losing my house and everything in it. And having to walk away from my job, since Julia's choice of lover had been my head of department.

'She'd have taken the lot if she could,' I said.

'I understand how you're feeling. But that's not true. I know Julia.'

'Did you know she was screwing Rupert?'

'People make mistakes. Julia . . . most people want the other person to get on with their life.' Jonathan paused. 'Or to forgive them, Martin.'

'Bit late for that.'

'Who's being vindictive now?'

'I think I'm entitled to feel a tiny bit put out.'

'All I'm saying is that she's not the sort of person who would leave you with nothing.'

'For Chrissakes, Jon. You don't know what she's like. I thought *I* knew her.'

'I'm starting to think I do know her better than you.'

There was a way to shatter his rose-coloured glasses. I took out my chequebook and wrote a cheque in Julia's name for the balance of my account.

'Fifty quid says she cashes it.'

'Don't be bloody ridiculous.'

'You said she wouldn't take it.'

'She wouldn't, but don't tempt fate.'

The idea had been spontaneous, but now it seemed absolutely the right thing to do. My entire net worth was on a small piece of paper that I could have screwed up and held in my fist.

'I'm not tempting fate. I'm tempting her. If she cashes it, I'll know I'm right. Fifty quid and no more of your "faults on both sides" crap.'

'No.'

'I'm going to send it anyway. That's a promise. So, fifty quid or not?'

'Make it five hundred. Julia's all right.'

Julia wasn't all right. But Jonathan was. He insisted on paying me the five hundred pounds, which covered my travel to France.

My sense of wellbeing carried me halfway up the long incline. I stopped to remove my woollen hat, and looked back to see that I was at an impressive height above the farmland. At 2 p.m., about five kilometres short of Tramayes, I stopped and finished the coffee from my thermos. I took the opportunity to check the cart's wheel mounting. I was experimenting with not using a split pin to secure one of the nuts, because I wanted as many of the parts as possible to be available from bicycle shops, which in Europe are thick on the ground.

I was feeling fresh and my map-less GPS told me that I was averaging four kilometres per hour. If I could hold this pace, I could keep going and make Grosbois by around 8 p.m. It would be a stretch, but I would pull back one of my lost days and complete a brilliant start to the journey.

I rang the bed and breakfast in Tramayes and cancelled. I didn't bother rebooking in Grosbois. I had previously reserved a room for this date, so I knew they were open. We could sort it out when I arrived.

Tramayes had the usual French small-town line-up of hairdresser, florist, *boulangerie, boucherie* and bar. There was also a hotel-restaurant with a few diners finishing lunch, and I decided I'd earned a proper coffee. The proprietor fetched her husband, in chef's hat and apron, to look at the cart.

'Do you see many walkers this time of year?' I asked. He had a front-row view of the Chemin.

'You are the second today. Maybe the second for the year. Most come in the spring and summer. Where are you going tonight?'

'Grosbois.'

He shook his head. 'It's a long way. Better to stay here.'

I was tempted. My legs had stiffened and I would have been glad to call it a day. What swung it in the end was the desire not to muck around my bed-and-breakfast host again. And to stay in another place in the same town would have been pretty poor form.

11
Zoe

When Keith died I was reading Camille's letter, on perfumed paper, the handwriting a tribute to years of knuckle-rapping by French nuns.

'Zoe.' I didn't recognise the voice on the phone at first.

'Jennifer? Have you got a cold?' I asked the girl who worked in the store with my husband.

Keith was the same age as me. At the funeral, I couldn't fathom why the universe had sent me this. I sat in the front pew in uncomprehending silence between my daughters, with Keith's mother on the other side of Lauren. Keith had no children of his own.

'Don't worry about anything,' Lauren had told me. 'You can stay with us and we'll give you plenty to keep you occupied.'

Tessa had just hugged me.

I expected I would make sense of it all in the coming weeks and months. I would pack Keith's clothes, go through all the photo albums and cry myself to sleep in sheets that would still smell of him.

It didn't happen that way. Albie, our accountant and an old buddy of Keith's, stopped by the day after the funeral.

'What do you mean, no money?' I said.

Keith had a shoe business. It was not big, but it had given us enough to pay the bills and the girls' college fees.

'Your joint account is frozen,' said Albie, avoiding my eyes. 'He's been in trouble for a while. He mortgaged the house to borrow money. You signed the papers.'

'I didn't . . .'

'He didn't want to worry you.'

'Do we owe people?'

'My best guess is that you'll be able to cover the debts—just. After you sell up. But I can't promise.'

I walked through the house and started saying goodbye to everything. I would miss it for the memories, the shared history. And I thought about the timing of Camille's letter—what message I should take from it.

It took me a week to tell Keith's employees they

were out of a job and get rid of all the stuff I didn't need. It took me another week to organise my immediate future. I checked my personal bank account, where I deposited my income from the wellness centre, the occasional massage client and the even more infrequent sale of a watercolour. The best deal my travel agent could get left me with two thousand dollars.

When I called Lauren to tell her I was leaving for France, she was speechless—maybe for the first time in her life.

'Albie is selling the house. You've got a key,' I said.

'Mom, you're losing it.'

'Right now, it's what I need.'

'You need to be with us!' She kept talking but my mind drifted. She was an events organiser—an *everything* organiser. She would love having children. I didn't want to be one of them.

'Lauren,' I said. 'This is a difficult time for us all. But I need space. Camille is an old friend.'

I had barely talked to the girls about the year with Camille at college and the issues with my mother. It took all my self-control not to beat up on their father, Manny.

If I told Lauren that I was walking the Camino, she'd be sure I'd lost it.

Though my third day on the road was as long as the previous two combined, the weather was mild and the terrain easy. The lighter backpack made a difference but there was no way I could do twenty-five miles in a day.

LA isn't a walking city. You drive to the store for milk, even if it's on the next corner. I finished the final uphill section into Grosbois feeling beat.

The light was almost gone, and for a moment I forgot my fatigue and stood at the gates to admire the château. Small, and faded—but I felt like I had walked back a few centuries.

There was a shout from the opposite end of the courtyard. Three teenagers were hauling bags out of a minibus. Hadn't the woman at the tourist office said there would be no one around at this time of year?

The château door was ajar and I stepped in, closing it behind me as the warmth rushed out. A middle-aged man with wispy fair hair almost bumped into me as he appeared from behind a curtain.

I managed to communicate that I was after a bed in the dormitory.

'*Ce soir, non, le dortoir n'est pas possible,*' he said slowly, shaking his head and pointing to the building where the young people were taking their bags. '*Mais j'ai une seule chambre.*' One finger raised, then pointed upstairs. '*Au cause d'une annulation.*' Mimed phone call, then a sharp horizontal movement with the hand, finger and thumb gripped together.

Dormitory not possible. One room available. An *annulation*. I'd have to go with the flow on that one.

I had hoped for something cheaper, but as I soaked in the bathtub after a day of healthy walking in my new gear and with an appetite for the three-course meal that was part of the deal, the scallop-shell charm still around my neck, I felt the universe was taking care of me.

12
Martin

As I hitched up the cart again in Tramayes, I heard a cry of *Bon Chemin* with an Anglo accent, and for a moment thought it might be Zoe, before realising she should be well ahead by now. When I turned I saw a couple. The woman was blonde and in jeans, boots and a long red coat. I waved back.

I pushed hard for the next three hours, wanting to leave as little distance as possible to do in the dark. The caffeine hit faded and I found myself pulling the GPS out regularly to check my distance.

I had done a couple of long training runs, out to twenty kilometres, but now I was looking at thirty-seven. The minor roads gave way to a steep muddy track which was mercifully short, but took a bit out of me. Then it was in and out of forests and farmland, over undulating country with occasional sections on the road. It was scenic enough, but I was focused on making time. I skipped the bar in the village of St Jacques des Arrêts, and missed the church and its frescoes, which the guidebook classified as 'unmissable'.

The light held until 7 p.m., when I had to strap my torch to my forehead. I proceeded slowly, not wanting to get lost or fall.

My GPS registered thirty-seven kilometres when I reached the town. A runner knows that the last few hundred metres, with the end in sight, can be the hardest. Then, as I bumped the cart up the steps to the church, I felt it collapse behind me. I unhitched, and turned to see the wheel tilted at an angle well in excess of what the suspension would allow. On Day One the cart had broken. In the final hundred metres.

I was too exhausted to take it in except as a wave of despair. No point trying to fix it here. I lifted the assembly onto my shoulders, using the straps, though the last thing I needed at the end of a long day was an awkward sixteen kilograms on my back. I hauled myself up the steps and into the street.

There was a sign—*Grosbois*. It was not until I was almost upon it that my light illuminated the digit underneath: *2*, and an arrow pointing uphill. I put the cart down, did some stretches and drank my remaining water. I reminded myself of the marathon. The ten kilometres I had done with a swollen knee had taken more endurance than would be required here.

I recalled that the rooms at Grosbois had baths. They also served dinner. I pulled out my phone to let them know I was on my way. No signal. Phone coverage in France is patchy, in part because the locals object to the towers. But there was a text message that must have come through earlier.

Good luck Dad. Love Sarah.

My problem was not luck, but judgment. With a modicum of that, I would have been sharing a glass of wine in front of a fire with the bed-and-breakfast owner in Tramayes.

I held on to thoughts of a hot bath and meal for the last stretch on a narrow, ascending track through pine forest. It was 9.30 p.m. when I arrived, utterly played out, at the château. In the large courtyard, a bus and two cars were parked.

I dumped the cart, knocked hard at the door of the main building and was eventually greeted by a short man of about forty-five, looking a little flushed with alcohol.

He frowned, shook his head, and said, '*Désolé—complet.*'

Full. How the hell could they be full? What about the dorm?

They had a school group staying. They remembered my booking, yes, but also my *annulation*—cancellation. And, *malheureusement*, that room was now occupied. The school had taken the whole dormitory. I could ask to join them, but it was their call.

I walked to the other building and dragged open the door. A crowd of kids were engaged in some sort of obstacle race.

I returned to the spot where I had dumped the cart. It was cold, and I suppose I could have walked back and begged a spot on the château floor, but I was beyond conversation.

As I laid out the tent, I heard footsteps and turned to see, in the light of my torch, someone that it took me a few seconds to recognise as Zoe. She was sporting a white fluffy jacket that might have looked excessive at St Moritz. It was hard to imagine a more inappropriate—no, surreal—look for the Camino. Paired with an antique pendant. Private room with bath, naturally, *madame*.

'*Bonjour,*' she said. '*Voulez-vous manger?*'

She thrust a brown paper bag at me. I took it and

managed a grunted *merci* before resuming work on the tent. I wasn't hungry but I would need to eat at some stage. After she left I realised that I'd automatically replied in French, and that she must have assumed I didn't speak English. It was easier to leave it that way.

13
Zoe

Leaving Grosbois, I found myself in a forest smelling of damp pine needles. Tentacles of white mist wound between the dark avenues of trees, and the stillness was broken only by an occasional water drip or birdcall. It was cold, and there were moments when the wind picked up that reminded me of my childhood in Minnesota, walking to the school bus in cotton socks and an oversized coat handed down from my brothers. But in the ridiculous Aspen number and thermals I felt quite snug. A sign told me I was at 915 metres altitude—three thousand feet. The hunter—who was apparently also a pilgrim—must be crazier than me to use a tent in this weather. Maybe he was doing some kind of penance. For shoplifting.

I walked for four hours alone in the mist, following the scallop shells, beginning to wonder if I would ever find a town. I tried recalling some of the inspirational quotes that were put up on the board each week at yoga and settled for Ralph Waldo Emerson: *Nature always wears the colours of the spirit.* It won just ahead of Alice being told it didn't matter which fork she took if she didn't know where she was going.

Just when the isolation was threatening to overwhelm me, I heard a voice. A soprano was singing an aria from *Carmen*—I couldn't remember its name. In the silence of the forest, it was unearthly, mystical. After maybe a minute, the singer emerged from the fog, a girl too slim for her voice, walking two huge mastiffs.

The dogs saw me first and strained at their leads. She stopped singing and motioned me not to touch. Like I was going to. I stood still and smiled as she continued on, resuming the aria a few moments later. Only when I could no longer hear her did I drink a little of the coffee that Monsieur Annihilation had poured into my thermos and begin walking again.

The fog lifted, and the beauty of my surroundings helped me realise how blessed I was, despite everything: the trail itself, its surface a soft mat of red-brown; the occasional ray of sun filtering through the trees to fall on frozen pine needles, drips forming on the ends; glimpses of rolling hills where forests were interspersed with distant houses and small villages.

I stopped at Propières. There seemed to be only one place to stay in town—a small hotel. I was not hurting, just tired, though I was not walking anything like four miles an hour. Nevertheless, I had an acute sense of relief when I put the pack down in the bar—a sports bar filled with men. One by one they stopped their conversation until they were all staring at me. The hostility was unmistakable. Two big guys rose from their stools. *Right.*

I crossed my arms and stared back, trying to look more confident than I felt.

'*Je suis* . . . looking for *une chambre.*' My French was slowly coming back.

'*Americaine?*' said one.

'*Oui.*'

Suddenly they were smiling, but not just at my accent. Their body language and head shakes were unmistakable: *she doesn't get it.* Meaning: *she thinks it's okay for a woman to walk into a sports bar.*

Screw them. France was a western country. Their culture didn't deserve special treatment.

I did my best not to be intimidated. I told them that in the US a woman could walk into a bar without having to deal with misogyny and that if their behaviour was representative of their country, then France had some catching up to do. Or at least I did to the extent that my French allowed.

'America *bon*,' I said and stuck both thumbs up. 'France *non bon*.' Thumbs down.

They responded by bursting out laughing.

'USA is shit,' said one, in English, and the others made it clear they agreed. Not just shit, but a laughing-stock.

Before I had a chance to channel my inner patriot, a woman appeared from the hallway and grabbed me and my pack. She pointed to the picture of the footballers. Not sexism, just team affiliation. I must have been the equivalent of a Yankees fan walking into a Mets bar. I guessed the 'shit' comment was referring to our soccer team. I could cope with that. I made a mental note to find out what team my backpack was supporting. And to keep working on my French so I wouldn't sound so damn stupid.

The hotel did a pilgrim meal, but the cost of my room and dinner was sixty euros, even after a discount because I didn't want the *canard*, just the vegetables. The soup was great, but since when was pasta a vege-table? I made up with cheese. How long would a vegan survive here?

The next day it rained. When I felt the first drops, I found shelter in a small chapel. Within a few minutes it was bucketing down, and about half an hour later the shoplifter came past, pulling a cart. My surprise at seeing him pressing on in the rain was overtaken by the realisation that I'd seen him and his cart the day I arrived in Cluny. I called *bonjour* but he just pushed on. Bringing him something to eat in Grosbois didn't seem to have changed his attitude to me. A seriously weird guy.

I couldn't find a hostel in Le Cergne, just a hotel with an upscale restaurant. I checked in and went in search of cheaper food. I was craving something hot. A lot of something hot. I couldn't remember being this hungry.

There was a pizzeria. As soon as I smelled the aroma, thoughts of every unhealthy topping imaginable flooded my mind. Particularly salami. I prided myself on being in tune with my body, and right now my body was asking for pizza with cheese, salami, bacon and all. I steeled myself to choose a vegetarian option. Our ancestors did a lot of labour but only the wealthy could eat meat.

'*Un grand*'—I said, using my hands to show that I meant big—'vegetarian.'

The owner shook his head and pointed to a mid-sized pizza plate.

I shook my head back. '*Maximum.*'

He looked surprised, but not as much as when I finished it and ordered another—this time just a medium. I'd learned that the *TTC* on restaurant checks meant that the tip was included, but I left behind a sketch of him sagging under the weight of a pizza he was delivering. He was pinning it on the wall, laughing, when I left. At least some people appreciated my efforts at creating good karma.

By lunchtime the next day I'd made Charlieu, the biggest town since Cluny, and found the tourist office.

'I'm doing the Camino.'

'*Credencial?*' asked the woman at the desk.

All right. They were serious about the rules if they would only service pilgrims. I pulled out my 'passport'. Instead of checking it, she stamped it with an impressive picture of the abbey and handed it back.

'Can you give me a list of places to stay?'

'You will find these in the guidebook.'

'Do you have one?'

'They come out in February.'

'I need somewhere cheap.'

'The hostels, they are mostly closed. It is not the season. A *chambre d'hôte*?' In response to my blank look, she added, 'Rooms in the house of someone. Bed and breakfast. Sometimes also dinner. For these accommodations, you make a phone call.'

Not with my level of French, you didn't.

She called for me. No answer at the hostel. But there was a *chambre d'hôte*.

And, when I found it after another two hours walking, it was wonderful. The bed was soft, there was a bathroom with an array of cosmetics and my host, a retired teacher, shared a vegetarian meal with me and spoke enough English for simple conversation. Then she gave me the bill. Fifty-five euros. Fair for what I'd got, but more than I could afford.

I could keep the cost of lunch to five euros a day. Bread was cheap. But every night apart from Richard and Nicole's—and the church in Sainte Cécile—had cost way more than my budget of fifteen euros. Either I would have to return to Camille's or find an English-speaking pilgrim who knew the ropes.

14
Martin

The night in Grosbois, I slept in my clothes. I woke, cold and ravenous, at 2 a.m. and opened Zoe's food package: bread, cheese and terrine. I wolfed it down, put on my fleece and was out to it until I heard the school bus driving away and then the voice of the man who had refused me accommodation the previous evening.

I poked my head out into a foggy morning, and he was full of apologies. Of course I should not have pitched a tent. Minus two degrees last night. Come in whenever you're ready.

I was stiff but not sore. I helped myself to a late breakfast—coffee, toast, jam and an omelette on the warmer. *Monsieur* joined me, and offered me the use of a room to shower and clean up. I wasn't going to say no.

The room had not been cleaned and the big unmade bed reminded me of what I had missed out on. On the desk was a sketch of the château. It was a well-executed drawing that flattered the old building. In the foreground was a caricature of my host which would have detracted if it had not been so good—the artist had captured not only his appearance but something of his essence.

I did a few minutes of stretches, then took a long shower. Another of Monsieur Chevalier's prophecies had come to pass: I had a blister on the big toe of my left foot. I guided a needle and thread through it, leaving the thread in place as recommended, then washed my socks and pinned them to the back of my bag to dry.

I could not delay examining the cart any longer. To my relief, the problem was the nut I had been experimenting with. It took only a few minutes to put the wheel back in place and tighten it with the ring spanner in my toolkit. Despite my fingers numbing in the cold, I enjoyed the work.

I took stock. I was coping. The first day was not representative; it was a double stretch. Today would be easier.

The proprietor, still apologetic for letting me sleep in the tent, packed me a sandwich, filled my thermos and added his stamp to my *credencial*. It was harder earned than any I had received at school.

I made a careful start towards Les Écharmeaux, a sensible twenty-four kilometres. My breath merged with the fog and, after a kilometre or so of following the scallop-shell signs, the stiffness in my legs dissipated.

The track led into pine forest, and a silence deep but not oppressive. I felt, once again, liberated, just me and my cart, the feeling enhanced by having demonstrated that I was not reliant on others for accommodation and had been equal to my first mechanical problem.

The cart rolled along behind without any issues, but there were some long ascents. I took them at the slow pace required to keep my breathing steady. As I reached the top of a long stretch, with a sign telling me I was at 915 metres, I stopped and checked my heart rate. One hundred and thirty-four. Bang in the middle of the cardiac-training zone. If I made Santiago, I would be fit.

In my preparations, I had not contemplated what it would be like to walk alone for most of the day, doing nothing else for three months of my life. I'd planned it as a business enterprise, but also realised that it would be an opportunity for reflection.

Now, I began to get a sense of what it was going to be like. The surprise was that I was not bored. More to the point, I was not going to be able to retreat into contemplation and let the miles roll by. The first time I indulged in a daydream, I was bumped back to reality by a realisation that the scallop-shell signposts had vanished. I retraced my steps, and, after ten minutes, felt the edge of panic. I pushed it back, but it was another five minutes before I found the fork where I had taken the incorrect path. It was a wake-up call. Walking required constant attention to the environment—not my greatest strength.

My unintentional detour taught me something. The scallop shells were fine until you missed one. Once off the track, it was harder to find the way back. Even if I succeeded in retracing my steps, I could still have a problem. The shells were placed to be visible walking *towards* Santiago. If I hit the track walking in the other direction, I might not realise I was on it.

I reached Les Écharmeaux as the sun was setting and checked into the hotel, where I logged onto the internet, loaded my maps, washed my clothes and hung them to dry on the heaters. In the hotel dining room, I ate an excellent meal of *boeuf bourguignon*, cheese, *nougat glacé* and a quarter-litre of Beaujolais—alone, surrounded by empty tables with the chairs stacked on top.

My third day, into Le Cergne, continued what I hoped would be the template for the rest of the journey. I packed lunch, walked steadily, if slowly, on the hills and took a break every five kilometres. The GPS was working well; I had it in and out of my pocket every few hundred metres, watching it track my path, checking the distance to the next waypoint and the day's destination, monitoring my moving-average speed—a respectable 4.1 kilometres per hour—and my overall average, which was a lazier 3.6 kilometres per hour.

The only negative was a deluge of rain, prompting frequent falls of ice from the trees, a couple of which landed on me. My jacket did well enough keeping me dry, but I couldn't do much to protect my face. At lunchtime, I found a flat tree stump a short distance off the track and forced myself to stop for fifteen minutes, in the interests of looking after my body, but sitting in the rain is never pleasant.

The weather was clearing by the time I got moving again. I had walked no more than two hundred metres when I rounded a turn to see a familiar white jacket. Its wearer was sitting under shelter on the steps of a small chapel eating an apple. She called and waved and I managed a wave back, but there was no point stopping now.

Perhaps I should have. By the end of Day Four, as the sole diner at a hamburger restaurant in Briennon, I was not yet lonely, but I was beginning to wonder how long it would be before I craved some company.

15
Zoe

I was now walking on rolling farmland between villages, the French countryside of postcards and
coffee-table books. The path was well marked, not only
by scallop shells, but by crucifixes. Small and large,
rustic and elaborate, Jesus at peace, Jesus writhing in
agony. They were hard to ignore on a route that went
past every church in every village. Modern pilgrims
might be more spiritual than religious but the Catholic
relics were set in stone.

I saw the intricately patterned roof of the ancient
church at La Bénisson-Dieu over hedges and the bare
arms of oak and elm trees. The village's only *boulangerie* had closed when I arrived at 1 p.m. What kind of
bakery closes for lunch? Until 4 p.m.?

Wandering around the church ramparts, I nearly

fell over another walker, sitting eating a pastry, back against the wall, with his legs out across the track. He looked young—all limbs, as teenagers sometimes are.

'*Bonjour*,' I said. Big eyes above prominent cheekbones peered up from under a beanie.

'*Bonjour*. American?'

'*Oui*. Zoe.'

'I am Bernhard. From Germany.' He thrust a paper bag at me. 'You are welcome if hungry. The bakery gives it for nothing. It is leftover and I am a *pèlerin*.' Good karma, paid forward. I felt an immediate connection.

When he stood up, he towered over me; there was more muscle to those limbs than I had thought. He was twenty-five, and had walked alone, five hundred kilometres from his home in Stuttgart. He had fallen out with his father over politics, lifestyle and his rejection of the bourgeoisie, and now, with neither home nor money, he had taken to the road. It was a story I could relate to, though I'd been younger when I fought those battles.

I was the first *pèlerin* he had seen, and whether it was loneliness or a chance to practise English, he was enthusiastic about walking with me. We talked about the Chemin and American politics. He was smart and well-informed. I had found the person I needed: a guy with weeks of experience of low-budget travelling.

'Where do you sleep?' he asked.

'Hotels and *chambres d'hôte.*'

'How much do you pay?'

I told him.

'Too much.' He was right about that. 'You are a *pèlerin.* Lodgings should be free. I go to Mary.'

'Nuns?'

'The official place. The *mairie.*'

The *mayor's* place. Civic offices. 'What do they do for pilgrims?'

'For *pèlerins* they find accommodation. I have slept with many women.'

I figured something had been lost in translation. 'Do you pay?'

Bernhard grinned and shook his head. There was something appealing about him and his light layer of chin fuzz. I could imagine women having their maternal spirit stirred by his smile.

In Renaison, Bernhard announced he would be stopping for the day. I decided to see if French women's generosity could be extended to the sisterhood. Bernhard disappeared into the bathroom to spruce himself up, after suggesting I do likewise.

'It is important to look good.'

Bernhard emerged with hair slicked back, and the top buttons of his shirt undone. I couldn't help thinking that Tessa and Lauren would have been impressed. The middle-aged woman in the *mairie* smiled at him and made a phone call. Her friend could put us both up.

Madame Beaulieu's home was only a short walk from the *mairie*. She had a neat room for each of us and insisted on washing our clothes. Dinner—after I had passed my chicken to Bernhard—was pasta, bread and cheese, and an apple tart to die for.

The only downside was the religious paraphernalia— and talk. My lack of French meant I was spared much of it, but Bernhard chatted enthusiastically as he helped clean up. Madame Beaulieu seemed to be caring for us out of a mistaken sense of religious fellowship: giving us an *accueil jacquaire*—a St Jacques welcome.

When we left the next morning, she kissed us and wished us *Bon Chemin*. Bernhard translated: 'She says to leave what you feel is right. For the works of the church.'

I was torn between my animosity toward religion and gratitude for Madame Beaulieu's generosity. There was no amount that I could put in her tin that didn't take something away from my integrity. I left fifteen

euros, but told Bernhard there would be no more Jac-
quarian welcomes for me.

The next day, the path wound up and down hills, often
on asphalt, which was tough on my feet. From the
rocky crags above the Loire I could see mist rising off
the water. The path descended to St Jean St Maurice,
with its tower high above the river.

I had started earlier than Bernhard but he caught
me, stayed for a while, then strode ahead.

He was waiting by the tiny church. 'We will use the
gîte—the hostel.'

Good: that was supposed to be the idea.

'Five stars.' Bernhard clarified that he was referring
to its online rating by *pèlerins*, rather than the system
that the Four Seasons belonged to. The rates at *gîtes*
varied, but they usually offered a good-deal evening
meal. Most also had kitchens. 'But do not take the
breakfast. Better coffee at the bar, and bread and pas-
tries are only one euro each. Or free.' I said I'd cook.

The municipal *gîte* was a small building near the
centre of the village. A woman of maybe forty met us
there and opened up. There was a tiny kitchen, a dormitory for six and just one bathroom, with two open
shower stalls. In the hall, the stove had a pile of wood

beside it. Ten euros per bunk bed, plus five to eat. Way cheaper than a *chambre d'hôte* or hotel, but my money still wasn't going to get me to the border. Maybe I would find what I had lost—peace of mind?—before then. So far, I had been too busy to do much thinking.

I hadn't shared a bedroom or bathroom with anyone other than my partner or children for twenty years. I tried to picture the dormitory full of pilgrims of varying ages, nationalities and genders, and a line for the showers with everyone in shorts and towels.

I went to put my pack on a bunk and the woman freaked out.

'You must leave the pack in the hall,' Bernhard explained, 'to avoid transporting bedbugs.'

'Bedbugs? You're saying they have bedbugs?'

'Probably not, but it is . . . preventative. *Prophylactique.*' He grinned at our host and then me.

There were baskets to unload our gear into. In the bedroom, I chose the bunk that gave me the most distance. About three feet. Bernhard spread his stuff over two other bunks.

The kitchen had a bulletin board covered in tourist information, cupboards full of chipped plates, and assorted pots and pans. I headed to the local *épicerie*—in this case a store attached to a gourmet restaurant—and bought pasta and vegetables for me, and a can of bolognaise sauce for Bernhard. When I got back, he had showered and was towelling his upper body in the dorm, wearing only a pair of tight briefs.

While I cooked, Bernhard got the fire going and uncorked a bottle of wine he had been given by the bedbug woman. The fire heated up the small hostel surprisingly quickly. With the table set for two, lit by a candle Bernhard had found, it could have been an intimate romantic dinner—had I not been with someone young enough to be my son.

Bedbug woman returned after we'd eaten. Bernhard was putting on the charm and I left them talking while I cleaned up and did a quick sketch. I made the woman a lot younger than she was, not that that was likely to worry her, but it did look like she was flirting. When I gave it to her the next morning over a breakfast of white bread and jelly, she blushed. I left Bernhard sleeping and walked out to find that night had covered the landscape with a dusting of snow.

16

Martin

S now was always going to be a risk this early in the year. I hadn't been aware of it falling as I slept in my riverfront bed and breakfast in St Jean St Maurice at the end of my sixth day.

The cart was not great on the slippery surface, but nor was it the disaster Maarten's golf trolley would have been. The large wheel gave it good ground clearance, and the narrow profile was essential as I negotiated tracks in the pine forest. The problem was at the human end: maintaining foot traction, particularly uphill. I slipped and fell twice, turning the cart over with me the second time. No damage done: the surface was soft.

Five hours into the day, I came to a village with a *bar-tabac* open. Seated on the curb outside was a lanky blond lad beside a large backpack. He jumped to his feet as I arrived.

'*Bonjour*,' I said, and added, '*Anglais*.'

He shook my hand and responded in English: 'I am Bernhard. From Germany.'

Bernhard refused my offer of coffee: he had his own full thermos. But he waited while I finished mine and used the time to examine my cart.

'Where did you buy this?'

I told him the story.

'That explains the poor quality of construction. I am not insulting you; you were forced to assemble it from components not intended for the purpose. Mass production allows for all components to be specifically designed.'

Thank you for the engineering lesson. 'It's a proto-type.'

'The single wheel is a mistake.'

'You think so?'

'I am sure.'

I let it go. He was almost a caricature of the arrogant German technician and it sat comically with his youth. I'd seen it before: international students—and tourists—struggling to assert their identity in a foreign place and exaggerating their supposed national traits. I'd probably done the same myself.

When we were back in the snow, I spotted footprints and pointed them out to Bernhard.

'Zoe,' he said, and we established that the two of them had spent the previous night at the same hostel, not for the first time.

Walking with a companion was a new experience. The narrow tracks and the concentration needed to walk in snow precluded conversation for much of the time, but there were stretches along wider paths where we walked side by side.

He was a talker, and had typical middle-class left-wing views, not dissimilar to those I had held at his age. His position on the pilgrimage was as rigid in its own way as Monsieur Chevalier's.

'There should be no charge at the hostels. Not for pilgrims.'

'What about the privately owned ones?'

'Hostels shouldn't be run for profit. It is the government's responsibility to provide accommodation for pilgrims.'

I had a certain amount of sympathy. Every French village, no matter how small, has a *mairie*, with associated administrators, even if it lacks any other services. Maybe some basic accommodation for pilgrims in the smaller villages as well as the bigger towns would be a sensible use of those resources. Not to mention a coffee machine. If you're going to have a socialist state, at least get the benefits.

We parted company when I stopped at a bed and breakfast. Bernhard was initially unimpressed that I was not staying at a hostel, but was convinced by the simple argument that I was putting something back into the rural economy. His political views did not seem to be any better founded than his opinions on cart design.

For the next couple of days, without ever making an arrangement, Bernhard caught up with me mid-morning, and we would walk together for a while until I took a break and he hared off ahead. He was cagey about his age, but I'd have guessed twenty. We talked about the day-to-day practicalities of the Camino, and he did his best to educate me on the politics of my own country. He was still staying at the hostels with Zoe, who was leaving an hour or so ahead of both of us each day. He mentioned more than once, heavy-handedly, that she and I should bunk up to save on accommodation costs. Apparently, she was keen on the idea.

17
Zoe

Bernhard was even more concerned about money than I was. In Pommiers, he offered to negotiate beds for both of us—in my case, without religious ties. He told me to wait outside.

'It is all organised,' he announced when he emerged from the *mairie*. He was not alone. 'I will sleep with *madame* . . .'

Madame was an attractive woman a bit younger than me. Beside her was a short man of about sixty, with sparse grey hair, sucking his belly in as he tucked his shirt into his pants.

'And you,' said Bernhard, 'will sleep with *monsieur.*'

'*On va manger au restaurant.*' The man smiled, broadly. Dinner included.

'*Parlez-vous anglais?*' I asked.

'A little.' His enthusiasm might have been infectious if I hadn't felt like Bernhard had just pimped me as a paid escort: a dinner date in exchange for a bed.

Bernhard's *madame* was locking the door. I grabbed him. 'You have to tell him I can't.'

Bernhard looked puzzled. There was a rapid conversation after which he told me it was fixed. *Monsieur* would pay for the meal. I gave up.

In the car to my host—Henri's—house, I discovered that he had more than a little English. He was a public servant—a *fonctionnaire*—and one did not attain such a position without a knowledge of English, though he had to apologise for being out of practice. He turned my backpack face down in his trunk.

'Not your team?' I said.

'Not my team.'

We arrived at a large rambling home, where he made coffee and showed me photos of his children and grandchildren, who lived in nearby villages. He was divorced and had moved here to care for his mother, who had since died.

I tried to explain I didn't need to eat out and was happy to cook. Even pasta. '*Je suis* vegetarian.'

'It is my pleasure that you accompany me. The vegetables will be no problem.'

We drove to the restaurant in an old car whose passenger door didn't open from the inside. The upholstery smelt of cigarettes.

It took us half an hour to reach our destination: St Jean St Maurice, where Bernhard and I had stayed the previous night. We parked outside the gourmet restaurant where I had bought provisions for dinner.

The host knew Henri: hugs and kisses and rapid French. I picked up the word *végétarien*. '*Poisson?*' he said, looking at me.

I sometimes ate fish when I needed protein. I'd done enough walking to deserve some. I nodded.

Henri explained that he had left the menu to the host, who was the restaurant owner. He returned with a bottle of white wine. A young server with a fresh outbreak of acne brought bread and an appetiser of three teaspoon-size servings of mousse: red, green and brown.

Henri was watching me like a parent watching a child open Christmas presents. Suddenly the craziness of the whole thing hit me: I was in a French restaurant with a friendly and intelligent gentleman, a *grandfather*, who had offered me hospitality and tried to put me at ease. It wasn't Monsieur Chevalier with his 'take what is offered' but Tessa in my head saying, 'For God's sake, Mom, loosen up.'

I smiled and let myself enjoy it.

The mousses turned out to be beet, apple and something I couldn't identify—rich and creamy, with a subtle taste that was hard to place. Then a tart packed with a variety of crisp vegetables, poking out like pins from a pincushion.

The fish was turbot, expertly filleted by the owner and delicious. A cart of cheeses followed: soft and hard, from white to red and then blue, some so furry that I would have thrown them out. And all great. Forget about being vegan: I was starting to think about opening a cheese deli back home.

Then, pastry and cream, and petits fours. I ate them without a trace of guilt. No matter how much I was eating, my clothes were getting looser.

On the ride back, Henri, who had kept me entertained through the meal with stories of his time in North Africa, was still fussing about the food.

'Was the appetiser . . . okay?'

'It was delicious. What was the brown mousse?'

'Foie gras. He makes his own. Not technically vegetarian, but only a small quantity.'

At his house, Henri poured me a glass of something strong. He wanted to keep chatting, but I was exhausted. He showed me the spare bedroom and I fell asleep as soon as my head hit the pillow.

I was woken by a knock at 8 a.m.

'*Café?*'

'*Dix*—ten minutes,' I called, scrambling to dress.

'Will you stay another night?' Henri asked over the coffee and a croissant still warm from the baker's oven. I could tell that he didn't expect me to say yes.

I had felt bad enough at the restaurant. As I left, kisses on both cheeks and coffee in my thermos, I made a decision that I would not take advantage of anybody's loneliness or religious duty again. I could not begin each day expecting that charity would get me through. Le Puy was four days away. I wouldn't get much further unless I could find a way of financing the rest of my Camino.

Bernhard caught up with me at lunchtime. 'A good time last night, *oui?*' From his expression, it looked like his had been. His beanie had ridden halfway up his head, making it look elongated and alien.

'*Non,*' I said firmly. I poured him the remains of my coffee.

'Louise cooked an excellent *saucisson*. Tonight—'

'Tonight I am staying at the *gîte*.'

'I have a better option. This afternoon I will see the other walker and find where he is going. You can share a room with him. For free. Zero.' He made a circle with his thumb and forefinger.

'What other walker?'

Bernhard frowned. 'You know him. Buggy Man.'

Great. Sharing with a French shoplifter—I'd probably wake up without my passport. It was awkward enough with Bernhard, but at least he spoke English and was safe.

'No—I need to be alone.'

Bernhard finished his coffee, and took off toward the next village and its *madame*.

18
Martin

Despite the tracks in the snow and reports from Bernhard, I had not seen Zoe since I passed her on the church steps outside Le Cergne. But I did not want for companionship. I had abandoned lonely hotels in favour of *chambres d'hôte*, which were mostly run by women. My evening routine consisted of washing my clothes, sharing a home-cooked meal with the proprietor, checking emails, a blog entry and as many phone calls as were necessary to secure accommodation three days ahead. It hadn't become dull—but I still had a long way to go.

I made up names for my *hôtes*. Without some handles to hang my memories on, the days might have merged into one hazy experience.

There was Madame Damp, a woman of perhaps sixty

whose demeanour was in keeping with the unlined shed that served as my bedroom on a rainy night. Drying my washing on the radiator can't have helped.

Madame Miserable I dubbed not because she seemed sad—though the sun hardly shone from her countenance—but because she was miserably tight. French bed-and-breakfast establishments were regulated—no surprise there—and there was a consistency in certain things: the glass of cordial on arrival, the quarter-litre of wine with dinner, the stamp for the *credencial*. Dinners were simple but well executed and generous. There were only two possible answers to the question: what do you want for breakfast? *Tea* or *coffee*. Bread and jam were standard and sometimes supplemented with fruit, yoghurt or croissants.

Madame Miserable delivered what must have been the bare minimum to pass inspection. After twenty-four kilometres walking in the cold, a single sausage, a few strands of spaghetti masquerading as a vegetable and a carafe of anaemic plonk did not a meal make. Dessert was an apple. Even my towel was undersized.

And, perhaps inevitably if one does this kind of thing long enough, there was Madame Chaud Lapin. *Hot rabbit*: an expression from my book of French colloquialisms that I was never going to risk in actual conversation.

She was perhaps early forties and quite attractive—black fringe, big brown eyes, nothing of the gaunt look so common in Parisian women of her age and beyond. Chatty, quick to laugh and interested in my personal story.

A bottle of Saint-Amour replaced the usual quarter-litre of anonymous Gamay and she opened a second as she served the cheese. *Décolletage* is a French word, and the amount showing in the overheated room could not have been an accident.

It had been almost a year since I'd split with Julia and I had no reason to feel guilty, no one to be accountable to except myself. Tomorrow, like the subjects of so many popular songs, I would be on the road, moving on. I had held the moral high ground with Julia. Sleeping with the Hot Rabbit would mean letting go of some of that superiority. Moving on.

We managed only half of the second bottle, but the Hot Rabbit poured *marc* and invited me to call her Aude. We were well on the way. A hand on my shoulder confirmed it, and marked the last point where I could have politely declined.

We adjourned to her bedroom and matters followed their expected course. It wasn't the best night of my life, but it was by no means the worst, and any shortcomings were on my side. Tired, drunk and sated, I fell asleep in her bed, and was woken by the sound of her preparing breakfast in the kitchen. In the morning light, I took in the room properly, and realised that I was not the only person to have shared it in recent times. On my bedside table was an alarm clock—fair enough, except that there was one on Aude's side as well. I opened the drawer: coins, pills, cufflinks. A quick look in the armoire confirmed my suspicions—dresses on one side; shirts, jackets and trousers on the other.

I needn't have bothered with the detective work. Over breakfast, Aude invited me to stay another night. Her husband would not be back until late the day after. Had it been like this for Julia—wild sex followed by practicalities? Martin's working late again tomorrow? Cup of tea before you go?

I loaded my cart and Aude appeared with my filled thermos, a packed lunch and a look that managed to convey that the previous night had been less about lust and more about some deeper need she'd seen in me. I walked into what remained of the snow feeling distinctly sad.

Mid-morning, I stopped for a breather after a tough ascent. The wind was blowing hard, and I was focused on pouring my coffee, so by the time I saw my cart moving of its own volition, it was out of reach and gathering speed on the slope. I sprung to my feet, splashing hot liquid over my jacket, then set off after it, back the way I'd come, downhill in snow in heavy boots. I thrust a stick in front of me and almost snared the cart as it seemed to slow over a bump, then stumbled and lost it again. If anyone had been watching, they'd probably have found it hilarious, in a slapstick sort of way.

There *was* someone watching. At the base of the hill was Bernhard, making no attempt to disguise his mirth. The cart came to a halt just a few metres from him and I duly joined it.

Bernhard pulled a paper bag from the inside pocket of his jacket and offered it to me. The croissant was still warm but I waved it away. 'You should install a brake,' he said, and crouched by the cart. 'Here . . . to lock the wheel.'

'I'm sure I can work it out,' I said, then, realising I was sounding churlish, changed the subject. 'Where did you stay?'

'I slept with a woman,' he said, grinning. 'How much did you pay for your *chambre*?'

'Forty-six euros.'

'You're crazy.'

'What do the hostels charge?'

'We are finished with hostels. We go to the *mairie*. We choose villages where there is no hostel open.'

He explained his technique, which Zoe had also embraced. The previous night she had extracted not only a bed but a restaurant meal from some lonely middle-aged mark.

'If you can afford forty-six euros for a room, you should invite Zoe to sleep with you. She can pay you maybe ten euros—maybe five, it doesn't matter. It costs you nothing and . . .' He shrugged.

'You've run this idea past Zoe?'

'Better for you to ask. Why would she have a problem?'

'Maybe she doesn't want to share a room with a man she doesn't know.'

'It's the way of the Camino. I told you, I slept with her already.' Grin. The little bugger knew exactly what he was saying, and was doing it to get my goat. 'Young people understand this. We meet, we share a room, no problems. You talk like my parents.'

I decided I was close enough to being in loco parentis to give him a bit of a serve, at least about the exploitation of generous villagers. We parted on frosty terms when I stopped for another break and he pushed on.

19
Zoe

The Montverdun *gîte* was located in a ninth-century priory. The *Ami* of the priory, in the information booth at the entrance, gave me the key as she closed up. 'There is only you tonight. In the morning, drop the key in the box if you leave before I arrive.'

I creaked open the huge door and stood in awe. There was something about the worn patchwork of brown and black stone walls and the eeriness of having this ancient place to myself that transcended religion. I thought of all the monks who had walked the stones, the pilgrims who had come in sickness and despair, and rejoiced at how blessed I was.

After I'd dropped off the groceries in the kitchen, with its big cooker and long tables that could have sat thirty, I made my way to the church itself. It seemed to be several degrees colder inside, but I paused under the inner dome and looked up to a faded painting and wondered about the person who had painted it, and all those to whom it had given solace.

I was pleased to have a break from Bernhard. But it was not Bernhard I found myself thinking about.

When Keith first asked me out, I had been divorced from Manny for six years. He came into the vegetarian restaurant where I worked occasionally. I said no. A month earlier I had been dating Shane, an Australian studying games design at UCLA. He had returned home but we had planned to vacation together in Bali. If it worked out, I'd be thinking about packing up the girls and going to live with him in Perth.

After Shane left, I had doubts. He was younger than me and hadn't had a real job. Manny wasn't much of a father, but if I took the girls to Australia they would never see him or his parents. His mother had been a big support from the moment I had found myself pregnant, early in the relationship. The more I thought about it, the more Shane seemed a risk—and too much like Manny.

On the last day that I could buy a cheap fare to Bali, Keith tried again, and I said yes. Writing an email to Shane turned out to be harder than I expected.

Then the Bali terrorist bombings happened right

when we would have been there. Fate had delivered me a safe choice at every level. Keith had inherited the shoe business when his father died. He supported the girls and insisted I stop working to pursue my art. His mother welcomed me into the family.

Pre-teen Lauren was not so accepting. 'Mom, you don't need him!'

And, incredibly, Camille: 'But your Australian? I thought you were in love.'

I loved Keith too, but our relationship was only briefly passionate. He was an average-looking, average-living guy who was happy with being . . . average. He wanted a wife and kids, and, though we never managed to have children together, he happily took on Lauren and Tessa, never wavering through Lauren's teenage tantrums and never badmouthing Manny. He was the guy every woman should want. But I came to realise that he had wanted to rescue me.

The solitude of the priory was a relief. A few of the dried chilli peppers I'd been carrying since the supermarket in Charlieu, along with my hard-earned hunger, turned my *penne con ratatouille* into a solo feast and I felt calm and centred after a glass of cider. I had to dash along corridors and across the square in the icy wind as I went between the heated kitchen, bathroom and dormitory, but there was something magical in history's whispers.

My life in LA seemed a world away. I rubbed my hands over the rough stone walls and willed them to tell me their secrets; instead, they told me I was in danger of freezing. Once again I was being forced into practicalities. But as I lay in the bunk I'd chosen beside the heater, under three blankets, the only person in a dormitory that slept ten, I knew I could do this myself, without anyone's help.

20
Martin

I was an hour past Montarcher and descending what I
hoped would be my last hill for the day when I saw,
off to my right and below me, a small figure. She—and
I knew it was *she*, because no one else on the Chemin
wore a white hooded jacket—was perhaps half a kilometre away. Heading in the wrong direction.

On the road into Montarcher, the GR3—one of
the Grande Randonnée hiking trails that criss-cross
France—overlays the Chemin, but then the GR3 goes
ahead while the Chemin deviates right. Zoe had missed
the turn.

It had been snowing off and on all day, and I was
trying to make the most of a break in the weather. I
had just two and a half days to go on the Chemin de
Cluny before I reached Le Puy and joined the busier

Chemin du Puy, where I could expect a wider choice of accommodation and food. The previous night, my bed-and-breakfast host had directed me to the bar for dinner, where I dined alone—again—on the pilgrim's menu of charcuterie and potatoes. No complaints about the quality, but the only green component of the meal had been the complimentary *verveine* liqueur.

I would never catch Zoe while I was pulling the cart, so I parked it—securely—and took off at what I hoped was a sustainable jog. For the last hundred metres, I was yelling, but she didn't hear me until I was almost on top of her.

'You're going the wrong way,' I said.

She just stared at me. Was she that confident in her navigation or just amazed that I had appeared from no-where, *sans* cart?

'You . . . speak English.'

'I'm quite good at it. Comes from being English. You didn't know that?'

I could see her casting her mind back to the outdoors shop, the café with Monsieur Chevalier and my tent at Grosbois, when I had been conscious of her speaking to me in French and had not enlightened her.

'Surely Bernhard told you . . .'

'We don't spend all our time talking about you.'

And, having finally established that we had a language in common, she didn't deign to say anything further.

She looked back at the hill, facing the same situation as I did—a climb she could have avoided. I could see that she was pissed off, presumably with herself for taking the wrong turn. No doubt discovering I was an Englishman, the current nationality of choice for villains in American movies, added to the effect.

'The marking was hopeless,' I said. Actually, there had been a bloody big sign.

Climbing without the cart was easy and I offered to take her pack. Scowl. I smiled inwardly. Where, I thought, was Monsieur Chevalier—the Knight of Cluny—when she needed him? Where was her German confidence man? Where was help of any kind, except in the form of Martin Eden of Sheffield, England?

We walked together, quietly, in the snow until I reached the turnoff for my bed and breakfast.

'How far have you got to go?' I asked her. 'You could maybe stay—'

'I'm fine, thank you.'

'No, seriously, the weather's pretty shitty.'

'I can manage a mile by myself,' she said. And kept walking.

I realised I was smiling.

21
Zoe

I reached Le Puy by literally opening a door to the city. *Pèlerins* enter a garden at the top of the hill through a wooden door in a stone wall, then wind down a path through woods to catch the first glimpse of a city dominated by two huge rocks: one topped by a monastery built by a monk returned from the Camino, the other bearing an oversized Madonna and child, like Christ the Redeemer overlooking Rio. If you forgot about the Madonna, Le Puy was a pretty town nestled in a picturesque valley.

I had completed the first big stage of my journey, but there was more than double that distance to come. My money was not going to last another week. Not exploiting the *mairies'* hospitality the previous two nights had meant a *gîte* in the boonies and a hotel room in Bellevue la Montagne.

Why not finish up in Le Puy? After fifteen days, I had nothing to prove, certainly not to a Brit with a buggy and his smug 'you've got yourself lost'. And the French masquerade, which Bernhard must have been in on.

As the trail weaved between the two rocks, I was drawn to the monastery perched above me. I marvelled that anyone could be inspired to undertake such a difficult construction in the days before cranes and heavy machinery.

Was this the sort of inspiration I was looking for? My experience of the last two weeks was of finding comfort in the simplicity of the daily routine, of having no time to think about anything but staying on the path, finding somewhere to sleep and washing my change of clothes—not even having to choose what to wear. I had rediscovered the pleasures of food, and of sleep that comes from exhaustion and leaves no room for rumination. The Camino existed on a different frequency to the rest of life—but part of me relished the difference, embraced it like a lost friend.

Le Puy was modern enough to have a *cybercafé*. I had been out of touch with my daughters—and Albie the accountant and the mess I had left him—for two weeks.

I was surprised at how long it seemed and how little I had missed home.

There were several emails from Lauren and Tessa—*Where are you? Are you okay?* Albie had sold the cars but the house might take a while. Camille wanted to know when I would be back—and had I met anyone interesting? If I needed help, I must call. *Promise me.*

I told Camille I was enjoying the walk and replied to the girls: doing fine, no need to worry. I had hit *send* before I realised I still hadn't told them about the Camino.

The hostel in Le Puy was bigger than any I had stayed in, and I was not alone. There was a photography student, Amaury, beginning a two-week project on the Chemin, and some Germans who had walked from Geneva on the Jakobsweg route. They would be back next year to do another two weeks. Four women I never saw had taken over the room beside the dormitory: Brazilians, the manager said, starting their Camino. They were at Mass—apparently, there were still religious *pèlerins*.

It was an early night for most of us but I had my first taste of communal sleeping. The Brazilians came in late and kept us awake with loud chatter until after midnight. Nevertheless, I felt a sense of being a part of something.

In the morning, I decided I would walk until my money ran out.

22
Martin

Thirteen days and 320 kilometres after leaving Cluny, I descended the winding road into Le Puy en Velay, home of green lentils and meeting point of three of the Chemin feeder routes, arriving only minutes before the tourist office closed for the day. I bought the thick *Miam Miam Dodo* guidebook for the five-week section to St Jean Pied de Port and discarded my orange booklet. Stage One down.

If my cart and I could survive this far, over the toughest terrain on the route, there was no reason we could not keep going for another sixty-six days. I was running to budget and there would be more hostels from here on if I needed to economise.

I had booked a mid-range hotel and felt out of place as I arrived in the mirrored foyer, with its reception desk and registration procedures. At the cheap hotels between Cluny and Le Puy they would throw me a key on arrival, and sort out the bill and a stamp on my *credencial* when I left. No passport required, cash preferred.

I contemplated my reflection. I had not shaved since the night of the Hot Rabbit. My walking trousers, tucked into heavy socks, were streaked with mud and the red mid-thigh-length jacket was looking less fresh. Scott of the Antarctic. The contrast with the businessman presenting his passport ahead of me could not have been more dramatic.

In my room, I showered in the pristine bathroom. A change into my cashmere vest and a finger-comb restored me to something like the engineering academic I had been two weeks earlier, but I kept the beard. After examining my feet and the remains of punctured blisters, I decided there was nothing to lose by taking Monsieur Chevalier's advice and investing in lighter boots.

The town was well served with outdoors shops—all of them closed on a Sunday afternoon.

Back in the hotel, I spent a while updating my blog, then headed out to dinner, expecting I would have a good range of eating options. The camping shops should have given me a clue: the streets were almost deserted. I used my phone to google restaurants. A long walk—relatively speaking, of course—brought me to a couscous restaurant which was open, but not for eating. 'The chef has gone to Spain.' They directed me to the competition on the other side of town, which was, unsurprisingly, full.

I joined a tall handsome woman, perhaps a little older than me, her short dark hair streaked with grey, to make a queue of two.

'English?' she asked. Did I have a Union Jack painted on my forehead?

I nodded.

'Good,' she said, with what I guessed was a Spanish or Italian accent. 'My French is terrible. Have you seen three women?'

I shook my head. 'Sorry.'

'They went to Mass. All of them. I'm Renata.' She shook my hand, firmly.

The maître d' waved us in as a couple departed. A table for four was not yet available, and I invited Renata to join me while she waited.

Her English was excellent, and we established that she and her missing friends—all Brazilian—were beginning the walk from Le Puy to St Jean Pied de Port the next day. She was from São Paulo, a historian. I liked her and hoped her friends didn't find the restaurant.

We had made a start on a carafe of red and a mezze platter when her fellow walkers arrived. There was a blur of introductions, dominated by a woman of about forty, platinum blonde in a tight white dress, bare legs and heels.

How far had I walked? From where? Carrying how much? My God, for three hundred kilometres! Her admiration was a bit disingenuous, given that she and her friends had eight hundred kilometres of their own to walk. But in the flirtation stakes, she would have had the Hot Rabbit for breakfast.

She invited me to join them, but they appeared to be gearing up for a big night and I was conscious of having a big day in front of me. My new guidebook warned that the stage from Le Puy to St Privat d'Allier was deceptively tough.

23
Zoe

The climb out of Le Puy was no big deal: I'd been doing hills like this for two weeks. But something had changed: the number of people. I was no longer the only carrier of a scallop shell—most of the walkers had real shells tied to their packs, some with painted red crosses or pictures of St James. I chatted with them before I powered past. There was a couple pushing a child in a stroller, a guy in running gear taking a break and a group of four with a dog. All on their first day. Many Europeans, I found, did two weeks at a time, starting from where they had left off the previous year. None I met were going as far as St Jean Pied de Port. Four days earlier I had sensed that I had graduated to another level of fitness, and that feeling had not gone away. I hadn't bothered getting a guidebook—I'd done okay without one so far.

Keith would never have taken on the Camino. Aside from business—and, it now seemed, money—having gotten in the way of vacation plans, he wouldn't have seen the point. Too much walking; not enough famous sights.

The Camino was more me. Not the physical me, whose hardest exercise back home was yoga. But being in the moment, having space and peace, taking each day as it came. I didn't want the *autoroute* of pilgrims I had heard about in the tourist office in Cluny, but neither did I want to be alone all the time. Now it looked like I would have company, and it would be good to meet a bunch of different people.

The walking got tougher. The Camino route was following the GR65 trail, and its red and white bars painted on trees and posts had mainly replaced the scallop shells. I missed the sense of being guided by the saint's spirit. After the screw-up in Montarcher, I was wary of tracks overlapping then separating, and kept a lookout for the occasional scallop.

My work was rewarded with spectacular views across the valleys to rolling hills. I rested for half an hour. After the break, the muscles in my legs and shoulders seized up. All day, my senses had been directed outwards, and I'd forgotten to be mindful of my body. Some yoga stretches helped, but then my feet started to hurt. I was moving at maybe half the pace I'd started at. *Long is a mile to he who is tired*, said the Buddha.

In mid-afternoon, the sky turned to fierce shades of grey and black, and the sun's rays illuminated my destination for the night: the hilltop town of St Privat d'Allier. *Hilltop* meaning *climb*. It was thankfully short.

As usual, the church dominated, in this case a formidable structure with what must once have been a monastery. The word at the hostel in Le Puy was that there were plenty of beds and I passed two *gîtes* on my way to the tourist office to find out which was cheapest.

I had forgotten it was Monday: the office was closed. In the main street was a bar that advertised rooms. I stepped inside and, sitting alone at a table, laptop open with a cup of coffee beside it, was the Buggy Man. The *Englishman*.

He now had a light beard. He looked more like a walker, rather than the hunter I had once imagined him. Not an unattractive look—but out of all the pilgrims now on the trail, why him?

The Camino changes you, Monsieur Chevalier had said. Maybe the Buggy Man was working on his personality. He *had* saved me from walking an extra twelve miles and I hadn't thanked him. I could at least show him I was civil.

24
Martin

Zoe stopped when she saw me. Our last encounter in the snow had been chilly, but I was prepared to put it down to her being embarrassed at getting lost and annoyed at having to retrace her steps. I'd have felt the same.

We hadn't got off to a great start back in Cluny. Her collusion with Bernhard in taking advantage of local generosity had not advanced her cause, but we couldn't have exchanged more than a dozen words. I should at least give her a chance to speak for herself.

I beckoned her over and she stood, still wearing her backpack, looking like she'd done a hard day.

'*Bonjour,*' she said. That one word was laced with enough sarcasm to support a longer statement: Thanks for letting me assume you were French when I might have felt a bit less lonely on the trail if I knew there was a well-informed fellow walker of roughly my own age who spoke my language.

I kept it light. 'Lost again?'

'Screw you.' She turned around.

'Hey, where are you going?'

'To McDonald's for a burger and a shake. Where do you think I'm going?'

'I imagine you're planning to walk around until you work out what I can tell you now. Only one hostel open and it's full.'

'And you know that how?'

'I've got a guidebook. Quite useful. I'd recommend it.'

'This café . . .'

'Hasn't got around to updating the sign.'

'I'm sure there's something.'

'I suppose every village has some lonely old chap . . .'

Even as I spoke the words, I regretted them, not just because it was a crass thing to say, but because at that moment I stopped believing Bernhard's story. Zoe's face was a combination of anger and mortification. Whatever had gone down, it hadn't happened the way Bernhard described it. For a moment, I thought she was going to burst into tears, but anger won.

'You conceited . . . prick. *You're* telling *me*—who

was it sending messages that he wanted to share a room with me, no charge, just . . .' This time, she was the one who trailed off. 'The little shit.'

Neither or us said anything for a few moments as I, and presumably she, reflected on how much of what we knew about each other had come from Bernhard.

Zoe looked down at me. 'Just to be completely clear, did you or did you not suggest we share a room in a bed and breakfast—on your dime?'

I looked straight back. 'No. I didn't. Bernhard said you were paying.' It took her a moment to realise I was joking. I offered a friendly grin to confirm it.

'You are on thin ice,' she said, but she took off her pack and sat down. 'I'll have a coffee. Where are you staying, then?'

'I'm not. I'm moving on. The hotel across the road is supposed to open at 6 p.m. but it's a Monday. I don't want to walk in the dark if it doesn't.' I had called ahead to Rochegude, the next village, and confirmed the hostel was open. The stretch was classified as steep and rough, but I would make it before sundown.

'I'm not walking any more today,' she said. 'If the hotel doesn't open, I'll try the hostel—the one that's full. I figure they'll make space.'

'And if not?'

'You know, one thing I've learned in life is that sometimes you have to trust fate.'

'If it's on your side. Otherwise, you're glad you packed a tent.'

She laughed. Paused. 'Did I get your room at Grosbois?'

'I assume so. Sorry I was a bit taciturn.'

'A *bit*?'

'I was stuffed.'

'The owner said you hadn't eaten.'

'*Stuffed* meaning *exhausted*. I appreciated the food. You don't draw, do you?'

'Sometimes.'

'I saw the sketch you left. You know what you're doing.'

'Thanks. The owner showed it to you?'

'No, he let me use your room for a shower. It was still there.'

'I could have told Bernhard we'd shared a room already.' She grinned.

'Do you still want that coffee or can I get you a beer—or a wine?'

'Beer's good. And you could tell me your name.'

'Martin. You didn't know?'

'A few days ago, I thought you were French. And a shoplifter. I'm guessing you're not.'

'Why? Because I'm an Englishman named Martin?'

'No, because I've been wrong about everything else so far.'

I fetched two beers, and she said, 'That'll give you a lift for the last stage.'

I drank half my glass in two swigs. 'I'll take a chance on the hotel.'

Six o'clock came around quickly. With a second beer down and the sun about to follow it, there was no sign of the proprietor. Zoe was right: the hostel could probably be persuaded to provide a place on the floor, and I always had my tent.

Our conversation hadn't departed much from the Camino, and I sensed she had also missed having someone to talk to. On my blog I was focused on delivering a commercial message, and my chats with Bernhard had suffered from me trying to hold my tongue and him looking for openings to score a point. I'd sent only a couple of bland emails to Sarah and her replies had been similarly brief.

Across the road, a van pulled up. I settled the bill and caught the proprietor as he was unlocking the door.

'The hotel is open?' I asked in French.

'*Bien sûr, monsieur et madame.*'

We were fortunate, he explained, as there was just one room remaining.

'Only one room left, apparently,' I said to Zoe. Shit—it sounded like I was making it up, following Bernhard's script. I held one finger up: 'Only one?'

Zoe laughed. 'That's what he said.'

'It's okay, you take it,' I said.

'We can share and toss a coin for the sofa.'

'You sure? But you can have the bed. I've got a sleeping mat.'

'I'm not going to argue.'

'Why don't you have a shower and I'll get some drinks? What's your poison?'

I mentally kicked myself. A fellow walker had generously offered to share her room, and I'd responded by sounding like a lounge lizard.

'Another beer or a glass of white wine would be great. I'm not much of a drinker.'

I was giving the room key to Zoe when Renata, the tall woman from the restaurant in Le Puy, walked in, again the advance guard. She looked more wrung-out than Zoe had done. Day One. The veteran and I exchanged knowing smiles.

Zoe headed upstairs and, in response to Renata's raised eyebrows at the single key, I explained that we were sharing only because of room availability.

The remaining Brazilians arrived a few minutes later. The blonde woman who had flirted with me the previous night had exchanged her dress for unusually tight walking pants, but not lost the makeup. They headed upstairs and were back, changed, before Zoe had reappeared.

Blondie, in the short dress again, was apparently in charge of the social programme.

'We are in France. We drink Ricard!' No point explaining that we might be in France but we were not in Marseille.

She slipped behind the bar. The proprietor came running over.

'Tell him it's okay, we buy the whole bottle.'

Monsieur was not convinced that this was a good idea. But he had his hands full.

'How much?' I asked him, quietly, in French.

'For the bottle, fifty euros,' he said. 'This is not a super-market.'

'Sixty euros,' I said to Blondie. '*Sessenta.*' I suspected the proprietor would have earned the tip by the end of the night. She had him take a photo of the group—on all of our cameras and phones—with the two of us front and centre, arms around each other.

She poured five glasses. One of the women—about the same age but the polar opposite in grooming and manner—made an attempt at refusal, but Blondie was brooking no party poopers.

25
Zoe

After a long soak in the bath I felt like a new woman; the beer may have helped. It had also mellowed me toward Martin. I figured that his attitude was just a national trait. I made use of the tub of water to wash all my clothes, and it was only as I began putting my underwear out to dry that I remembered I would be sharing the room. I put it all on one radiator and draped my coat on top. I could uncover it when Martin went to sleep. And try to wake up before him.

When I made it downstairs, four women were in the bar. One, dressed for a party in a tight white dress and bare legs, was almost in Martin's lap. He stood up, quickly. 'Have some Pernod,' he said, taking a bottle from Party Girl and pouring me a glass. It was the stuff I had seen bereted men drinking in bars at

11 a.m. The aniseed smell was strong enough to knock me out. A conservative-looking woman was looking at her glass like Alice contemplating the Drink Me bottle.

I took a sip and felt the alcohol burn. I held the key out to Martin.

'I've got it sorted,' he said. 'The room's all yours.'

Party Girl was smiling. Right.

'I am Margarida,' she said as Martin walked away, I guessed in embarrassment. 'Like the cocktail, only with a *d*.' Her mother must have been given a sign when she named her. 'Fabiana and I will share.'

I should have remembered that stereotypical British-ishness included being a gentleman.

While Martin was upstairs, I introduced myself to the other women. I figured they were the Brazilians who had kept me awake at the hostel in Le Puy. The tall woman, with a bone structure like Grace Jones, was Renata. The conservative—pious—looking one was Fabiana. She seemed to have decided the Pernod was safe to drink.

The group leader was Paola, a motherly woman of maybe fifty who organised a private tour each year on a section of the Camino. After reaching St Jean Pied de Port, she was going to take a three-week break before leading a second walk from somewhere in Spain to Santiago. Her three customers planned to rejoin her, along with her teenage daughter.

Paola had a wealth of knowledge but needed a lesson from Nicole the Australian—the pack sitting at her feet looked bigger than the one I had started out with.

'My knees are not good,' she said.

'I can't help with knees,' I said. 'But I do feet and shoulder massages.'

'How much?' Paola asked.

I took a breath. 'Five euros for ten minutes of either, seven for fifteen minutes of both combined.'

Keith would have fallen over if he'd heard me.

Margarida told me that they were all taking the *pèlerin* menu. I was welcome to join them. Chicken and pasta. As I dug my fingers into Paola's shoulders, the barman hauled her pack upstairs.

I was finishing Margarida's feet when Fabiana walked over. Margarida refilled her glass from the bottle beside her.

'Do you think this is okay for pilgrims?' Fabiana asked me.

I wasn't sure if she was talking about the drink or the massage.

'I think,' I said, 'that the ancient pilgrims would have taken what was offered.' Margarida added that if her feet were no good then there would be no pilgrimage. It got me another five euros.

Massaging someone, even if it's only their feet, creates a connection. I sensed that Fabiana was carrying a lot of emotional baggage, perhaps guilt. Margarida was closed, shutting me out of her space. I didn't find their energy totally negative, but a little at a time would be enough.

If there were enough pilgrims around with sore feet, I could finance my way to St Jean Pied de Port—and feel good about how I was doing it.

Then Bernhard arrived.

'Zoe! You and Martin?' He must have seen the cart. 'I will have a massage too.'

'Twenty euros,' I said. 'Per foot.'

Martin was unpacking his cart when I came downstairs after cleaning up from the massages—and rearranging my drying clothes. The Aspen jacket now had brown stripes on the inside. 'Bernhard's eating with the Brazilians. The other side of the restaurant looks good to me.'

Martin had spoken to Renata in Le Puy, but didn't know the other women's names. He didn't need to point to them.

'Bashful,' he said.

'I was thinking Pious. That'll be Fabiana.'

'Mama.'

'Too easy. Paola. She's in charge.'

Martin hesitated a moment as if he'd forgotten Party Girl. 'The other one.'

'Camino Barbie?'

Martin laughed.

'Margarida,' I said.

'Wine?'

I'd already had a beer and the glass of Pernod. I'd only earned nineteen euros, and had a hotel room to pay for. I shook my head.

'My shout. Treat. I insist. You made the right call, waiting for the hotel.'

I ordered salad and French fries—*frites.* Martin ordered duck. And a bottle of local wine. It was good: I could see myself getting used to it. Not such a great lesson to take home from the Camino.

'So,' said Martin, 'the most important thing you haven't told me about your walk is why you're doing it. Besides the call of the scallop shell. Why are you in France?'

'Don't underestimate fate.'

Martin raised an eyebrow.

'Look,' I said, 'there are plenty of people in the

world who believe our destiny is in the hands of some old white guy sitting above us dealing out rewards and punishment like . . . some old white guy. What I believe makes more sense than that. Some things are meant to be. Fate, destiny, karma—whatever you want to call it. The universe has plans—we just aren't smart enough to know how it works.'

'So why do you think fate sent you on this journey?'

'My husband died. Suddenly. Five weeks ago.'

'Christ. I'm so sorry.'

I felt a sudden wave of emotion. I looked away and took a gulp of wine.

'I haven't really confronted it yet.'

'A lot people walk the Camino to grieve,' he said after a moment. 'You've got a long way to go yet.'

'I'm only going to the border.'

'Still a long way.'

Dinner arrived. My hot goat-cheese salad had a heap of greens—topped with bacon bits. I drank more wine and unloaded the bacon into my paper napkin. Reluctantly. The *chèvre* was the best I'd ever had.

Martin explained his relationship with Jim the realtor and asked how I knew Camille.

'We were roommates at college in St Louis,' I said. 'I was studying art and she was doing languages; she'd already done a year in Japan.'

'And you got on—connected?'

'Actually, I didn't like her at first. She was crazy—a total drama queen—and men ran after her anyway. Sharing a room was like living in the eye of a tornado: moments of calm but then you knew the storm would move and . . .'

He laughed. 'So, what happened?'

'She got into trouble.' I was back there, picturing my roommate's face, the beautiful, confident, sophisticated European sobbing like a child. I had realised what an act it had all been.

'She was in love. But he dumped her. The *crétin*—that's what we called him. In the end, we both dropped out. She went back to France, and I got married and had children.'

'But you helped her?'

'She . . . couldn't handle the picket line. There was a lot of pro-life activism happening in St Louis. She freaked out, and in the end the only physician I could convince her to trust was out of town, so I took her there.'

Bernhard and Margarida were laughing loudly across the room.

'What about you?' I asked him. 'What do you think about in all your quiet time?'

'How far to the next village; whether it's going to rain; where I'm going to eat.'

If I hadn't been walking the Camino myself I'd have thought he was avoiding the question, but truth was, I spent a heap of time thinking about everyday stuff.

'So, what are you trying to leave behind?' It was an instinctive question. I'd drunk a lot of wine.

Martin looked surprised, then shrugged. 'Done that already. No problem with Cluny, but . . . time to do something different.'

Now he was holding back. I sensed he was hiding a lot of pain. But he wasn't going to share anything emotional. Typical man. Typical *fucking* man.

I closed my eyes and felt my anger giving way to an overwhelming sadness. 'Excuse me.' I got up and went to the restroom. And fell apart.

Great sobs heaved through my body and the tears didn't want to stop. When I heard someone outside—there was only one stall—I forced myself to concentrate on my breathing until I was calm enough to walk out.

When I did, I found Martin standing there, looking concerned and kind, and that started it again. He put both of his arms around me, gently, surely trying to be caring. I couldn't deal with it. I pulled away, said, 'I'm sorry—I've just had too much to drink,' and fled upstairs.

26
Martin

Thank God—or Renata—I had my own room. I'd have pitched my tent rather than follow Zoe upstairs after making such a fool of myself. 'I've had too much to drink,' she says, and Martin—*What's your poison, baby?*—moves in. That must surely have been how it looked to her.

I waited for her in the morning, apology and explanation ready, but she didn't appear. The proprietor told me she had skipped breakfast—and town. She couldn't have made it any clearer that she wanted to put distance between me and her. Half of me wanted to set things right: I'd enjoyed the chat, and had felt we were on the way to some companionable walking and perhaps meals together. The other half was relieved to escape the complications.

The twenty kilometres to Saugues included the hardest climb so far: five hundred metres over just a few kilometres. My guidebook had a story that the postman at Saugues used to wait at the entrance to the town with cardboard boxes for the pilgrims to fill with all the kit they'd decided to send home.

Steep ascents were the cart's *bête noire*—or at least mine. Rough terrain, even snow and ice, it handled well, but climbing was like pulling a plough. I took it in fifty-metre bites, watching the GPS register each metre of elevation until I could stop for five minutes, sip some water and regroup. Even with the thermometer on my jacket zip showing six degrees, I was down to just a T-shirt.

Shortly after noon, I reached the top of the final crest and looked back over the valley. Someone had provided a bench to sit on. I waited a few minutes for my breathing to steady, drank some water and surveyed the path ahead, looking for a white jacket. I couldn't see anyone, and a cold wind chilled the sweat and had me reaching for my fleece.

I arrived in Saugues mid-afternoon, propped at the first bar and settled down to watch the pilgrims arrive. I was about to leave when Renata appeared—alone, again. She was happy to share a beer and a can of olives.

'How did you find the climb?' I asked.

'Not bad. I have been training for three months. The others, not so much. And I am carrying only this.' She indicated her daypack. 'The taxi carries our packs. After the first day, the others agreed to it. It was a democratic decision.' Democratic but not unanimous, said her expression.

'Where are the others?'

'They walked past while you were getting the drinks. Anyway, tell me about your . . .'

'Cart? It's a long story.'

'I like long stories. You can tell me at dinner.'

I suppose some men would have prepared for the first time they had been asked out by a woman with a visit to the local tailor. Instead, I went looking for hiking boots. I found an outdoor-equipment shop, well located to serve those who needed to review their kit after two days on the track.

The moment my feet slipped into a pair of Gore-Tex hiking shoes, I knew that I would never wear my heavy boots again. As I was paying, I spotted a familiar pack behind the counter, or at least a familiar design: the 2010 French football debacle souvenir. I slipped my glasses on and had a closer look. It was obviously not new. Too much of a coincidence.

'Tell me, what is that backpack?' I asked in French.

It was not a smart move. My English accent must have been obvious. The moustachioed man serving me whisked it away and made it apparent that no further enquiries would be entertained. I tried anyway.

'Was there a woman?'

He wasn't having any of it. He handed me my credit card and receipt, and didn't bother putting the boots in a bag.

Had Zoe thrown in the towel and sold her gear to buy a bus fare back to Cluny? Had revisiting memories of her late husband, perhaps confronting them for the first time after literally running away, been too much? Or, worse, had it been my clumsy effort at comforting her?

Thoughts along these lines persisted through an otherwise delightful dinner with Renata. She ate meat, worked for a living and was a paid-up atheist. She had no children and had recently ended a long-term relationship. They had split the assets without recourse to lawyers and remained friends. She had prepared for the walk.

'I was worried I would not keep up with the younger people, but it is they who cannot keep up with me.'

'You seem to be doing this almost by yourself.'

'A little. But I did not want the effort of planning.'

She was not keen to discuss her companions, and I respected her discretion. Instead we talked about the history of the walk, and its connection to her research at the University of São Paulo on the current relationships between South America and the colonising countries.

'Where are the others eating tonight?' I asked.

'I don't know. I didn't tell them either.' She smiled.

I walked her back to her hotel, and she kissed me goodnight, reasonably chastely, but not before telling me that they would be stopping in St Alban sur Limagnole the following night and then Lasbros. I had resumed booking in advance, and had the same itinerary.

In three weeks on the Chemin, I'd had three dinners with interesting women: Renata, Zoe, and Aude, the Hot Rabbit. It occurred to me that Monsieur Chevalier's multiple pilgrimages might not have been entirely for religious reasons.

It was only 9 p.m. so I went looking for Zoe. The municipal *gîte* was closed and the private hostel had locked up. If she had decided to abandon the walk, as I was now feeling must be the case, she had no reason to hang around.

27

Zoe

A tough day's walk into Saugues helped take my mind off the previous evening. I had breakfast in a bar at the bottom of a cliff where I could see the trail ahead switchbacking up. I sat for a while wondering why I was doing it—I didn't have to keep walking just because I could afford to. I thought of my daughters, of the familiarity of home. Of talking over last night's debacle with my girlfriends and letting the rawness heal.

I rubbed my scallop-shell charm and Keith's gold heart touched my fingers. Was it trying to tell me something I didn't want to hear?

Meanwhile, the universe was giving me a less subtle message. The wind was bitterly cold, and my hands were in danger of freezing. Ahead of me was the Aubrac plain, likely to be colder still. I needed gloves—proper gloves—before I could walk on. Or I could call it quits, maybe sell my gear, and take a bus to Paris.

The climb into Saugues felt like an ending, and I began to imagine myself tucked into a seat on the plane home. Then, walking down the main street, I saw a camping store. The message couldn't have been clearer.

I was waiting in line, starting to have doubts about whether they'd want any of my stuff, when a guy behind me shrieked.

'*Horreur!*'

I dove to the floor—I didn't have time to think how unlikely it was that a terrorist would target Saugues. The employees looked at me in bewilderment as I got up. The negative energy from last night's experience must have left me more unsettled than I had realised. The weapon that had unleashed the horror seemed to be my backpack.

'*Je suis désolée,*' I said—sorry—though I probably didn't sound it. '*Je suis un pèlerin et le pack libre . . . gratuit.*' Free. So, get over yourselves. Did this team have *any* fans?

Three staff had an animated conversation and one, an older guy with a moustache, smiled.

'*Madame,* we have a backpack for you. Superior.'

His colleagues disappeared into the back room and returned with a pack.

It looked similar in size, grey and red, with a burn mark on the top flap. They were safety-pinning a miniature American flag over it.

'I don't need another pack,' I said. 'I need . . . I need gloves.'

'Also, gloves!' He grabbed a pair from the table.

The private hostel was a home with rooms leading off each other and a clothesline across the back garden. Amaury, the photographer I'd met in Le Puy, was there and he went out to take shots of the town, after a massage. We managed a basic conversation—my French was getting better—and decided that the best hostel options for the next day were in St Alban sur Limagnole, twenty-seven kilometres away. It would be my longest day so far.

There was also a Swiss woman, Heike, in her fifties. She was walking with her partner, Monika, who was hitchhiking back to their starting point to collect their mobile home. Their plan was to walk to the destination, then take turns to hitchhike back and retrieve the vehicle. They wanted to avoid hassles from pilgrims or hostel staff in rural France taking the Catholic line on their relationship. No problem so far, but it was only Day Two. The hostel was for dinner and companionship.

The Brazilians never showed. They seemed to be using a variety of lodgings. Martin might be seeing more of them than I was.

I had learned that there were three types of mud: sticky, sucking and slippery. Walking to St Alban sur Limagnole, I got all three. It was almost impossible to rid the bottom of my shoe of the two- to three-inch layer without getting the other foot stuck or falling on my butt.

I caught up with Fabiana and Margarida an hour into the day. Both had taken their boots off and Margarida was laying on the ground out of the wind behind a stone fence—under an umbrella.

'Gringa!' Margarida said. 'How ya doin'?'

'Good,' I said, meaning it. 'Where are the others?'

'Renata is ahead,' said Margarida. 'Always.'

'And Paola?'

'Bad knee,' said Fabiana. 'She meets us in the next town.'

I walked on, secretly pleased that I didn't need to stop. I was eating way more food than usual, but maybe not enough protein. My clothes were loose and I felt fitter than I'd ever been.

I tried to figure out why I had fallen apart at dinner with Martin. I guessed he'd seen my tears as female weakness, which was annoying—I didn't cry often. Not even at the funeral. I'd got stuck on how the minister Keith's mother had insisted on had not captured anything about him. Though not as badly as the pastor had messed up my mother's funeral.

My mother. I could never understand how my mother could disown her daughter for the sin of caring for someone else. It still ate away at me.

As I reached the top of another hill I was greeted with clapping. A barrel-chested man about my age and height was sitting on a rock, backpack beside him.

'Well done, honey. That was one big mother.'

'Honey?'

The American grinned. 'Stars and stripes on your backpack. First person from home I've seen. Ed Walker from Houston. Name is destiny, right?'

Huh?

'Walker. Should be Dead Walker. One more of those hills and I may be.'

'Zoe Witt,' I said. 'Not much destiny there.' If there had been, I might have thought of a witty response to 'honey'. 'I used to be Waites, but I didn't do too much of that. I got married at twenty—so I was Rosales for a while.'

'Bed of roses?'

'Not exactly.'

'Nor was mine . . . Took off, and took the money and the kids with her. Now I've taken off.'

'How old are your kids?'

'Ten and . . . You don't approve, do you?'

'Not my business.'

'Thought I might learn something about myself on this walk. So far all I've learned is I hate walking. So, teach me something. Tell me what you're thinking.'

He asked for it. 'Kids need their parents. Both of them.' I almost added, 'Which is why I gave up a man I loved,' but stopped myself in time. Where had that come from? Was it even true? Instead I said, 'Children blame themselves for everything that goes wrong.'

'You think I walked out on them?'

'Doesn't matter what I think. That's what they'll think.'

'I should go home?'

'How often do you call them?'

'I've only been walking three days. What do you think of the food? Supposed to be the best in the world. Not so far, it isn't.'

'We're not exactly in Paris.'

He laughed. 'We're up high. Edge of the Aubrac plain. Did they tell you it gets snowed in?'

We both scanned the sky: no signs of a change in weather. But it was a reminder to get moving.

The terrain had changed. Between the pine forests, there were now broad plains traversed by powerlines. I needed the gloves. With my hands out of my pockets, I could use my arms for balance as I crossed the slippery terrain.

St Alban sur Limagnole was built around a château that was now a psychiatric facility. The hostel was down the hill, attached to a hotel. Church bells welcomed me.

Paola, Renata and Heike were already there. I offered to cook and Paola insisted on buying the groceries.

An hour later, I had a pot of vegetarian chilli simmering. Monika, the other half of the Swiss couple, showed up with the mobile home and two bottles of wine.

Bernhard arrived and I sent him out for more beans.

Three others joined in: two elderly French sisters and an Italian man with a bad hip. His priest had told him that cycling the Camino was not enough penance for some domestic sin, and he was repeating it on foot from Le Puy. He wasn't seeing much of his wife—maybe that had been the priest's intention.

While the chilli bubbled, I switched from cook to masseuse. Margarida, both sisters and the Italian hip-man lined up. Bernhard hovered as I did Margarida's shoulders. Fabiana went to Mass.

Someone had set the table with an array of mismatched plates, and Margarida plugged her iPhone into the hostel's boom box. Our appetiser of nachos smothered in guacamole was eaten to the sounds of what I guessed was Brazilian rap. By the time the chilli hit the table the music was more like reggae and we were all—Fabiana included—bopping along.

As we started on the chilli, the group fell silent. Heike and Monika were sweating. The French sisters were gulping water between mouthfuls.

'Have I made it too hot?' I asked.

'No, no,' said the Italian man.

'This is not hot,' said Bernhard. 'In fact, it is . . . weak.'

'You're right,' I said. 'Anyone beside Bernhard want more before I spice it up?'

The Brazilians were up for the hot version.

I retrieved the packet of chilli peppers that had already rescued a couple meals from blandness (Zoe's Camino lesson: pack peppers), and crushed a dozen into what remained in the pot. I put it back on the table and helped myself.

At my local Mexican, it might have scored three red-chilli symbols. Bernhard took one mouthful and his eyes bugged out of his head. He gulped water, then went to the kitchen, returning with a full bottle of milk. Then, as everyone watched, Bernhard ate the whole plateful, and drank most of the bottle of milk, tears running down his face. The Brazilians seemed to enjoy the food and the show as much as I did.

28
Martin

I caught the unmistakable aroma of Central or South American food as I came downstairs to dinner. Seated in the dining room, I realised it was coming not from the hotel kitchen but from the adjacent dormitory. On the blackboard, the sole offering for tonight's sole guest was lentils and sausage—fine, if I couldn't smell the alternative.

With a bottle of Kronenberg and my computer for company, I worked on my blog. There was only so much to say about the cart each day and I had been making my posts a little more personal. Likewise, the comments back were increasingly focused on my journey. The major Camino website had added a link.

As the proprietor-waiter-chef was bringing my bill,

a second guest bowled in, a stocky, balding chap of perhaps forty.

'Cognac—double,' he said in American-accented English as he intercepted our man. He raised two fingers to translate the second word, then added '*merci*', thankfully not calling him *garçon*.

The result was two individual cognacs.

'I think he took double to mean two glasses,' I said.

'I figured that. Hey, buddy—you're Australian?'

'English.'

'Near enough. Ed Walker from Houston, Texas. Name is destiny, right? Should be Dead Walker. You been walking too?'

I nodded. 'Martin Eden from Sheffield.'

'Famous name there.'

'More in the US than the UK,' I said. Only Americans and literary types knew the Jack London novel.

'The American dream. Start from nothing, work your way up.'

'My parents didn't know it. Any name but Anthony, as far as my dad was concerned.'

'There's some problem with Tony?'

'Anthony Eden. Tory prime minister.'

I may as well have been speaking French.

'You want this?' he said.

I smiled and he passed me the second cognac. 'You having dinner?' I asked.

'I ate already. Burger in my room. Had to make some calls.'

'They made you a burger?'

'I just kept saying "hamburger", and he kept showing me the menu in French, and in the end I won.'

I hoped he didn't take this single experience as representative of the French approach to commerce.

'You walked from Le Puy?' he asked.

'Cluny. I've been walking eighteen days. About two hundred and fifty miles.'

'Jesus.'

I let his response run over me for a few moments, basking in it. 'What about you?'

'Le Puy.'

'Going to?'

'St Alban sur Limagnole. Here. The end of the line.' He raised two fingers again to the proprietor, who brought the half-full bottle over and left it on the table.

'I thought I'd do this to find myself. Don't say anything. I know what that sounds like. But I had a crappy divorce and I figured some time out would be a smart thing to do.'

'But you're stopping?'

'Like I said, I wanted to work out who I was, what I wanted. Took me three days.'

'If it's not a rude question, what did you learn?'

'Not rude at all. I learned I don't want to bust my balls for no reason, I don't like being alone, I like to work with my head not my legs.' He took a sip of his Cognac. 'And I've been an asshole to my kids since the divorce, and I'm gonna go back and do something about it instead of wandering in the fucking wilderness.'

He topped up our glasses. 'You been married?'

We finished the bottle. The proprietor had gone. It would have been a good time to stop, but Ed commandeered a half-full bottle of *eau de vie de framboise* from behind the bar, leaving two fifty-euro notes in its place. Spending like a drunken sailor on his last day of leave.

We finished it about 1 a.m.—a very late night for me on the Camino—and staggered up the stairs singing 'Shiver Me Timbers', Tom Waits and Joe Cocker on a bender.

I forced myself to drink two big glasses of water before collapsing, clothed, on the bed.

The twenty-three kilometres to Lasbros the next day was tougher than the thirty-nine I had done on my first day. I didn't just feel hungover: I felt poisoned. My conversation with Ed about divorce and kids had dragged up some stuff that was still running around in my thumping head, so I had that to deal with too.

I didn't need a night of partying with the Brazilians. I cancelled my room, bought some bread and cold chicken in Aumont Aubrac, and pushed on another five kilometres before pitching my tent and crashing.

In the morning, I got up late and walked the remaining two kilometres to Lasbros, where the hostel owner let me make coffee and toast, and checked the weather. A twenty percent chance of snow in the afternoon. Eighty percent tomorrow. I had planned to stop in Nasbinals, leaving the seven kilometres of exposed plain until the following day, but it made sense to knock it over before it became impassable.

A night in the fresh air had cured the hangover. In Nasbinals, which was probably a pretty town when they weren't doing roadworks, I bought a roll and sat on a bench contemplating the weather. It wasn't looking great, but it was only going to get worse if I hung about.

29
Zoe

'You are finishing here today, I hope,' said Paola, as I slid my pack off.

The Brazilians and I had stayed in different hostels the previous night in Lasbros, but I had shared a glass of mulled wine in front of a roaring fire with the Swiss women, given them both massages and had a good night's sleep.

After arriving in Nasbinals, I spent an hour in the tourist office looking at the maps showing ancient paths from all over Europe to Santiago. Including mine. Buzzing with positive energy, I set off to the hostel but Margarida ran out of the bar and pulled me in.

The Brazilians had pushed tables together and there were other familiar faces: Heike and Monika, Bernhard, Amaury the photographer.

'The next section is the tough bit, right?' I said.

'Someone got lost on the Aubrac plain last year,' Amaury said. 'They had to send a search party.'

'How old was he?' said Bernhard. 'It is only nine kilometres.'

'In bad weather it's difficult for anyone, experienced or inexperienced,' said Paola. 'Unfortunately, we have bad weather coming. Tomorrow we take a taxi.'

Her tone said: *no argument.*

Bernhard was tone deaf. 'Renata will walk with me. And Zoe, if she is not afraid.'

'No one in my group walks unless I say it is safe.'

Though I was no zealot—and I was learning that there were many on the Camino—it felt wrong to get a taxi, perhaps because I had walked this far without using one. I could hole up until the weather cleared but that would add cost and put me behind my companions. Or should I trust Bernhard's judgment over Paola's?

Margarida brought me a 'special beer' and I was greeted with the taste of blueberries. It was different, but good. As I took a second sip, I saw Martin outside, poles in one hand while he ate a piece of bread with the other. It seemed he was walking on. I jumped up. 'I might try and do it tonight before the snow,' I said, and rummaged in my jacket to find money for the beer.

I looked up just in time to catch Bernhard mimicking my action, half jumping from his chair with his tongue out like a puppy dog.

'Screw you, asshole,' I said. 'If you want to hang out with grown-ups, grow up.'

Bernhard smiled and looked around for support: *she's snapped and I'm staying cool.*

I could fix that. By the time I hoisted my pack and walked to the door he was struggling to find obscenities to scream at me. And I was still shaking when, a minute later, panting, I caught up with Martin.

30
Martin

I was more than surprised to see Zoe: I'd resigned myself to the conclusion that she'd given up in Saugues. And, after the awkwardness in St Privat d'Allier, I certainly hadn't thought that she would be looking to me for emotional support again.

But even as she asked if it would be okay to walk with me, I could see there was something wrong.

'Are you all right?'

'Not really. I just emptied Bernhard's pack on the floor and poured a blueberry beer over it all. He was a bit upset.'

'A *bit*? You're sounding like an Englishman. *Bernhard may have been a little put out.*'

She started laughing, almost hysterically, at my lame impression of an upper-class twit, stopping occasionally to add detail that set her—and me—off again. His sleeping bag soaked in beer, him snatching away the porn magazine, stuffing it back in his pack and then realising that there were things still inside that he'd now made beery.

We were half a kilometre out of town before we both calmed down.

'I'm losing it,' she said. 'He's just a kid. And back in the restaurant in St Privat . . .'

'I owe you an apology . . .'

'*You* owe *me*? I don't think so. You were just trying . . .'

'I was a klutz. You'd just told me about your husband, and I was a bit wrong-footed . . .'

'I think there's something wrong with me. It's almost six weeks since he died and I've hardly cried.'

'You don't have to explain that to an Englishman.'

'Stiff upper lip, right?'

'You put a lid on it and after a while it breaks through when you're not expecting it.'

'I wasn't trying to put a lid on it. I'm Californian. We talk it through.'

'You haven't had anyone to talk it through with.'

'I did have . . . my friend Camille. But . . .'

'You walked away. Maybe there's something you're not ready to deal with. Yet.'

She didn't ask me to elaborate. Fortunately. I was at the limit of my psychoanalytic abilities, and there were more immediate matters to attend to.

'Do you have a smartphone?' I asked.

'Sorry, why?'

'Wanted to check the weather. My battery died; I was in the tent last night and couldn't charge it.'

'You want to go back?'

'No. I think this weather app just spins a wheel every hour anyway. Last time I looked it said thirty percent chance of snow. It's not snowing now and every kilometre without snow is one more down. But I'll go back with you if you're not comfortable.'

'I'll come with you. Thank you.'

31
Zoe

At first, the track looked no different than others I had walked, and there were just a few patches of snow at the side, but it soon took us high into the hills. On the ridges, we were at the mercy of a wind that seemed to be coming from the Arctic and threatened not just to chill us but to knock us off our feet.

A weathered scallop shell on a post directed us across wet muddy fields where progress was slow and there was no clear path or anywhere to paint or hang the markers. Martin was checking his GPS a lot.

As we passed Martin's cart over a fence, my foot slipped and my ankle twisted. I stepped carefully and it took my weight.

'Sorry,' he said. 'I usually strap it on my back to do that. We'll be sitting beside a fire in a couple of hours.'

Then the snow started. The large white flakes were pretty and a little magical at first, but within minutes our visibility was down to a few feet. My nose, which had been cold, was now alternating between pain and numbness. I tried to bury my head in the fluff of my hood—not so easy when I needed to see what my feet were landing on, and where I was going, even if the chance of seeing a scallop shell in the blizzard was next to zilch. The wind whistled past my ears.

Martin had somehow turned his hat into a ski mask. He had the GPS in his hand all the time now, and gave me a thumbs-up as he pointed ahead, then spoke into my ear, over the noise of the wind. His breath was re-assuringly warm.

'There's a hut ahead. About half a kilometre. Keep your eyes open.'

It was hard to do with snow blowing right at us, but I couldn't afford to lose sight of Martin. It had been years since snow had been a part of my winters, and on days like this we had stayed indoors—and I was a town kid, not used to snow in the middle of nowhere. This kind of weather was an annual event in North America and featured in the news regularly. Blizzards that killed people. For the first time in my life, I felt the malevolent force of nature up close—and it was terrifying how insignificant and small I felt.

Every story I'd ever seen on the news was running around in my head—if nature was wearing the colour of my spirit, then I was in bad shape, and no other meditative message was able to drown out *bodies found after thaw* and *storm kills entire family*. My body being dug out, frozen solid. Hadn't the scallop shell been destined to get to Santiago? Maybe the girls would sell it to a pilgrim to help pay for my remains to be sent home.

'We're lost,' I yelled, coming up beside Martin.

Martin looked at me, then put his arm around my shoulder in a clumsy hug—clumsy because of backpacks and carts and poles and jackets and gloves.

The wind and snow didn't let up and we barely seemed to be moving. My ankle twinged as I slipped again.

Then I saw the hut. We almost bumped into it: a few yards either side and we would have missed it. Martin nodded but seemed as relieved as I was.

'Well spotted. Nice work. Do you have something warmer you can put on?' He was shouting over the wind.

I nodded.

'Be quick about it.'

It was a relief to be out of the storm. Martin waited outside while I took off my jacket and fleece and put my sweater on underneath. My fingers were frozen and white—I didn't think I would ever get it done.

'Not far,' he said, when I emerged, and it must have only been half an hour before we staggered onto the road. We could make out the town of Aubrac ahead.

'I didn't think I'd ever be so grateful to see a church,' I said. Martin looked at me as though I needed to say something more.

'We wouldn't have made it without your GPS.'

'You should get one. They're standard on smart-phones these days. Then you'd have a phone too.'

I was getting to know this guy and his sarcastic defence. I put my hand on his shoulder. 'Thank you. Okay?'

He smiled this time.

I took off almost at a run, and arrived at the hotel before him. In the empty bar, we peeled off layers, snow and water dripping all over the tiled floor, then fell into chairs in front of the fire.

'Bloody hell,' said Martin.

'Holy crap.' I was trying to massage feeling into my fingers. We ordered drinks and I took off my boots. My feet were tingling, which I hoped was a sign that I wouldn't be losing any toes. Martin was talking to the bartender.

'Dinner,' he said, when he returned with a steaming coffee and an icy-looking beer, 'is at 7.30.'

'Probably is at the *gîte* too.'

'It doesn't open till April.'

'You're kidding me. How much vacation do people need in this country?'

'There's one in St Chély. It's only a couple of hours' walk.'

Oh God.

Martin sipped his beer. 'You were looking so full of energy that last hundred metres, I can understand you're keen to knock it over.' He didn't wait for a reply. 'Don't be bloody silly. Tonight's on me.'

'I don't need you to take care of me.'

'Just drink your drink.'

I was hungry, tired and being offered a good deal. I'd worry about my problems with being rescued tomorrow. Without doing massages, I wouldn't be able to pay for the dinner or the room. And I sure as hell wasn't massaging Martin.

The room had a bath. I soaked for half an hour until every part of me felt approximately normal. I took a moment standing in my room, with my own bed, listening to the wind outside, to feel humble and remind myself how blessed I was, before dressing for dinner.

Except dressing for dinner on the Camino means putting on your one change of clothes: leggings, a long top and no bra. Camille would have slit her wrists rather than go out like this—to say nothing of my red nose, which looked like it was going to swell and peel. No cosmetics to cover it.

Martin's meal smelled great, and mine was a well-balanced salad with hot goat cheese for protein (no bacon, as requested) and a fruit tart that had to be healthy.

I still didn't know much about Martin. He told me he'd had an ugly divorce, but I sensed that he didn't want to go there. Instead, we talked about our daughters and shared our worst teenager moments.

'I'm not sure what I did to deserve an Aries and Taurus,' I said.

'Star signs?'

Not everyone was into astrology but did anyone have better answers?

'I'm Sagittarian,' said Martin. 'What does that tell you?'

'If you hadn't told me I would have guessed. The knight in shining armour. With or without the GPS.'

'Not to my daughter, I'm not.'

I waited.

'We text,' he said. 'Not perfect. But it's better than her being ferried between two warring parents.'

'Is that what she wants?'

'I don't think seventeen-year-olds have much of an idea of what's best for them.'

'Bet you did.'

Martin looked uneasy. 'She's got her mother,' he said finally. 'For all my problems with her, she's been all right with Sarah.'

'I had to do it alone for years before I remarried. It was tough.'

Martin was looking beat. I figured the cart took a lot out of him. Maybe it was the weight of what he had in it, but he had seemed to be working harder than I was.

'I'd better crash,' I said.

Martin insisted on a last drink. Keith hadn't done after-dinner drinks and always went to bed early; I had adapted to his rhythm. Now there was no need.

'To surviving parenting,' said Martin, lifting his glass of green liquor.

'And to surviving the walk,' I said. 'Thanks to your GPS.'

32
Martin

Jon: Don't know if it was the cold or missing a night's charge, but your GPS let me down today. The one time I needed it. Flat battery in the middle of a snowstorm on the Massif Central. Had to use the little compass on my jacket zip and keep pretending to look at your bloody device so the American woman who had put her trust in it (rather than me) wouldn't panic. Wouldn't want it to happen in Afghanistan. It'll be in my report. M.

I sent the email and followed with a short message to Sarah, letting her know I was alive. Zoe's advice about parenting was nothing new: Ed Walker had given me much the same message two nights earlier.

Almost immediately there was a reply. *Miss you Dad xxx.*

I knew she missed me. I was trying hard not to miss her, trying to do the right thing. I knew from experience—bitter experience—that one loving parent was better than being in the middle of a constant fight between two. Yes, Zoe, I did know what I needed at seventeen. I guessed she disagreed with what I'd done. She didn't know Julia. Or my parents.

In the morning, we shared breakfast at the hotel and set off together.

The landscape and buildings were covered in snow. The wind had died and, off the plain, navigation was straightforward. There was nobody about and most of the time the crunch of our footsteps was the only sound.

'Winter wonderland,' I said. It came out without the irony that I would normally have given to those words. Zoe smiled and, had we not both been wearing gloves, I'd probably have taken her hand.

'I'm booked in Chély tonight,' I said, 'and I'm inclined not to change it. Just walk an easy eight kilometres and have a break.'

'Works for me. But I'm staying at the hostel. No more freeloading.'

'Meet you for breakfast?'

'Sounds good.'

I had a quiet afternoon in Chély, washing clothes, checking the cart and going over my plans. I was running exactly to schedule, even with the delayed departure from Cluny.

After dinner, I pulled out my phone to text Sarah. There was a message from her already.

Hi Dad. Where r u?

Chély, southern France.

In a hotel?

Yep.

By yourself?

Yep.

How far did you walk?

Today of all days. *8km. My shortest day. I average about 25.*

In miles.

Work it out. If you're still planning to do science.

Thinking about medicine. Probs won't get the marks. Don't say anything.

Who was I going to say anything to? Julia and I had not spoken since I left England. Another message came before I could reply.

Who are you walking with?

Different people. Mostly alone.

What about today?

Why the interest?

Guessing woman.

You're not guessing. You read my blog. BUT, husband just died. And American ;-)

American!!! Is she nice?

Believes in astrology. Vego. I had exhausted my negatives.

What's her name?

Candy ;-)

Yeah, right.

Have to go to bed.

It's only 9!!!

10 here. Early start.

Goodnight old man. Love you.

I sent xxx and shut down.

It wasn't actually an early start. Breakfast at rural hotels in France never began before 7.30, and sometimes as late as 9 a.m., and I'd learnt not to depart on an empty stomach in the hope of finding something in the next village. French shops had a long list of reasons for closing: certain days of the week, lunch, annual holidays, obscure public holidays, family reasons and the all-purpose *fermeture exceptionnelle*.

We got away at 9 a.m., aiming for Espalion. The weather had cleared, the sun was shining and we were both rested.

Zoe was a pleasant walking companion. She chatted about her daughters, and it was reassuring to be reminded that all teenagers had problems and that hers had turned out fine, even without their father on the scene. Keith, the late husband, remained absent from most of the stories and she deflected questions about her parents and siblings.

Five kilometres out from Espalion, I called a break. Some days my feet lasted longer than others, but even with the new shoes they were usually sore by twenty kilometres, particularly if I had been walking on bitumen. A few minutes' rest was remarkably effective at restoring them.

While I was checking my GPS, Zoe came up behind me and, without warning, put her hands over my eyes.

'What do you see?'

'Nothing.'

'Right. What did you see before I put my hands over your eyes? Describe the landscape for me.'

'It'd be easier if I could see.'

'You've been standing here for ten minutes.'

'Grass, trees, clouds . . . I'm just not that observant.

I don't notice much outside my head.' I said it lightly, but it was true, though not as true as it had once been. I had become accomplished at spotting scallop-shell signposts, and had not wandered off track since the second day in the pine forest. But, as an artist, she must be acutely conscious of the environment, while my mind was turning over the same things as it would have if I was drinking alone in a Sheffield bar.

Zoe removed her hands and rose to her feet. She had made a point about our difference, but it had been made with her hands on my face and her body pressed against my back.

We shared a mandarin and she asked where I was staying.

'Haven't decided.'

'I'm staying at the hostel. If you feel like slumming it. And eating healthy food.'

The sun was still delivering some warmth when we arrived, but it was hardly sunbathing weather. So it was a little surreal to find two women stretched out on deckchairs on the porch, sipping cocktails through straws. Doubly surreal, because they were Margarida and Fabiana, who we had left behind in Nasbinals. Triply, because Margarida had an umbrella, functioning as a sunshade.

They greeted us effusively. 'Caipirinhas?'

Where did they get Brazilian cocktail ingredients in a French village? How had they crossed the Aubrac plain and arrived here ahead of us?

They hadn't. Paola had considered the Aubrac too risky and they had taken the taxi to within a few kilometres of Espalion, leaving only a short walk for today. She had given a pass to Renata, who had crossed behind us, in the company of a male Danish walker who had arrived after we set out, and they had done the extra nine kilometres through to Chély while Zoe and I were recovering. No matter what you do, there's always someone to top you. I toasted Renata, making my views of the others apparent by default.

After dinner—a surprisingly tasty vegetable stew cooked by Zoe—it was party time. Margarida dragged me up to dance. She was wearing an off-the-shoulder red dress, which seemed an extraordinary thing to bring on a long-distance hike. Unless, I supposed, you saw it as a rolling party, in which case you would naturally pack high heels, cocktail makings and audio cables for your phone. Maybe she had a mirror ball stowed away somewhere.

I did my standard shuffle on the spot, but Margarida grabbed my hips and did a passable impression of stand-up sex. I wondered what Zoe, and Renata, who was dancing by herself, were making of it. I suspected that Margarida was all show. Regardless, the chemistry was not there.

I peeled her off, and caught Zoe looking pleased. If Margarida was using me to make an impression, we were square. I tried a couple of times to turn down the music, but Fabiana, of all people, turned it up again. She was dancing too, although she stopped short of making a move on me.

There was an element of repetition about the walk. Every day finished with washing, eating, blogging, photo and video back-up, and battery charging. I had bread and coffee for breakfast, fruit for morning and afternoon breaks, and the coarsest-grained bread I could find for lunch with tomatoes and salami or cheese. If there was no fridge, I parked my salami on the window sill overnight. I had a final checklist of stuff I might have left lying around before departure: CPGS—computer, charger; passport, phone; GPS, guidebook; sticks, salami.

Zoe and I got away ahead of the Brazilians the next day and shared a huge *escargot* pastry from the local patisserie. Her idea, and fair enough. No need to count calories when you're walking twenty-five kilometres up and down hills every day.

'So,' I said, 'party again tonight?'

'I don't think so. I asked Paola where they were staying. So I wouldn't be.'

'Where?'

'Keen to see your girlfriend?'

'Girlfriend?'

'*You wanna dance, Marteen?*'

I spread my hands. Was it my fault?

'Anyway,' she said, 'I've forgotten where they're staying, but it's not Golinhac. Which is where I'm going. Does that work for you?'

Winter was turning into spring, and I might not have noticed without Zoe drawing my attention to the flower buds and butterflies. With spring came rain. The skies opened, big hailstones beating down. It only lasted fifteen minutes, but that was enough to soak both of us. Zoe's ski jacket looked like it had been in the washing machine: limp and lifeless. She burst out laughing.

'I'd just been waiting. I was so worried about getting soaked, and then . . . what does it matter?'

We took belated refuge in Estaing, in the church opposite the château, which overlooked perhaps the most picturesque town I'd seen on the Chemin. Two couples from Zoe's homeland were talking loudly. As they do.

'Says here it's Gothic. I thought that was a kind of novel.'

There were three different interpretations offered—all wrong.

I wandered over. 'It's an architectural style. Originated in France, middle of the twelfth century through to mid-sixteenth. Which was when most of this building would have been constructed.'

'So, what makes it Gothic? I mean, how do you tell?' One of the women was asking and they all seemed interested. I gave them a little illustrated lesson, conscious that Zoe was listening and being careful not to show off for her benefit.

'You don't know what these squiggles mean, do you?' asked the man with the big camera, kneeling at the gates protecting the altar.

'Tetragrammatons. The name of God in four Hebrew letters. YHWH.'

'Yahweh.'

'You got it.'

'If you don't mind me asking, how do you know this stuff?'

'My job.' And because his expression demanded elaboration, I added, 'Architecture.' Near enough, but Zoe raised her eyebrows.

'What about this picture?' one of the women asked.

'That's St James on the left and St Roch on the right.' I could read the inscriptions under the wooden statues. 'St Roch is the patron saint of pilgrims.' I gave them a short summary of the pilgrimage.

'I was wondering about the picture itself.'

I could have said the obvious—the man in the middle was Christ and the others his disciples. But Zoe stepped up.

'It's a great example of Pentecostal art,' she said. 'More typical of the period before the fifteenth century. It shows Christ and his disciples receiving the Holy Spirit. The light radiating from the dove is the sign of the divine illumination. Can you see the flames above their heads?'

'I guess . . . Now that you point them out.'

'They're to show the entry of the Holy Spirit.'

They looked closer, sounding as enthusiastic as if they'd been in the Louvre viewing the *Mona Lisa*.

'Not a bad team,' Zoe said after they'd thanked us and wandered out.

'The religious upbringing wasn't all wasted.'

'That was art school. Mostly. And since when were you an architect?'

'I didn't want to sound like a wanker—people don't

take any notice if they think you're showing off, but they'll listen to someone who does it for a crust.'

'Doesn't explain how you know so much about it.'

'I'm just a knowledgeable chap.'

'*Now* you're showing off. *Wanker.*'

'Careful with words you don't understand. When I was young, I wanted to be an architect. Didn't work out.'

'Go on.'

'Left school. Worked in a machine shop. Got a scholarship for engineering. End of story.'

As we came out of the church, the Americans were looking in the window of the art gallery opposite.

The camera guy came over. 'Let me take a photo of you two. That's *my* job.'

He posed us on the stairs, with my arm around Zoe, and her leaning into me, and was surprised when we gave him separate email addresses for the photo.

We picked up the key from the *mairie,* and there was a sense of being on an adventure together, of a different kind than navigating the snowstorm on the Aubrac. There were two dormitories. I dropped my bags in one and turned on the heating. Zoe peeled off her wet jacket and hung it on a drying rack in front of the heater.

'Dining in or out?' I asked.

'I need vegetables,' said Zoe. 'So, in.'

'Leave it to me.'

'I don't think so, Mr Carnivore.'

She checked the kitchen cupboards for staples and stuff left behind, then wrote a list.

I gave it a quick scan. 'That little shop won't have brown rice.'

I had to find a supermarket to get wine anyway. They had brown rice in the Bio section. I bought some marinated vegetables for starters and a small tart for dessert. Plus a bottle of local red and a half-bottle of Chablis to go with the entrée.

When I returned, Zoe had changed into tights and her long top. I dumped my purchases, put the white wine in the freezing compartment of the fridge and headed for the showers.

Zoe had laid out the antipasto more artistically than I would have and uncorked the red. I pulled out the Chablis and poured two glasses. We clinked and she gave me a huge smile.

We had put a dent in the wine by the time she dished up the vegetable curry. She did a bit of probing about my post-Julia personal life and I told the story about the Hot Rabbit coming on to me. I stopped at that: she could work out where things had ended up.

I was watching for any indication beyond that initial smile that she was feeling any empathy with the Hot Rabbit. Too close to call. The giggling could be put down to the amount that she had drunk. And the same isolation that had created the sense of intimacy would make any unwanted move on my part seem threatening.

I took the bed at the opposite end of the dormitory. There were two heaters, so even our drying clothes remained decently separated.

33
Zoe

Walking with Martin was different than walking alone. For one thing, I knew where I was and where I was going. He took time to talk me through the route on the map.

'The path diverts from the direct line to St Jean Pied de Port, going west rather than southwest.'

'Let me guess. There's a church.'

'There is indeed. The Sainte Foy abbey at Conques.'

'Never heard of him.'

'Her. Third-century martyr. Tortured to death with a brazier, aged twelve.'

'You're not making me feel any better about the church.'

'It wasn't the church that did it. The opposite.'

Near Conques, Martin stopped and checked his GPS for about the hundredth time. 'Celebratory drink tonight. Five hundred kilometres from Cluny. Three hundred miles, in your language.'

'I'll take the five hundred. I think I should celebrate that my body held out.'

'Still three-quarters of the way to go.'

'Halfway for me.' And still no peace of mind. Or even clarity that peace of mind was what I was seeking. Monsieur Chevalier's 'finding what I had lost' had sounded prophetic, but I was never going to get back the most important thing I'd lost. Keith wasn't going to be there to congratulate me at the end.

We had been climbing, and I was expecting that at any moment the trees would thin and we would emerge to see the town. Instead, the trail turned downhill through a wood thick with trees and undergrowth. And then, when we got our first glimpse, it looked like just another pretty village, different only because it was nestled into the side of a mountain. A little further on, we got a better view and at that moment something stirred in me.

The abbey rose from below the level of the road we stood on to tower above us. The rest of the town merged with it, born of the same era and stone. A single red tulip along the path swayed gently.

Martin unhooked himself from the cart and put his hands over my eyes. 'Your turn.'

'Um . . . red on bleached canvas. An amazing abbey, pitched slate rooftops . . . spires, a path that goes around the church and leads to a square building which must be the monastery.'

It was hard to concentrate on anything except the warmth of his hands on my cheeks, the hardness of his chest behind my shoulder where he had manoeuvred around my pack and the tingling sensation that went through my body.

Martin uncovered my eyes and delivered a lesson on eleventh-century architecture, still standing close behind me. When he'd finished, I turned to him and he looked at me intently, as though he was trying to see something or make up his mind. He kissed me on the lips, quickly, then turned back towards his cart. It wasn't there.

It took us only a moment to find it, resting against a stone wall where it must have rolled, taking out the tulip on the way. We walked over to it and he checked for damage. All okay.

'Good lesson,' he said. 'I need to design a brake.'

Then he hitched it up, threw his sticks on top and took my hand.

We walked down a narrow cobblestone street, which wound past bars and souvenir shops, and then back on itself. I followed it toward the monastery hostel, leaving Martin to check into his hotel. Walls rose above me on either side. At the entrance to the monastery, several people with pilgrim hats and packs and the occasional traditional wooden stick had congregated and were talking to a man in a long fawn robe, who introduced himself as Brother Rocher.

I checked in and climbed the huge staircase of worn stone to the dorm; it seemed like the monks of the ninth century had just departed and, for a few moments, standing alone in the silence, I felt I was somehow connected with all the souls that had gone before.

'You know Compostela means "field of the star"?' said Martin. After exploring the town, we had climbed a flight of uneven wooden stairs to the rooftop bar of his hotel, and were bundled up, drinking local red wine. We had a perfect view of the abbey as dusk settled.

'As in Santiago de Compostela? Not a word I ever needed to use in Spanish.'

'The story is that a star led a hermit to the remains

of St James, buried in a field. Over a thousand years ago. They're now in a silver coffin in the cathedral at Santiago de Compostela. Now you know why you're walking.'

I could see the first of the stars high in the sky and, for the first time, I allowed myself to imagine Santiago as a destination. There was something romantic about the story, however misguided—literally—the ninth-century hermit had been. We were all shown signs. It was just that we usually missed them, or misinterpreted them.

'I love the bells,' I said. 'Not just here. In every village, chiming us in or out. How many people over the centuries have heard those bells, and here we are . . .'

'You know the Edith Piaf song? "The Three Bells"? A bell for birth, a bell for marriage, a bell for death. The church was the centre of everything back then. The abbey here took a hundred years just to rebuild in the eleventh century. People would have spent their whole lives working on it and never have seen the end.'

'I guess they were earning their ticket to heaven.'

'Quite,' said Martin. 'Their lives had purpose.'

'That doesn't make it right. The church was taking money and labour from poor people who didn't know any better.'

'They believed in what they were doing. Who are we to say what is and isn't a good life?'

'Not being tortured to death with a brazier. Or burned at the stake. While the Pope puts another Michelangelo on the wall.'

'Or the ceiling,' said Martin, laughing at my intensity. 'You should be pleased that the church patronised the arts.'

'I can't believe you're defending it.'

'I'm not,' Martin replied. 'Just putting it into historical context.'

'It's still going on today.'

'Hard to change centuries of beliefs.'

'Because people are selfish, because they're indoctrinated and threatened with hell and . . .'

And Martin was being annoyingly reasonable.

'Go to dinner with the monks. Maybe go to the blessing,' he said. 'With an open mind—*judge not, lest ye be judged*. Come back for a drink afterwards.'

Martin assured me his own mind was already open, so I left him to eat while I joined the Brazilians and the monks at the hostel.

Renata's view of religion made mine look mild. Researcher or not, she was having nothing to do with the Catholic Church. 'The feeling is mutual' was her only explanation, and I wondered what she might have done—or published—to earn their wrath. After dinner, she stayed behind drinking beer with the older Danish man she had been walking with.

The interior of the Sainte Foy abbey, with its five radiating chapels, was as impressive as the exterior. The roof of the nave was a high barrel vault, divided into bays by massive stone blocks. Above us were galleries from which choirs would have sung. I took a moment to check out some of the artwork on the columns: palm leaves and monsters competed with scenes of Sainte Foy's short life. In one spot, I could still see a trace of the colour that must once have brightened this huge stone interior.

Fabiana was looking stricken; she pulled me aside as we made our way to the front pews.

'Do you think God knows I try?'

'God is supposed to know everything. If you believe, I guess the answer has to be yes.'

'But I make so many mistakes,' she said. 'Not from hate, from love. Do you think that makes it less . . .'

I wasn't the best person to ask. Maybe that was why she had chosen me. I thought of a guru I had spent a weekend retreat with and tried to channel him.

'The path is not a straight line but every step takes you closer,' I said. Wisdom all the way from Fresno, California.

Almost as soon as we sat down, the bells rang. There was dead silence as we listened—and then in the stillness came the sound of men singing without accompaniment. Five monks, including Brother Rocher, filed in. They were wearing cream cassocks over long pants, all but one in shoes and socks. At maybe forty, Brother Rocher looked the youngest; one of the others must have been ninety, wizened and huddled over his prayer book.

I had no idea what they sang. I guessed it was all in Latin but some could have been French. I didn't need to understand the words to have them touch me. I don't know whether it was the acoustics, the song, the beauty of the singing or the conviction behind it, but there was grandeur and hope in every note.

The frescos flickered in candlelight and stained-glass men looked down upon me benevolently as the monks' singing brought pieces of me apart. Maybe this was why I had come, why I was meant to be here. I saw tears running down Fabiana's cheeks.

Brother Rocher asked in French and English for those wishing to be blessed to come forward. I sat and watched the three Brazilians and half a dozen others move forward in turn. There was a final chant and everyone filed out. Except me.

Centuries of singing, service to others and dedication

to something bigger than twenty-first-century materialism had created a peace that permeated the walls. Whatever issues I had with religion were not relevant here. The stillness and austerity gave me a strange sense of comfort, and I seemed to be moving toward some sort of clarity.

A voice startled me. 'You are most welcome to stay,' said Brother Rocher emerging from the front of the church. 'But if I can help?'

I wiped the tears that had been trickling down my cheeks. 'Thank you. I'm okay.'

'You have a large heart.'

'I have had some losses—a loss,' I said. 'And I . . . haven't been able to grieve.'

'Some wounds heal quickly; some wounds heal more slowly,' said Brother Rocher. 'What matters is that they are healing.'

'I didn't get blessed,' I blurted out as he turned to go. Inexplicably, I felt that I should be.

Brother Rocher turned, smiling. 'Come tomorrow night. I will be happy to bless you, if you are ready.'

As I made my way up from the abbey to the hotel, on stones worn from centuries of pilgrims' footfalls, I wondered at my change of heart.

'It isn't the church I'm angry at,' I told Martin. He pulled out a chair, but I didn't want to sit. I didn't need a drink and certainly wasn't ready to pursue the feelings that had flashed through my mind when he kissed me earlier.

'I'm staying an extra day,' I told him. 'Or as long as it takes. I think . . . I have found why I am on this walk.'

Martin went to say something, then stopped himself.

'I mean, I know I have to grieve for my husband . . . but all this *anger* isn't me.'

'No? I seem to remember being told to screw myself when I teased you about losing your way in St Privat d'Allier. And the blueberry beer . . .'

'Not taking shit is something else. I'm talking about the religion. The crosses and the . . .'

I sat down. 'After I helped Camille . . .' How to put into words the look on my mother's face? The judgment she had handed down not just on Camille, but on me? 'My mother said I was no longer welcome in her house.'

'Because of her religious beliefs.'

'Yes—or the pastor's, though he was damn forgiving of my father.'

'Violent?'

I nodded. Martin looked at me for a while. 'You've never forgiven your mother.'

'She never forgave me.' I wiped a tear from my cheek. 'And she's dead now, so she never will. But I guess I've been doing a lot of thinking. Something you said helped, actually. *Judge not, lest you be judged.*'

'Wise words from you-know-where,' said Martin.

'My mother might never have forgiven me, even if she'd lived. But I have a choice about how I judge her now.'

'I'm pleased for you.' Martin hesitated, then squeezed my hand, and kept holding it. 'But sorry I'll be losing my walking partner.'

Could I ask him to stay with me? I stopped myself. He had a deadline.

'Maybe I'll catch up with you,' I said. It was unlikely. Once he was one or two days ahead, under more time pressure than me, we wouldn't see each other again unless something slowed him up.

I kissed him goodbye on the cheek. 'Stay in touch with Sarah, okay?'

I spent the night thinking about my mother. For the first time in years I remembered some of the positives: the stories she told me, decorating the tree at Christmas with ornaments we had made together; how she made soup and cut up my toast and put on extra peanut butter when I had a cold.

I thought of how hard her life had been with my father, and with her father before that. She had never believed in herself enough to survive without husband and religion, and who was I to judge that? She had been raised in different times. I was grateful instead for the love she had given me when I was young and how that had helped me be a better mother to my own daughters. And that, despite all the negative energy in our home, she had somehow given me the strength to follow my own path.

I was outside the abbey the next morning, with Brother Rocher, when I heard a faint bell in the distance.

'Where's that coming from?' I asked.

'The chapel on the hill opposite, along the Chemin toward Santiago.' As Brother Rocher spoke the bells from the abbey chimed. 'And that is the church bidding farewell to the pilgrim who rang it.'

'The pilgrims ring it themselves?' I asked.

'Yes, and we always reply.'

I asked if I could see the bells of Sainte Foy abbey, huge thick domes once rung by a long rope from below, now controlled electronically.

'Does the bellpull still work?' I asked, thinking it was more romantic to drag on the cord that coiled in front of me than to push the button.

'Oh yes—the traditional way is still good.'

I heard another bell in the distance. Then another. Three in all. *The three bells.* My skin tingled, just as it had when I had picked up the scallop-shell charm. I was sure it was Martin standing there, across the valley, saying goodbye not just to Conques but to me.

'Can I ring it back, the traditional way?' I asked. He seemed to understand and gave me the heavy cord to pull, and I was able to say goodbye to Martin. If Brother Rocher thought it was strange that I had tears streaming down my face, he didn't say so.

34
Martin

*H*ow was Conques?
    Awesome.

I was using the word in its proper sense, but I knew Sarah would be amused.

What's her real name?

Who?

Candy.

I'm not walking with her anymore.

Poor u.

Too many assumptions. Bad habit in science.

Speaking of . . . Can u do calculus?

I can do calculus.

Got time to talk?

I opened Skype and pressed *call.* Sarah answered—without video.

'Hi Dad.' It was the first time I had heard her voice for six months.

'What's the problem?'

'Integration by parts. I don't get it.'

'Probably because it's not easy.'

'So it's not just that I'm a moron.'

'Not just.'

'Dad!'

'Have you got paper? It's not *that* hard—it's just the way they teach it.'

Decazeville, where I was holed up in my hotel room with a flaky internet connection, was less than hospitable. Perhaps in the right season and the right mood it was a pleasant town, but I did not catch it under those circumstances. Winter had returned and the hotelier denied having taken my booking before eventually giving me a room.

I spent half an hour talking Sarah through integration techniques, then, while I waited for her to try it out, reflected on her prodding about Zoe.

I had work to do—not least, getting my finances back into shape—before I could allow myself to be pulled into a relationship. Which, I had to acknowledge, was what had been happening, at least on my part.

'Minus $x \cos x$ plus $\sin x$. Plus c,' said Sarah in Sheffield. 'Looking it up now. Corrrrect! You're a legend.'

'Glad someone thinks so.' It was out before I had a chance to suppress it.

'You broke up.'

'Nothing to break up.'

'Yeah, right.'

'Sounds like the voice of experience.'

'A bit. I'm trying to focus on my exams. Not get messed up.'

'Good thinking.'

'I better finish these examples.'

She hung up, then sent me a message. *Thanks Dad. Love you.*

I typed back: *xxx. Text me if you get stuck.*

Figeac, the following day, was a different story: a big and pretty town on the river Célé. As I sat in a bar, enjoying my post-walk beer, I watched a curious drama unfold at the hotel opposite. A taxi arrived and unloaded half a dozen backpacks. And three women—Paola, Margarida and Fabiana. But rather than follow the packs into the hotel, they crossed the street to the bar. They saw me straight away.

'Marteen. Where is Zoe?'

'She stayed in Conques.'

'For how long?'

'I don't know.'

The barman came over.

'Mojitos?' asked Paola.

'*Oui, madame.*'

Three fingers went up.

'Bar no good at your hotel?' I asked.

The exchange of glances confirmed my suspicions.

'We don't go in right away, or they know we come by taxi and don't give us the stamps,' Paola said. 'We have a sore knee.'

All three of them pointed to a knee. I wished I could share the moment with Zoe.

'Yesterday,' said Paola, 'was a long walk. We took the short cut to avoid Decazeville and stayed at Livinhac le Haut. Which was *haut.*'

'Renata?' I asked.

'Renata walks,' said Margarida. 'She—'

Paola cut in. 'I have been walking the Camino for twelve years. Everyone walks for their own reason. We make our rules—not an old man in a hostel or some *fonctionnaire* from the tourism office selling *credencials.*'

The mojitos arrived and Paola smiled. 'Every walker is different. Some people are too sick to walk all day. Some people want only to walk a short way.'

'And who is having the most fun?' said Margarida.

'You will eat with us tonight, of course?' said Paola.

'There is a little restaurant—not too expensive but very good.'

The restaurant delivered on Paola's promise. As we walked back to our hotels, I fell behind with Renata.

'I will buy you another drink?' she said.

'Just one. I have to call my daughter. They won't notice you missing?'

'They know me. I do what I do.'

The bar was still open at my hotel.

'So,' said Renata, 'you and Zoe. What is happening?'

'We were walking together but she stopped back in Conques. That's the way it works on the Camino.'

'Bullshit.' She laughed. 'You ran away, right? Scared of women.'

'Something like that.'

'I don't blame you. You are divorced, right?'

'Right. And you told me that you are too.'

'Effectively. I am impossible to live with. But I need a man.' It wasn't clear if this was a general statement or one that related to the present moment. I suspected both.

'You're not afraid to say what you want.'

'It is difficult to get what you want. More difficult if you don't ask for it. Which way are you walking after Figeac?'

'I'm following the Chemin.'

'There is an alternative. It is in the *Dodo*.' She was referring to the food and accommodation guide, the *Miam Miam Dodo*, the title of which translates roughly as *Yum Yum, Goodnight*. 'From Figeac I am taking the Variante du Célé. I will meet the others in Cahors.'

She walked me to my room, and outside the door kissed me goodnight. For about five minutes. It would be a lie to say I didn't enjoy it, but when she walked back towards the stairs and I scurried into my room, my feeling was of having escaped.

I fired up my computer and posted an entry on my blog.

Richard from Tramayes had posted a query: *Have you seen an American named Zoe?*

I replied to the effect that I had walked with her into Conques, but that we were now on different paths. Another writer had asked: *I read that the Camino Francés is a party. Is this true for the Chemin in France?* The enquiry was from Brazil. It was impossible to resist. I uploaded the photo of me with the Brazilians, drinking Ricard, my arm around Margarida.

Then there was a truly uplifting Skype message. *Integration by parts test. 94%. One dumb mistake. Thanks Dad.*

I decided to take the Vallée du Célé variant.

My reasons were more complex than pursuing Renata, and I hoped that if we met up she would not interpret it that way. I wanted to put some space between Zoe and me, if only to get my head straightened out.

The Célé route also looked flatter. There had been a steep descent into Figeac and I had been forced to zigzag like a skier to protect my knees. I did not want to endure another operation. Nor did I want to send out a message that the cart was hard on knees. Many potential buyers would be interested primarily because it put less strain on them than carrying a backpack.

The following day I was in my *chambre d'hôte* at the oddly named Corn by mid-afternoon. If this was the flatter alternative, I was grateful not to be on the main Chemin. *Madame* took my washing and I sat in my room in a towel, blogging and marking my route for the GPS.

Sarah popped up on Skype with a two-word message. *Zoe, right?*

?

That's her name, right?

She had obviously been reading my blog and Richard from Tramayes' query. I was about to compose a defensive parry when an alternative occurred to me—an alternative I would have thought of earlier if I hadn't been so self-centred.

Who's the one giving YOU grief?

What makes you think there's someone?

Give me a break.

There WAS someone.

And now?

Don't go there.

But he's still in the frame?

Whatever that means. Mum hates him.

Tricky. Fortunately, I didn't have to reply. She added another message.

I think you'd like him.

Why?

Engineering student.

Good start ;-) Maybe.

He's 22.

No father can imagine any boy suitable for their daughter. I knew plenty of engineering students. There were worse cohorts to draw from. But something told me that there was more to it than the age gap. Julia hated him, and while she might be miffed that Sarah had chosen someone in my image, I didn't think that would translate into hate.

And?

Long pause.

He's got a girlfriend.

And?

He can't leave her.

Because?

Baby.

For the first time since it all went pear-shaped, I felt some sympathy for Julia. Sarah was having an affair with someone who was effectively—perhaps actually—married. And Julia had lost the right to take the high ground.

You want to talk? I hoped she would say no. I needed to think.

No. Thanks Dad. Then, *You think I'm an idiot.*

Relationships are difficult.

Really? Then, *Night Dad. Love you.*

xxx

What was she thinking? The simple answer was probably the right one: Julia and I had been focused on each other during the break-up and divorce, and then I had been out of touch. We had sent her a message: crises get our attention. Now she had created one of her own. The smart thing was to give her attention but not as a response to this sort of behaviour. The maths coaching was doing that.

It was easy to perform this situation analysis sipping an aperitif in the south of France. It might be a little harder for Julia, sharing the house with a teenager in the throes of exam pressure, a messy relationship and the aftermath of divorce.

In respect to the last of these, Jonathan had sent me an email: *Thought I should let you know that Rupert and his wife are back together, more or less. Julia's had a tough time. Hard to find winners in this one.*

I was feeling like I should be following Dead Walker's example and going home to fix things up. But that would have taken me straight into a fight with Julia, which would have done none of us any good. I was making better progress on my relationship with Sarah at a distance.

Dinner at the *chambre d'hôte* was exceptional, both for the food and the company. Renata had arrived after me, and we had a meal of restaurant quality—good-French-restaurant quality, cooked by Madame Laundry's husband. I'd have wagered that he had spent most of our tariff on the ingredients. He was obviously not doing it for the money and we both sensed that the best repayment was praise, which we heaped on him lavishly.

He was perhaps sixty-five and, after dinner, over glasses of Armagnac, explained that he was retired, and that he and his wife ran the bed and breakfast for pleasure: for the company and the conversation of people like Renata and me. They had a modest house in an isolated village, but they seemed to have made a good life for themselves.

Renata and I agreed on breakfast at 8 a.m. and I assumed we would walk together.

It was another tough hike to Marcilhac sur Célé. At around the twenty-kilometre mark there was a steep and rough ascent. The cart handled the terrain well enough, as it always did, but halfway up I had to call a break.

'See you at the hotel,' said Renata, and walked on.

When I arrived, she was in the bar, in conversation with the Danish walker she had crossed the Aubrac with. She introduced him as Torben. He was a compact chap, with that determinedly fit look of men in their sixties who have decided to confront age head-on at the gym. The three of us ate together, but when Torben called for coffee and after-dinner drinks I decided I was a third wheel, and beat a retreat.

As I was finishing my blog entry, there was a tap at my door. Renata, showing the effects of probably more than one digestif, stepped in and planted a full kiss on my mouth.

'Last chance,' she said, 'or tomorrow I am walking with Torben.' Then she kissed me again, as if to ensure my choice was an informed one.

'Perhaps we will meet again before Santiago,' she said, and left.

Yum yum, goodnight.

For almost three weeks I walked alone, passing through Moissac, Lectoure and Condom and any number of towns and villages between, across vineyards, orchards in blossom and unfenced fields of golden crops, staying in cheap hotels and *chambres d'hôte*. I had a table for one at a gourmet restaurant in Cahors, shared a pot of coq au vin with fellow pilgrims at a hostel in Lascabanes and cooked for myself from the array of preserves at a duck farm between Aire sur l'Adour and Uzan.

I was back on the main Chemin, and though I saw few walkers during the day, we piled up in the evenings at the bars and hostels. I guessed there were about a dozen on each section of the track at any time, about half of them French, most ·doing a two-week stage rather than the full Chemin.

Sarah's openness had ended; we were back to short text messages.

On Day Forty-three, after a longish day into Sauvelade, I had given myself an easier seventeen kilometres. Mixing up the distances, as I had learned to do in my marathon training, was working well. I was on schedule to reach St Jean Pied de Port, on the Spanish border, in three days.

I had phoned the sole *chambre d'hôte* listed in the guidebook. A voice message had informed me that the owners were on holiday, but recommended an unlisted alternative where I had duly booked.

Signs led me to the location listed in the guide. A handwritten note and map on the gate redirected me to the back-up, a less well-kept cottage down the road.

'You 'ere for the room?'

Those five words told me the owner's nationality (English), origin (Bradford), politics (Conservative or UKIP), likely reason for being in France (weather / house prices / bloody immigrants back home) and general attitude (chip on shoulder).

He showed me upstairs to what was the most

basic—or makeshift—accommodation I'd been offered in a *chambre d'hôte*. Two single beds were crammed into what had obviously been a child's room: Tintin on the curtains, toys on the shelves and no private bathroom. Wifi? No, though my phone detected a secured network.

The stamp for my *credencial* confirmed my suspicions: it had the name of the original *chambre d'hôte* on it. Steptoe and wife were filling in, making do and making money without making any investment. *C'est la vie.* I was done for the day.

Which was fortuitous. Because when I heard a knock on the door and slipped downstairs to see who might be joining me, it was Zoe.

35
Zoe

I was halfway through explaining who I was—in my
improved French—when I saw him.

'Martin!' I may have squealed. The short, older man
who had answered the door jumped back as if I had.
I dropped my pack, already hanging off one shoulder,
and threw myself at Martin.

'Oh my God—I found you! I've only got three days
to go and I'd almost given up.' I kissed him on both
cheeks.

Martin hugged me back and laughed: 'You're looking brilliant!'

I was feeling it. I'd had three weeks since my day off
in Conques to get my thoughts together, and my body
and head were in a better place than they had been for
a long time. It hadn't all been easy, but Conques had

brought me peace and I had lit a candle for my mother before I left. Though I had chosen not to forgive my father, or the pastor, I had accepted my past and was no longer tormented by it every time I saw a cross.

I felt ready to move on and was grateful to have had time in a beautiful country, living simply and health-ily. Any doubts about reaching my destination had been blown away by my first glimpse of the Pyrenees. The range of white-capped mountains stretched along the horizon as a marker of an impossible task almost achieved.

Camille had emailed and insisted on meeting me in St Jean Pied de Port and driving me back to Paris for my flight: 'A road trip, *chérie*.'

The universe was going to get me to the Spanish border, and home. And now it had brought me to Mar-tin. I'd seen his single-wheel track in the mud coming into Navarrenx. A fisherman on the river told me he'd seen Martin pulling the cart out of town an hour ear-lier, so I took a gamble and continued on.

I had bottled the things I wanted to share with him and now the cork popped. 'Have you seen the Brazil-ians? Did you stay with the religious guy who . . .'

'Whoa!' Martin was laughing. 'I think our host would like to establish if you're staying.'

'*Pardon, monsieur, je voudrais . . .* '

'We speak English 'ere.'

He did, but the accent was so strong I could barely understand him. At that point, another backpacker, a petite older woman, arrived. The owner looked at us both.

'I've only two rooms. You'll have to share.'

The other woman—who introduced herself as Monique—didn't speak English. Martin had talked with her a few times on the Chemin and interpreted as we followed the owner upstairs. Our room had a double bed and a lot of stuff—computer bits, books, clothes— piled in boxes. I turned to Martin.

'How big is your room?'

'Bigger than this. Two beds.'

What the hell. We'd shared a dorm in Golinhac. The hostess—a tall woman who reminded me of Margaret Thatcher, but with a weaker chin and an overbite— arrived with a towel, looked me up and down, and sniffed. 'Yer brother, is 'e, then?'

When I came downstairs, Martin was in the living room typing on his phone.

'Needed to text my daughter—Sarah. Now I'm yours.'

'How's she doing?'

'Who'd know? I'll tell you about it tomorrow. Right now, I want to hear about what you've been doing. You drink scotch?'

'I'm not really a whisky drinker.'

'The Camino will change you.' He said it with a French accent—a perfect impression of Monsieur Chevalier—and I found myself marvelling at how my feelings toward him had changed since that meeting in Cluny.

He disappeared for a minute and returned with two tumblers. He gave me one. 'Drink most of it. Leave a bit.'

I sipped cautiously. 'It's water, isn't it?'

'It's water. But you'd have thought I'd asked for Dom Pérignon.'

I stood guard at the door while Martin poured two slugs from the bottle on the sideboard. 'Cheers,' he said, and clinked my glass. 'We're entitled to an aperitif, so I'm helping Steptoe to comply with the law.'

I'd never drunk hard liquor before the Camino, but was getting used to it.

Martin sipped from his own glass. 'What's happened? I haven't seen the Brazilians since Figeac.'

'I caught them just after that. They lost a day because they separated from Renata and there was some confusion about getting back together. They're with Bernhard and the Danish guy—Torben.'

'Bernhard?'

'Apologised. So did I. I think Paola made him do it before she'd let him travel with them. Did you see the guy walking in the kilt? Scottish?'

'Scottish? Who'd have guessed?'

'Stop it. Seriously, he was walking the whole way in a kilt and he said he never washed it.'

'What about the Dutch couple with the dog who stayed in the same hotel every night?'

'The same hotel? How?'

'Bicycle and van. Drive to the day's endpoint, drop the bike—'

Our host interrupted to announce that dinner was served. As we moved to the dining room, Martin took my hand and squeezed it. I squeezed back.

Dinner was sausages, mashed potatoes and cabbage, and a jug of red wine. Monique took one sip and wrinkled her nose. '*Entrée?*'

'If you can get through that lot, I'll find you something more,' said the man that Martin had for some reason named Steptoe. I took some potato and carrots, but left the meat. Martin noticed.

'Don't suppose you'd have some fish for the lady,

mate? Can of sardies or something?' He said *something* like *summit*. If he was mocking Steptoe's accent, I hoped our host didn't notice. I could see he was about to say no but changed his mind.

'No problem, *guv.*'

In a few minutes, I had a piece of fried whitefish on my plate. The first bite brought back memories of childhood—it tasted *fishy*. I thought for a moment about how spoiled I'd been: in LA, we'd turn our nose up at anything but the freshest. Fish that had spent a few days in the fridge—after being frozen and thawed—hadn't hurt me as a kid and it was unlikely to now.

As I walked up to bed, I had second thoughts. I felt a wave of nausea. Maybe it was nerves. I remembered how I'd felt after Martin kissed me in Conques and my stomach did a somersault.

Had I been reading the signals wrong? I'd had a bit to drink. Did I want to do anything other than sleep? I hadn't slept with anyone but Keith in fifteen years. And Martin must have some issues of his own—or he'd surely have taken up the Hot Rabbit's offer.

Martin smiled, grabbed a toiletry bag and headed for the bathroom. I took the chance to get into my own nightwear—a worn T-shirt. Not what I'd have picked for a first night. And all the time I was thinking: this man isn't Keith.

Martin was in shorts when he came back. I forgot my nerves.

'Good to see you again,' he said.

'Likewise,' I replied, realising it was true.

He stretched an arm out and caressed my shoulder. Then he kissed me and I let myself go with it, savouring the physical closeness I had missed every night I had gone to bed by myself since Keith's death, pretending I was okay.

The kiss was long and unhurried, and I felt conscious of being older and wiser than when I had been dating, and more comfortable with myself, whatever might come.

Then my stomach heaved. It had probably been trying to send me a message for some time, but I had given myself over to something else. I only just made it to the bathroom. At least Monique wasn't in it. I sat in my T-shirt and underwear on the floor, with my head over the bowl, wanting to die.

It was at least fifteen minutes before I felt ready to come back. Martin mumbled a cautious 'Are you all right?' from his bed. I barely managed, 'I'm not feeling so good.' I wanted to cry. He didn't move and I couldn't think of anything else to say, so I crawled into bed and let tears trickle down my face as I spent another night alone.

I was aware of Martin waking in the morning before I fell asleep again. I had lost count of how many times I had been up in the night. I still felt sick, though not as badly, and quite weak.

Monique was packing to leave and said she had slept well. I told her I had been ill.

'*Le poisson*,' she said authoritatively.

She produced a bag from her pack with an array of pills in plastic bottles, selected one and handed it to me.

'Herbal?' I asked.

'*Homéopathique.*'

Downstairs, Steptoe was waiting and announced that Martin had 'buggered off without paying'. We had shared the room and eighty euros was due. Then, after I'd handed over most of my massage earnings, he produced the scotch bottle. There was a line marked about an inch above the level of the liquid.

'Your mate's a thief,' he said. 'I could call the police, but I'll settle for fifty euros.'

As I was reopening the packet that held my last hundred and eighty euros, feeling I'd do anything to erase the shame, Mrs Thatcher appeared. 'What happened to the fish I had for the cat?'

I put my money away. 'Call the fucking police,' I said.

I wasn't sure how long the pill would take to work, but I wasn't planning on sticking around. I hit the Camino with only one thing on my mind: to catch Martin and tell him what I thought of him.

He would try to put as much distance as he could between us. I should know—hadn't I run every time shit went down in my life? From Fergus Falls to St Louis, and then LA, and from LA to France. And after that meltdown in St Privat d'Allier.

This time, the shoe was on the other foot. Martin had told me he'd walked thirty-nine kilometres on his longest day, so I figured he'd shoot for a little more than that. Ostabat, one day short of St Jean Pied de Port, had his name on it. Could I do it? One thing this Camino had taught me was that I could walk. And, after watching Martin struggle with his cart across the Aubrac plain, I knew I could walk further than he could.

36
Martin

I planned to walk further than Zoe would be capable
of. The guidebook estimated forty kilometres to
Ostabat. I would start early, knock over the twelve kilometres to Lichos, and mentally start a twenty-eight-
kilometre day there. As a bonus, I would make St Jean
Pied de Port a day early.

Renata had accused me of running away from Zoe
in Conques. Whether or not she was right then, she
was right now. And I was doing Zoe a favour. Neither
of us would want to face the other after the previous
night's debacle.

I was under no illusions that she had left her dia-
phragm in the bathroom or suddenly been caught
short. Anyone with a modicum of sexual experience
knows the scenario: at the point where lust threatens

to take over, the person who isn't ready freaks out. Zoe had obviously not been ready.

A little while later, I'd heard her crying. I took the safe option and left her alone.

Forty kilometres was a big walk but I had plenty of daylight and was fit. I was in Lichos before 9 a.m.

After a leisurely breakfast, I bought bread, salami and tomatoes for lunch, plus mandarins and chocolate for the breaks. I had a flashback to flying to Canada for holidays and organising a treat to be opened every hour on the plane for six-year-old Sarah.

It was fine but cold: good walking weather. The Pyrenees looked touchable and the snow appeared to be east of my destination.

I was in Basque country. A herd of sheep blocked the trail for a good fifteen minutes as they were shepherded across and my feet enjoyed the break.

I arrived in Ostabat twelve hours after setting out. I would not have wanted to do any more, but was pleased with the accomplishment.

A bearded guy of about my age was sitting on the porch of the hostel playing guitar and singing 'Five Hundred Miles' in French-accented English to a small dog.

I unhitched my cart beside him.

'*Bonsoir.* I was hoping I might get a private room.'

'Bad luck. They were pre-booked by a walking club. But there should be space in the dormitories.'

'How much do I owe you?'

He laughed. 'I am not the manager. I am staying here too. In a dormitory.'

'You walk with that?' My image of the guitar-toting pilgrim had materialised.

'No, I drive with the dog. It is too hard for him. My wife walks.'

I pulled my cart inside, to find the place full of middle-aged French walkers pulling off boots. I added mine to the collection and went upstairs to snare a bed. I tossed my sleeping bag on a lower bunk by the wall. It was cold, and I would not have wanted to be relying on one of the cotton or silk bags that the hostel hoppers carried.

As I was coming down the stairs, I met Margarida bounding up. She saw me, broke into a hobble, then laughed.

'Taxi?' I said.

Oui. She pointed to her knee, but her expression told me she was only doing it for form's sake.

I had some sympathy for Paola and her contempt for the Monsieur Chevaliers of the world, who saw the walk as an Olympic event and themselves as the governing body. But after I'd busted a gut to make some distance, the taxi did seem like cheating.

The walking club had taken over the kitchen, and offered a deal for the rest of us—ten euros for dinner and wine. I put my contribution in the pot and applied my engineering expertise to the heating, which nobody could get working. The problem was straightforward: all the gas cylinders except the one for the stove were empty. Someone went off to fetch the owner, and I donned fleece, gloves and woollen hat.

The owner duly arrived, not with gas but with a bag. After collecting our fees, he produced three unlabelled bottles of clear liquid, which he plonked on the bench.

'Warm yourselves from the inside,' he said.

I dug out my harmonica and joined the folk singer on the porch, which was no colder than inside. He was happy to have me play along. A woman from the walking club brought us wine.

Renata arrived, greeted me like the old friend I was, and drained my wine glass. Torben the Dane followed a few minutes later.

The kitchen team brought more wine, pigeon terrine—a local specialty—big serves of cassoulet and a huge platter of cheese. This was the end of their two-day walk, and the shared meal in the hostel was obviously a big part of what it was all about.

Paola joined us, the singer pulled out his guitar again and we discovered that Fabiana had a pretty singing voice. There had been a bit of a transformation here: her hairstyle had changed and she had become an enthusiastic drinker.

We played for maybe an hour, with the walking club and Brazilians singing and clapping along, before the cold and dark drove us inside to a kitchen slightly warmed by the oven. I transferred the gas cylinder and got one of the heaters going. The walkers perched on every available surface, which for Fabiana meant the lap of a man from the walking club, passing the *marc* that our host had provided.

The scene was the cliché of hiking camaraderie I had not seen so far, and perhaps a preview of the Camino Francés, the main walking trail from St Jean Pied de Port to Santiago. Playing fills to 'Under My Thumb', with a belly full of wild pigeon and cassoulet and a glass of *marc* on the table, it seemed to me like a pleasant prospect.

Then I heard the front door opening and the sound of a pack being dumped in the entrance area. I turned to see Zoe. The guitarist stopped playing and Paola jumped up. Renata stopped her and looked at me, but I was already on my way over with my glass of *marc*.

She pulled back the hood of her ski jacket. 'You asshole!'

37

Zoe

All men were assholes: my father, my brothers, Manny, Bernhard, Martin. Keith, for dying on me. After I left the British bed and breakfast, the first two hours had disappeared, fuelled by fury. Martin could have at least stayed to see if I was okay. He must have thought I'd been leading him on. And then made me pay for the room when I didn't follow through.

But the sun was shining and the familiar routine lulled me into serenity. The blossom-filled orchards and farmland that I had grown used to gave way to green forests, where I passed *palombière* signs and large treehouses, way up high. *Palombe* means dove. Treehouses for pigeons to roost in—a sweet idea.

And the scallop shells. Since Cluny, they had accompanied me—not just the printed squares on trees and posts, but actual shells nailed to fences, shells carved into stone columns, big metal shells incorporated into the design of railings. Coming out of St Jean St Maurice, there had been a series of real shells with paintings by schoolchildren. All to guide pilgrims like me on our way. It was comforting—and humbling.

In Lichos, I managed to eat some bread and an apple, and I hoped it would be enough to keep me going. I was in rugged hilly terrain with neat villages. I may have been fitter than I had ever been, but my feet were aching and my legs were tired. There had been rain, and the ground under my feet was soft and occasionally slippery. I watched my step and the sheep in the fields watched me. Black faces, jaws in a constant chewing motion as another *pèlerin* passed by their paddock.

As I closed in on Ostobat in the failing light, I looked out for signs of a cart. Not that I had anything much to say to Martin anymore.

The previous night, I'd imagined us walking together, sharing what we'd done since Conques. The larder of wonderful preserves for guests at a *gîte* in Uzan. Finding an alternate route along miles of canal out of Moissac—the flat path would have been perfect for his cart. And the colours: the purples of wisteria on the houses, acres of brilliant yellow canola in the fields, the pinks of the sunset over the river bridge at Aire sur l'Adour. Had he seen them? It didn't matter now. Not worth worrying about.

Then I walked into the Ostabat *gîte*, where his cart was parked outside, and he was kicking back, playing harmonica with a glass in his hand. I guessed he hadn't given me or the eighty euros or the stolen whisky a thought, until I told him what I thought of him in two words.

The singing had stopped—now the talking did too. I didn't care. I was only interested in Martin. 'Didn't it occur to you I might be seriously ill? Like, you know, I might need to go to the hospital or something? You could have at least stayed to ask. But no, just because you didn't get what you wanted, you run and leave me with the bill.'

'*Merde*,' said the guitarist. Then, to Martin, 'This is what they are always saying about the English.'

I grabbed my pack liner and its contents, and headed upstairs.

I was halfway up the first flight when Martin caught me.

'What do you mean, leave you with the bill?'

'The eighty euros. For the room.'

Martin's expression was probably what mine had been when Steptoe had asked for payment.

'I paid when I got there. Forty euros.'

I sat down on the stairs and started laughing. 'I can't believe we paid a hundred and twenty euros so I could get sick on cat food.'

'What? You were ill?'

'What did you think? I've hardly eaten all day. And he marked the whisky.'

'Oh shit. I'm really sorry. I thought . . . What do I owe you?'

'An explanation. And I need to lay down.'

Instead, he offered me the glass in his hand. 'It's pretty crappy,' he said. 'Basically moonshine.'

I took a swig. It burned all the way down. I took another.

'I was embarrassed,' he said. 'I thought you would be too.'

So simple that it had to be true. I might have done the same if I'd woken first.

'Here,' said Martin standing up and grabbing my bag. 'Let's find you a bed and I'll get you some food.'

Paola was peering around the corner. 'I will bring food. You look after her.'

Martin put my liner bag on a bed. Fabiana appeared with bread and cheese, and a refill of *marc*. I took a few bites and a quick swill but my stomach wasn't up for anything more yet.

Martin finally spoke. 'You're always giving people massages. How about I give you one?'

I was barely able to move any part of me and it felt like slow motion as I looked up at him. He was apologising. I owed him one, too.

'I . . .'

'Lie down. Or lay down. Whichever you guys do.'

I lay down, and he ran his fingers over my toes and the soles of my feet. At first they protested, but I relaxed into it. He moved to my shoulder muscles. Firm enough to get to the sore spots but not so hard that I had to grip the mattress.

'You're a difficult person to understand,' said Martin.

What was there about being sick to understand?

My mind was as exhausted as my body, and the doubts that had hovered on the edge of my consciousness the previous night had evaporated. I gave in to the feeling of someone taking care of me and the tingling that made for goose bumps, quite separate from the wisps of cold air that occasionally accompanied the movement of Martin's hands.

I was going back, twenty or more years, my body remembering a time when sexual tension was the norm.

Martin edged me over and, still fully clothed, lay down next to me. He felt surprisingly warm and safe, smelling of *marc* and candle smoke and freshly soap-scrubbed skin. I turned toward him, his arms pulling me so my body melded with his. He was so unlike Keith physically: thinner, muscles harder and defined, shoulder blades and ribs evident even through a shirt and thermal. But the kiss, with the brush of the neatly trimmed beard, was all lust and lost youth. It had once been like this with Keith, a long time ago.

He was in no hurry, and neither was I. Perhaps it was because I was so exhausted, beyond tired, but minutes seemed to drift past, a wonderful suspension of time where I enjoyed the luxury of kissing without any urgency on either side.

We were interrupted by talking—the Brazilians. Martin kissed me on the forehead and slipped off the bed to his bunk opposite. Exhaustion should have sent me to sleep. Instead I lay awake listening to the usual giggling, packing and repacking, toilet flushing, and then the opera of snores. I was freezing, and pulled my fleece and thermals on.

Fifteen minutes later I was shivering, too cold to sleep. There was no snoring from Martin's bunk. I wondered if he was still awake. I had to do something. Martin seemed unsurprised. He unzipped his sleeping bag and took his fleece off as I discarded my sweater and slipped in with him. It wasn't easy to get comfortable, particularly as he seemed to want to kiss again.

After walking forty kilometres, all I wanted to do was sleep.

'How about a hotel room tomorrow night?' I whispered.

'I'll shout,' he said, and in my exhausted state it took me a few moments to remember the quaint expression.

I snuggled into his arms, surprisingly relaxed and comfortable, and fell asleep with the warmth of his breath on my neck. It was as if we had known each other for a lifetime, yet there was little chance that I would see him again after tomorrow. My Camino was ending, and he still had weeks to go.

38
Martin

I woke with a numb arm. I disentangled myself and tried to enjoy the moment, but instead found myself wondering how to persuade Zoe to continue to Santiago with me.

Around dawn, I felt her stir and unzip the sleeping bag and, by the time the masses had begun to rise in the makeshift sleeping outfits they had donned against the cold, she was bouncing around the kitchen trying to light the stove.

The gas cylinder was empty and there was no electric kettle, so we set off without breakfast. In lieu of a shower I sluiced myself from the kitchen tap, then used my phone to book a hotel room in St Jean Pied de Port.

The day's walk began with a steep hill, and we found a pub and an adequate breakfast at the top of it.

The rules of etiquette surely don't cover appropriate topics of conversation for a day's walk in the country when both parties have agreed it will finish with the consummation of their relationship. But there seemed to be an unspoken agreement to talk about anything except the elephant in the hotel room in St Jean Pied de Port, as we ambled our twenty-three kilometres.

I was happy with the way the previous night had turned out. I had shown what I hoped was an admirable level of restraint, and now there was a degree of tension in the air. A few kilometres along the road we stopped to shed our outer layers, and I helped Zoe off with her fleece. Before she put her pack back on, I kissed her, out in the open spring air, with nobody around.

This was Zoe's last day of walking, and my last day of walking with her. She seemed to be celebrating, almost dancing along.

'So, after today, it's back to LA?' I asked.

'I guess. Camille's coming to give me a ride to Paris. I haven't really thought beyond that.'

'You wouldn't consider pressing on a bit? If not to Santiago, at least into Spain?'

'I can't change my ticket. I changed it once and it was a big deal . . . My travel agent will go nuts if I ask again.'

The last few kilometres of the walk, as we approached the periphery of the town, were less attractive than the early part. But in mid-afternoon we arrived in a picture-postcard town, through the Porte St Jacques by the citadel and down an ancient stone street. The queue for information at the tourist office extended out the door. We were unusual. This was a departure point, not an arrival point, theories about walking only the French section notwithstanding.

There was a long list of registrants in the visitors' book, almost all just setting out. Most popular country of origin: USA. I'd seen just two Americans—Zoe and Ed Walker—in eleven hundred kilometres, but they were here in force. Then the Irish (Catholics), Australians and New Zealanders (ubiquitous), a mix from other European nations and a sprinkling from largely Catholic countries around the world. We had stayed ahead of Torben and the Brazilians, and there were no familiar names.

On the street, there was more evidence of pilgrims and the pilgrimage than I had seen anywhere else—camping shops, Camino souvenirs, people with backpacks drinking in the outdoor cafés, a melting pot of accents and languages. A French version of Kathmandu.

We walked past a boutique and Zoe pointed to a blue sleeveless dress.

'Margarida told me the pilgrims used to burn their clothes at the end of the walk and buy new ones to show they'd changed. I should buy that.'

'I think you'd look stunning in it.'

'It'd be different.'

'That's the point, isn't it?'

'I suppose.' She laughed. 'I guess it expresses the way that I feel different right now, but it's not exactly a spiritual change.'

'So—buy it.'

'I'm not even sure I can afford to get home.'

'Then keep walking.'

'Did you make that hotel reservation?'

'What do you think?'

'I thought you might have forgotten.'

Her expression suggested otherwise, and I sensed that this was a bit of an adventure. If she had been faithfully married for years, it probably was. She could count me in on that too.

I had booked a room at the Arambide. It was the top hotel listed in the *Dodo*, and a hundred euros for a double room seemed more than reasonable. But it was still a fine afternoon, and now that we had stopped walking I was inclined to stretch out the wait.

'Drink first?'

'If you're . . . shouting.'

I parked the cart beside an outside table and Zoe dropped her pack.

'Champagne to celebrate?'

'Depends what you're celebrating.'

'Finishing your walk. Eleven hundred kilometres.'

'I'm not much of a champagne drinker.'

I ordered a bottle of rosé, a wine I would not normally touch, and it seemed just right. We shared a big bowl of mussels—'I'm having to tell myself they're not fish,' she said—and though she was almost gushing with joie de vivre, I did not feel that she had mentally finished the walk. I was increasingly leaning towards trying to persuade her to continue with me, plane ticket be damned.

'So, where's this hotel?' she said.

'Patience, patience.'

'I'm just hanging out for a proper shower.' She finished her glass. 'And now that you've filled me with wine . . .' She looked straight at me and smiled, and I waved for the bill.

Zoe had to wait a bit for her shower. It seemed that she had been hanging out more for the second item on the agenda and we passed a very enjoyable half hour before she bounced towards the shower, inviting me to join her. All her inhibitions and what Julia would call 'issues' seemed to have fallen away, and I was seized by a desire to do something, to give something to this woman who seemed to have transformed herself.

'I need to get a guidebook for the next section before the shops close,' I said to her through the frosted shower glass. This was not exactly true. I was not going to walk out on a naked woman to buy a guidebook.

'Can I use your computer? I should skype Lauren,' she called from the shower. I set it up for her and headed out.

The young woman who served me was certain that the blue dress would fit, and was happy to take it back if it did not. She made a show of gift-wrapping it. My intuition is not brilliant, but I had little doubt Zoe would appreciate the present.

As soon as I opened the hotel-room door, I knew something was wrong. Zoe was gone, as was her pack. There was a note on the bed, on hotel notepaper. One word: *Sorry.*

39
Zoe

I got out of the hotel as fast as I could. I was acting on instinct, in no state to ask myself if it was the wisest thing to do. Does anyone, in the moment when their world falls apart?

But before I could process any of what I'd just learned, I had practicalities to deal with. Having arrived a day earlier than planned, I'd need somewhere to stay until Camille arrived. Fortunately, there was no shortage of hostels in St Jean Pied de Port. I went for the municipal *gîte*, where, for the first time in seven weeks, I encountered my countrymen and women en masse.

'Where are we eating? I don't want French food two days running.'

'What the heck is a *Miam Miam Dodo*? Some kinda bird?'

'Do they use pesos in Spain?'

It hit me how loud we—and maybe Brazilians—are, compared to Europeans. They had taken up the entire entrance hall, not because they were larger than the French, though that was true too, but because the locals would have been standing closer together.

Part of me wanted to run a mile, but another part of me recognised that they were offering me what I wanted more than anything else—home. I had the rest of my life to process the news that Lauren had given me.

I walked over to a curly-haired woman in her forties and introduced myself. Her handwritten name badge announced that her name was Donna and she was a guest of Americans on the Camino.

'You walking to Roncesvalles tomorrow?' she asked.

'No—I've been walking seven weeks and I'm done.'

'Seven weeks! Mike, you hear that?' Donna and Mike dragged me over to join the group.

There were about a dozen of them, all name-badged for the getting-to-know-you drinks.

'Have you seen where we're supposed to sleep?' Barbara was still standing—she didn't look like she thought it was safe to sit. I remembered my first night sharing with Bernhard and the first time I'd slept with a bunch of other walkers, five weeks ago in Le Puy. I'd come a long way since then.

'It's only one night, honey,' Larry said. 'After this, it's all hotels.'

'They wanted us to experience one of these,' Donna told me. 'Get it done early. Some people stay in places like this every night.'

'Why are you walking?' I asked.

'Same reason everyone does, I guess,' said Larry. 'Saw the Martin Sheen movie.'

'What movie?'

'*The Way* . . . You're saying you haven't seen it? So, you heard about the Camino . . . how?'

I gave them a summary. With questions, it took about a quarter of an hour, and I found myself as staggered as they were when I reviewed what I'd done—and for reasons no more substantial than theirs. And wondered: why had I bothered?

'Where's your bags?' asked a skinny redheaded guy without a name badge, the youngest of the group by at least twenty years. He was checking out my backpack.

'This is it.'

'You're kidding me.'

'If you can live without it, don't haul it. This is all you need, believe me.' His pack looked like he had emptied a camping store into it.

'I'm not with these guys. I'm walking by myself. My name's Todd. So—'

'So, you want as little as possible. I'm walking alone too. *Was* walking.'

'Seven weeks,' said Donna. 'All by yourself. Did it change your life? What did you learn?'

If she had asked me yesterday I would have told her I had resolved all my life issues. Now, I only knew I was an idiot. I didn't want to disillusion her: she might do better than me.

'I've learned . . .' What had I learned? I thought of how their Americanness had assaulted me minutes before, just as the Frenchness of France had disoriented me at the start.

'I've learned,' I said, 'that there's more than one way of doing things, I guess—and not just the right way and the wrong way.'

'Sure, I get that, but for example?'

'*Entrée* means starter. So, don't complain if it's too small.'

'You're kidding. I mean, not just a different word, but a word that means something else. It's like they're being confusing on purpose.'

'You'll be out of France tomorrow. But everything seems to be closed when you need it open. No service culture as we know it. Drives you crazy at first. But, you know, maybe it's about putting a value on stuff besides commerce.'

'What about the walking?'

'I've learned to listen to my body and to trust it, to live in the moment, and that food and wine taste better if you've walked hard and are hungry, even if it's not something you would ever have thought about eating. And that a bed in a dorm—like this—even with snorers, not enough heating and shared restrooms, is pretty good if you're wet and cold.' I could have added, 'And if you have someone to hold you,' but I was already blinking back tears.

I looked at Todd and his huge pack. 'And I'm learning about what to hold on to and what to let go of.'

When Martin left me in the hotel room, I had sat down to face the music with my daughters. It had been more than two weeks since I'd touched base with them. If I had taken a moment to think about my reluctance to connect with my life—my real life, back home—maybe what came would not have been so much of a shock. But the walk had lulled me into a sense of calm and competence, and I had pushed away any thought that threatened to take me out of that space.

It was morning in New York: Lauren would be at work. I clicked on the Skype link and she answered right away. She was relieved to hear from me. I waited for the next bit, about how irresponsible I was and how worried they were, but the universe had sent me something else and, as my world crashed around me, I realised that I had known all along. *This* was what I had been running from and refusing to face.

After I clicked the *end call* button I stared at the screen, knowing I didn't have much time. I felt an enormous wave of sorrow that I was going to let Martin down, because I had chosen to ignore the signs. I had just wanted to fall in love and make things right again. I had blamed the church and gotten myself tied up with my mother's death—old problems—rather than confronting the bigger issue. Even when Martin had suggested something was blocking me, I hadn't looked to see what. Now he was going to be collateral damage. Would he ever trust a woman again?

Keith had died in a car accident. He had been driving alone, during the day, sober; he was a careful driver, a responsible stepfather, a loving husband. He had hit a tree. I had decided he must have had a heart attack. Except the report now said his heart had been fine, the cause of death head trauma. There were no other cars on a road he had no reason to be on. Nothing mechanical had gone wrong with the car.

'Mom,' Lauren had told me, while I was still taking in the autopsy report, 'he took out an insurance policy. A million dollars. Two years ago. They're saying they won't pay.'

My husband had killed himself.

40
Martin

*S*orry. That was Julia's word. She must have said it a hundred times, as though it would somehow make things right. My reaction to Zoe's note was different. I felt sorry for *her*. I could guess what had happened. A Skype call to her daughters would have brought back all the grief she was running away from. 'Where are you staying, Mom?' 'In a hotel about to have sex with a Brit I met on the road. Yes, I'm over your dad. Only took two months.' Hardly.

My immediate thought was to find her. She would have likely fled to one of the hostels, and I could reassure her that I would be happy to just buy her dinner, to talk . . . But my computer was on the desk, still turned on, and I logged into my own Skype account, after noting that Zoe had indeed called Lauren. I also had a daughter who I had not been in touch with for a while, thanks to three successive evenings dancing around Zoe.

Hey there.

Sarah's reply came straight back. *I thought you must have died.*

No wife.

Huh?

Wifi, I typed more carefully, glad Sarah wasn't studying psychoanalysis.

Seen Zoe?

Seen the engineering student?

He's being pathetic.

. . . (My best impression of a therapist's 'mmm'.)

I told him I didn't want to see him. Not forever, just while I swotted for this test. And he went pathetic.

Meaning?

You know what I mean. Calling all the time, texting, just being pathetic.

Guys can be like that. How did the test go?

Tomorrow. Studying now. Zoe?

What about her?

Have u seen her?

She's finished her walk.

When?

Today.

So you're celebrating.

Yep. Maybe see her at dinner. There'll be a lot of people celebrating the end of the French section.

Have fun. Gotta study.

xxx

Love you, Dad.

xxx

Scouring the hostels for Zoe might have been a bit pathetic, so I decided it would be better to run into her in a bar or restaurant. If not, I could be pathetic in the morning.

There were perhaps a dozen bars in St Jean Pied de Port, many of them with outside seating. It took me just a few minutes to establish that she wasn't in any of them. No surprise. She wasn't much of a bar person and I'd seen what a couple of drinks could do to her. She probably wasn't going to risk it.

Back in my room, I did a little research. The tourist office's website listed several hostels, and it wasn't going to be practical to cruise their kitchens at breakfast looking for Zoe. But there was an interesting announcement: a seminar on the Camino the following evening, taking advantage of the presence in town of a distinguished expert on its history, Dr P. de la Cruz, who would be joined by one J. Chevalier, from Cluny.

As I was noting details of the presentation, which I thought Zoe would have a good chance of attending, my email window popped up.

It was the German hiking-gear distributor. They had a business meeting in San Sebastián in nine days. Would I consider taking the coastal version of the Camino, which passed through that city? If so, they would be delighted to inspect the cart in advance of the trade show, with the possibility of making a pre-emptive offer. Accommodation would be provided at the Hotel Maria Cristina, and they would contribute two hundred euros to compensate for the change of plans.

I hit the internet again and found the alternative route. I would have to take a train to the coast to pick it up. Alternatively, I could negotiate the GR10 walking path—along the line of the Pyrenees and the French–Spanish border. Either way, I would join the Ruta de la Costa, also known as the Camino del Norte—the Northern Camino—at Hendaye, on the Atlantic seaboard.

Both options were feasible, but I would be using almost all my contingency time. I could make San Sebastián in a week—less if I took the train—but I would have to wait for the Germans. The journey overall would be about a hundred and forty kilometres longer.

In its favour was the opportunity to develop the relationship with my potential investors, a chance to prove the cart on a mountain trail that might well attract a different type of walker, and a handy two hundred euros. It would also enable me to escape the rolling party and unruly scramble for rooms that I had been anticipating on the Camino Francés. I was not in the mood for either.

I emailed to accept the offer.

I spent a good part of my anticipated two hundred euros at the hotel restaurant. Good luck came in threes: Sarah's suggestion that she might be offloading the married boyfriend, the German offer, and a mix-up with the wine that had me drinking a fine Bordeaux for the price of the more modest one I'd ordered. Our mistake, sir. Enjoy.

I decided I would stay another day in St Jean Pied de Port and catch Monsieur Chevalier's lecture.

41
Zoe

I was in the tourist office, emailing Camille to let her
know I'd arrived, when the Brazilians and Bernhard
came in.

'You will have dinner with us before we go to Madrid,' said Margarida, linking her arm in mine.

Paola looked at me. 'Someone is looking for you. I
think you should talk to him.'

'No. Martin and I—'

'Not Martin—Monsieur Chevalier, from Cluny.'

'He's here?'

'Come to breakfast at our hostel—he will be there.'

I went back to their hostel, where they had a room
for four, worked on Margarida and Fabiana's shoulders,
then scored three more takers. Camille wouldn't make

it until tomorrow night, and I'd need the money for my bed and something to eat.

Back at my hostel all the walkers were just starting out, so there were no takers for a massage. It had been a long day but if I went to bed I would lie there turning the same thing over and over in my mind. I got out my sketchpad. There were only a half dozen sheets left.

Todd was talking to his fellow walkers but caught me glancing at him a few times. He came over to check out what I was doing and whistled. An obvious Todd—big smile, teeth and ears, with a schoolboy grin—was dwarfed by a pack that had his knees wobbling.

'Awesome! Can I buy it off of you? My folks would love it. Is twenty euros enough? Make it twenty-five?'

'It's okay. You can have it.'

'No way.' He peeled off the notes and handed them to me.

'Can you do one of Mike and me too?' asked Donna. She already had a fifty-euro note out.

It seemed that fate had not given up on me entirely. Two hours later I curled up in my bunk, a hundred and twenty-five euros in front. American deal-making would pay for the gas on my ride to Paris.

The next morning, Todd had his stuff, most of it new-looking, spread across the dorm. He'd taken my advice—or my sketch—seriously. I went back to the Brazilians' hostel, where Monsieur Chevalier was sitting in the back courtyard with a mug of coffee, wearing a wide-brimmed hat.

'*Chérie!*' he cried, kissing both cheeks. There was something comforting about his presence. A guardian angel, maybe. His eyes went to the place where my scallop-shell charm had hung. I saved him from asking the question.

'I'm done,' I said.

He insisted on buying me a coffee, which came with an observation. 'You are still troubled.'

If he had said this twenty-four hours earlier he would have been right, but I wouldn't have known it.

'Tell me about your Chemin,' he said. 'What have you learned?'

The same question twice in twenty-four hours. I didn't think Monsieur Chevalier was after my take on French culture.

'That I can walk,' I said.

Monsieur Chevalier nodded as if I had said something profound. 'Then keep walking,' he said.

It was my turn to shake my head. 'I've walked seven hundred miles and I just found out I'd been running all the time, refusing to face the truth.'

'But,' said Monsieur Chevalier, 'what do you expect when you are only halfway?'

I stared at him. Was I about to run away again?

He patted my hand and spoke with quiet certainty. 'What you seek will be on the road to Santiago. You must not give up too soon.'

I had chosen St Jean Pied de Port as a destination on nothing more than the parochialism of the woman in the Cluny tourist agency—and because I thought I could walk it in a month. The shell had sent me toward Santiago. Monsieur Chevalier had said I wouldn't find what I was looking for until the end. Walking into the town with Martin, part of me had wanted to continue.

Crossing the Pyrenees. The *autoroute* of pilgrims. Sharing my experience with the newbies. I had nothing else to do with my time, and the grief would be with me wherever I went. Lauren and Tessa were more worried about me than about Keith's death. They didn't need my help.

It still didn't feel right. I shook my head. 'I've been able to avoid seeing the truth by enjoying everything else about the walk. The Camino Francés feels wrong.'

'The Camino Francés is the . . . king, the peak of the

Caminos. This is the perfect time to walk it; even the Meseta, which some find boring, is green with crops. There is much support and company, well-marked paths, bars every few kilometres and *albergues* for all pilgrims. The first day is hard for new walkers, but not for you. And after that . . . easier than what you have done already.'

I shook my head more forcefully this time. I didn't need easy. 'No. I need solitude.'

Monsieur Chevalier muttered something in French, then, 'It is possible that you are right.' I could see it took an effort. He had wanted to be my guide, but above all he was philosophical and spiritual, and I respected him for that.

His next words surprised me. 'You must still go to Santiago. There is a path through the Pyrenees, but it is difficult walking, not so well signposted. It is not part of the Camino; there is only accommodation for hikers and vacationers. So, you take the train via Bayonne. At Hendaye, on the coast, you will find the Camino de la Costa. It is longer and more difficult, one of the oldest ways, used in the Middle Ages to avoid the bandits. Only the last two days are shared with the Camino Francés.'

He was still holding my hand. Longer and more difficult. Good.

'Maybe it's what I need,' I said. If fate had sent Monsieur Chevalier all the way from Cluny with a message, I would listen to it and worry about the flight home later.

He hugged me and kissed my cheeks. 'I will see you in Santiago,' he said. '*Bon Chemin.*' Then a smile. '*Buen Camino.*'

'Camille?' Margarida had loaned me her cell phone.

'Zoe! Soon I will be there, just some hours. Then *Paree*. We will take two days to drive there—a road trip in France—then a day for shopping.'

'Camille . . .' I felt bad for her, hoped she hadn't driven too many miles already, but I had to do this. 'I'm sorry to mess you around, Camille, but I had to change my plans.'

After saying goodbye to the Brazilians, I returned to the hostel and discovered that all the packs had been moved, mine included.

'Where are they?' I asked the hostel supervisor.

'People leave. They take their packs. Or have them transported.' She saw my alarm. 'There was a bus that took the Americans' packs. It is possible . . .'

'Where?' I could feel panic welling up.

'I do not know. The bus takes the walkers to the top of the mountain, so they only walk down. No climb. The backpacks are going to their hotel. Maybe Roncesvalles. They are travelling to Santiago in one week, so it is possible the bus will take them further.'

My pack must have been swept up with the rest. The stars and stripes on the top wouldn't have helped.

If they were using transportation, they wouldn't be limited to hotels on the track. They could be going anywhere. When would they work out they had an extra pack? Would anyone recognise it as mine? Maybe they'd send it back to the hostel. The supervisor let me use the internet to track down details for Americans on the Camino but all I could find was an email address and phone numbers for the US. It was after midnight on a Friday in LA. I sent a message, but whatever happened it was going to be a while before I saw my stuff again.

I did a stocktake. I was in walking clothes, but sneakers, not walking shoes. I had started the Camino in these and they had been okay. I had no change of clothes but I could wash what I had every night and wear them wet if I had to. But no sleeping bag or wet-weather gear. I had 275 euros in my pocket and no money in the bank.

'One of the Americans,' said the hostel woman, interrupting my thoughts, 'left some things here. The young man is carrying his pack. Unlike the others.'

Looking at what Todd had discarded, I wondered if he had bought the sketch as an explanation to his parents. There was a down sleeping bag—'Too hot for Spain,' said the supervisor—a sleeping mat, T-shirts, Chicago Bulls sweater, thermos, deodorant, sunscreen, shampoo and conditioner, insect repellent, a bottle of bourbon, two boxes of Oreos, a whistle, large flashlight, metal mess kit, two pairs of walking socks still with their tags and a pair of sandals. And three books on the Camino.

'Keep the books and the sandals,' I said. 'I'll take the rest.'

I used the hostel's computer to email my travel agent. She had said my ticket couldn't be changed a second time but I had to try—and I had a bigger favour to ask, as I would now need to fly out of Santiago. I went for the last day of my visa: May 13. Friday the 13th. Great. I scanned a cartoon of me begging, in pilgrim gear, and hoped she was religious. Or had a sense of humour. Then I wrote a short email to the girls, assuring them that I was getting plenty of help and support, and not to worry about me.

At the Pèlerins' Boutique, I spent half of my money

on thermal leggings, a basic pack, and a poncho to cover it and me. Back at the hostel, I stuffed it full of Todd's leftovers. The hostel supervisor looked at me sympathetically. 'Stay here, for free, tonight,' she said. 'Perhaps the backpack will be returned.'

I thanked her but the thought of spending a night with another group of enthusiastic Americans was more than I could bear. Their journeys would be different than mine, though maybe, along the way, they would learn tough things about themselves. Right now, I had my own tough things to deal with.

42

Martin

A day of wandering around St Jean Pied de Port produced no signs of Zoe. In the evening, in the interests of improving my mind and, I hoped, running into her, I fetched up at the Camino seminar, in a meeting room at the Office de Tourisme.

No sign of Zoe, but the seminar turned out to be a treat in itself, not only for its educational value but as a dramatic performance. I had assumed Dr de la Cruz would be Spanish and, to my shame, male. In fact, she was Brazilian—our Paola, the tour leader. And it was apparent that she was the senior player. She had written two books on the Camino, and walked several of its variants and feeder paths. When the tourist-office manager introduced her, he used the word *walked*, and

I smiled inwardly, thinking of her tumbling from the taxi in Figeac.

Monsieur Chevalier spoke first, in keeping with his role as support act. As Dr de la Cruz was the expert on the history of the Chemin, he would confine his remarks to the practicalities, and in particular the insidious lowering of standards as the walk had become more popular. He enumerated the travesties: packs carried by taxi; certificates of completion awarded for a mere hundred kilometres; people walking for non-spiritual reasons; and widespread cheating by pilgrims doing the minimum distance, which had led to a requirement that they collect two stamps per day in the final hundred kilometres.

No doubt he regretted the demise of sackcloth robes as standard pilgrim attire and the use of penicillin in cases of infection. Then, in what was surely a targeted remark (he had definitely seen me), he confided that he was concerned at the recent appearance of unconventional approaches to carrying provisions. He was not yet ready to make a definitive ruling on carts, but the original pilgrims did not have access to carbon-fibre technology and computer-designed suspension. I wished I could have recorded him and his implication that dragging the cart was easier than wearing a pack.

There were many times I had doubted this basic selling point. He received a good, if perhaps slightly guilty, round of applause from the thirty or so walkers and tourist-office staff.

Then Paola ripped him to shreds. In what must have been something of an embarrassment to her hosts, she pulled no punches. In excellent French, she stopped short only of attacking Monsieur Chevalier personally. People walked for different reasons. No one owned the Camino. Why should it be restricted to the athletic, the religious, to those who could afford six weeks away from earning a living or healing the sick? She, for one, had abandoned Catholicism, and gratefully accepted money for guiding others on their journeys without regard to their reasons. And yes, sometimes she took taxis. This must have been the final blow for Monsieur Chevalier—but, to his credit, he kept a poker face.

After her minute or two of destruction, Paola segued into an erudite and entertaining history of the Camino. And, at the end, she thanked Monsieur Chevalier— *Jules* Chevalier—acknowledging his vast experience and right to his view, then pulled him to his feet and embraced him warmly.

I bailed him up as the audience dispersed and we shook hands. I did not sense that my making it as far as St Jean Pied de Port had improved his impression of me.

'I enjoyed your talk,' I said.

'*Merci.*'

'You were right about the boots. I have lighter ones now.'

'Very wise. You are continuing to Santiago?'

'Via the Camino del Costa.'

'You should complete the traditional route before attempting the variants.'

'I have a personal reason for taking the alternative,' I said.

He seemed unimpressed. 'You must walk, then, the GR10. I believe it is very beautiful, many pleasant places to stay.'

'Thanks,' I said, keen to keep him on side for the question I really wanted to ask. 'Have you seen the American woman?'

'There are many American women walking.'

'Zoe. She was there when I collected my *credencial.*'

He performed a poor impression of a man scouring his memory, then shook his head. At that point, Paola joined us and embraced first me, then *monsieur.*

'Wonderful talk,' I said. 'I was just asking Monsieur Chevalier if he had seen Zoe.'

'We said goodbye to her this morning,' Paola said. 'After Jules had breakfast with her. She is planning to return to America.'

I let him stew for a few moments.

'Did she say when she was leaving?' I asked.

'I think she has left already.' He extended his hand in dismissal, but I fancied I saw a trace of gratitude.

43
Zoe

The weather looked threatening as I walked out of St Jean Pied de Port in my old sneakers, wearing a heavy pack and without my scallop-shell charm. I hadn't considered taking the train. I had no guidebook telling me how far I had to go, but I could follow the red and white stripes of the GR10 and walk twenty-five miles in a day if I had to. I forced aside the mundane things that had kept me distracted until now. And thought about how I had killed my husband.

When I met Keith, he was focused on making a success of his business, but he took time out to pursue me with a determination that eventually wore me down.

I guess he saw me as someone to be rescued. Even though I had coped for six years by myself, looking after the girls, I had little money and no qualifications that were going to get me a well-paid job, unless you counted a half-completed fine-arts degree and a three-quarter-completed certificate in massage therapy. Manny was unreliable and my family was no support.

Keith and I were opposites in many ways, and not always in the positive sense of yin and yang. There were times when he had to restrain himself from exploding at my take-it-easy approach, my Leo on the cusp of Virgo exerting its influence. There was a Thanksgiving dinner when I invited his extended family and hadn't done the math. Some of us had to sit on crates, and we stretched the food with packets of pretzels and chips. So? We were having fun and I figured that being together mattered more. After that, Keith organised the family gatherings.

When he died, I hadn't wanted to deal with it. If I had, even for a moment, I would have kept my mind open about what really happened. It took Lauren's story about the life insurance to force me to confront reality. I didn't know he had a policy, and it seemed he hadn't even told Albie. There was no way he would have paid the premiums when he was in financial trouble and without discussing it with anyone unless . . . Two years. Had he been planning it that long, all the time hoping he'd find a way through, but unable to turn to me for help because he thought I wouldn't cope? When had he given up? Where was I at that moment?

The only hint of trouble had been in postponing our French vacation. He hadn't asked me to cut my spending, maybe because I didn't spend much. He hadn't looked for support of any kind from his wife of twelve years. He had preferred to die rather than face me as a failure.

I saw now how the differences between us had played out, and how our relationship had been eroded by misunderstandings and miscommunication. In hindsight, it had been hanging on by a thread when he died. That was why I hadn't felt the cosmic shift.

I wasn't sure if I was crying for him or for me. I felt raw, like I had been attacked with a steel pot scourer. When the rain started I barely noticed. I had told Monsieur Chevalier I could walk, and that was what I did.

Hours passed, and if there was beauty in the landscape I didn't notice. The wind picked up and blew my poncho wildly, the plastic flapping in the wind. I was chilled to the core. I embraced the suffering as I stumbled along the rough track. Penance.

It was dark when I arrived in St Étienne de Baïgorry, grateful for Todd's flashlight.

I couldn't find a hostel, so I went for the cheapest

hotel. It was about as welcoming as a dentist's chair. The manager seemed to have no French or English or Spanish. More likely, one or both of us didn't understand the other's version. No, he didn't need to pay me for help with anything and the room would cost forty euros. I was the only guest, so no massages. I ate some of the Oreos and crawled into the sleeping bag, where my head filled with images of Keith's last moments. It was only after two big swigs of Jack Daniel's that I got any sleep at all.

44
Martin

It was time to move on, physically and metaphorically. Zoe was gone, and there was nothing I could do about that. Perhaps I could track her down in Los Angeles when my walk was over. I had plenty of time to decide whether that would be a good idea. I had seven weeks to make Santiago in time to take the train to the trade show in Paris, assuming the Germans didn't make me an offer too good to refuse.

I did a little research on the GR10 route. The first two days, ending in Bidarray, involved 'up and overs'— tough mountain trekking. The good weather that had greeted us in St Jean Pied de Port had given way to intermittent rain, not unpleasant, but always an inconvenience. By road, Bidarray was an easy twenty-six kilometres. I embraced Monsieur Chevalier's advice to enjoy a pleasant walk and took the D route.

Traffic was light, my jacket dried off between showers and I found myself feeling buoyant. Not quite singing in the rain, but in much the same mood as when I had left Cluny.

In almost twenty years of marriage I had never craved freedom. The grass is supposedly greener on the other side, but I had been happy on my patch. Yet now I was feeling what was surely some sort of relief at having escaped even a one-night stand a long way from home.

On the highway, navigation did not require any concentration, and I indulged in a little reflection. Truth was, I did not see Zoe as a one-night stand. I saw her as the beginning of a return to what I had before. And, like her, I was not ready for that.

My feet had begun to hurt from walking on the sealed road when a Saab swerved across to the left-hand side, where I was walking, and pulled up in front of me. The driver, a middle-aged Swede with excellent English, wanted to see the cart. The woman in the passenger seat was giving him a hard time, and rightly so, as they were parked on a bend, and she would have been the one to take the hit if someone appeared from either direction—or both.

'Where are you staying?' he asked.

'Bidarray.'

'Which hotel?'

'I haven't booked yet.'

'Stay with us.' He turned to his wife. 'Draw him a map.'

Mrs Saab gave him a dirty look but found paper and pen, and sketched a simple diagram.

'See you tonight,' said Mr Saab. He pulled back across the road just as a lorry came the other way and squeezed us all into single file.

The location marked on the map was a couple of kilometres past Bidarray but I avoided the climb into town, or at least deferred it until the next morning, when I would have to retrace my steps. Zoe would have said that the universe was speaking to me. I decided to listen.

The hotel was more of a resort, complete with golf course and buggies to drive from the gate to the accommodation. I walked it, pulling the cart and feeling distinctly out of place.

But I received a warm welcome at reception.

'Monsieur Carte,' the young woman said, and laughed. 'Mr Cart. You prefer English?'

'French is fine.'

'Herr Nilsson reserved your room, but did not know

your correct name. He will meet you for a drink at nineteen hours.'

She pushed me a registration form, and I dug out my passport.

'You are in the main building—here. Herr Nilsson has taken care of the room and breakfast. May we have a credit card for any extras?'

The decor was upmarket but in keeping with the rural location and not ostentatious. I could not have been the first hiker to stay. I would get away with not having a jacket at dinner.

Two nights in a row in fancy hotels. My room was huge, with a claw-footed bath and a full selection of creams and cosmetics. Zoe should have walked one more day with me. After rinsing my clothes and putting the electronics on to charge, I had a soak in the bath and cleaned myself up.

The evening felt out of time—more so than the previous night, when I had other things to occupy my mind. An oasis in the desert, a few bars of popular music in the middle of a jazz performance, a quiet moment in the eye of a storm. But it was the walk that was the anomaly in my life. This night was a reminder of the way I had lived before it, and would presumably do again.

My host's name was Anders, and he was a director of a diverse marketing and distribution business—in other words, a generic businessman. But he had a background in engineering and was fascinated by the cart. His wife, Krista, was delightful company once the threat of being killed by a French lorry was gone, and we sat on a deck overlooking the mountains drinking white Burgundy as the sun set on an almost perfect day. I was living the life of Riley—or perhaps the life that Zoe had enjoyed in that first week on the Camino when fortune had delivered her hospitality and guidance.

We disposed of the ostensible purpose for our meeting quickly, to Krista's obvious relief. The cart's mechanics were not complex, and Anders was more interested in its performance, which translated, at least for Krista, into an interesting travelogue. It was good to recap, but I found myself talking it up. Selling wasn't my style, and I was reminded that I had a lot hanging on this. I didn't have a job to return to if I couldn't find an investor.

Anders knew the German company that was bidding for the cart. They were reputable but tough businessmen. 'Don't deal with them without a lawyer,' he said.

As the meal progressed, I wondered if there was a deeper motivation for their generosity, an envy for what I was doing, shackled only to my cart. Anders would be back at his desk next week as I ambled along the Atlantic coast.

In my room, I took advantage of the big dry space to unpack everything and review my kit. It was getting warmer and I thought about sending some of the clothing and the thermos back to Jim once I was out of the Pyrenees. He might wonder about the blue dress, which I had chosen not to return to the shop. As I unpacked the medical kit, with its now-unneeded blister treatments and condoms, a small object fell out. It was Zoe's scallop-shell charm.

45
Zoe

My second day in the Pyrenees was worse than the first. My pack had gotten wet under the poncho and not dried, and it was still raining. And I was hungry. The local bar served me bad coffee, and pointed me in the direction of the track with the sort of boredom that came from too many annoying hikers having asked too many annoying questions.

I couldn't tell how far I'd walked. Before, I'd had an idea of my pace but now I was in mountains, with a heavier pack. The landscape was barren, rocky and windswept, with views forever of mountains covered in rocks and dirt. I paid it little attention. I collapsed into another uninviting hotel, without dinner, unless Oreos counted. I finished them.

I didn't feel any better the next day. I started to

wonder if I had bedbugs. I was itching all afternoon, scratching myself like the tourist agent in Cluny when she was trying to describe them to me. The idea terrified me. It would mean I was a liability in hostels, and as far as I knew the only way to get rid of them was to burn all your stuff.

'Are you happy now?' I screamed at the sky, at fate, at God, at my dead husband. 'Is this what you wanted?'

The answer I got was what had to be the most tasteless crucifixes I had ever seen, and I had seen plenty in the last seven weeks. Not one, but three, life-size. Jesus with the thieves beside him, all contorted and looking a lot like I felt.

'Screw you all!' I yelled, but my words were lost in the wind and rain and my tears.

If the ascents were bad, they were nothing compared to the descent into Ainhoa. It took me three hours and, for a while, I had to walk backward to relieve my muscles and knees. Which made me trip and fall into the muddied side of the mountain.

When I saw Ainhoa, a real town, I wept harder. I wanted to go home. But I was miles from any airport and who knows how far from an international one. Not that I had a ticket anymore. I walked along the main street, where there were plenty of expensive-looking hotels. On an outside table, out of view of the restaurant interior, a full glass of rosé had been abandoned. Such a waste. On an impulse, I picked it up and drank it.

'All right,' I said to Keith. 'You told me so. You told me I should plan and I didn't, because you always did it for me and I never had to.'

The tourist office directed me to a *gîte*, where sixteen euros bought me a bunk bed in the dormitory.

I was alone. I had wanted solitude; now I had it, and I hated it. I wanted my children, Martin, Monsieur Chevalier, anyone. I hated myself, I hated Keith and then I hated myself some more. He thought he had failed me, but I had failed him. I had accepted him as the provider because that was what he wanted to be. But I was supposed to have been the one in tune with the emotional landscape, the one in charge of keeping things on an even keel, in balance with the universe. I had let us both down.

My passiveness, my failure to say, 'It's okay, I don't need a vacation in France or a big house—I'm happy to live with what we have,' had meant he had never been comforted by my perspective and balance. He had thought I needed money more than I needed him. The sheer craziness of the idea made me shake with rage.

I cooked some sad-looking vegetables, ate until I could eat no more and packed up the leftovers. Afterwards, I drank enough of the bourbon to make sure I'd sleep for a while, then washed everything before I crawled into Todd's sleeping bag. It might have been too hot for the Camino Francés, but it was perfect for the Pyrenees. I was feeling less certain about the bedbugs and wondered if I had an allergy. Maybe my whole body was trying to purge itself of grief: the only comfort was a sense of connection with all the souls who had suffered over the centuries as they had walked and died along the Camino.

I woke with a sore head from the whiskey and felt some sympathy for my father. Well, some understanding. Of the need to obliterate yourself and how it added to the problem. I left the half-full bottle behind.

The hostel owner told me I had a short walk to Sare, a long walk to Biriatou, and then I would reach the coast at Hendaye, on the French side of the Spanish border. My spirits lifted a little. I was nearly in Spain.

I crossed the border sooner than I'd expected, but not in the right place. I had now not only lost my way spiritually, but physically. After some distance with no red and white stripes I saw a building on a river and made for it. To my surprise, it was a bar. Even more surprisingly, they didn't speak French and not because they were being belligerent. After five minutes my Spanish started to flow more easily, though we both struggled with accents. The younger man drew me a diagram to supplement his rapid-fire directions. It led me back to red and white stripes, but it got dark before there was any sign of Sare. I was going to have to spend the night on the trail, in the cold.

I consoled myself that it wasn't raining. There was no snow, and the temperature was probably above freezing point. I had a cold-weather sleeping bag and a poncho that could work as a tent. Things could be worse.

At 3 a.m., they were. I woke to find that rain had been dripping down the back of my neck. Todd's sweater hood had been functioning as a miniature reservoir. I spent fifteen minutes finding a way of keeping the hood from squishing against me, and another ten refixing the poncho. To keep dry, I had to curl into the foetal position.

I fell asleep again—for an hour or two. When the sun rose on a damp and misty day, I ached in the way I imagined I might in old age, but I wasn't thinking of the future. My mind was stuck on ruminations about how I had failed Keith. I deserved this.

46
Martin

Whether or not the scallop charm had any influence, I found the Pyrenees less daunting than I'd expected. There was a fair bit of climbing but not too much to bother the cart. I met a few other walkers, most just out for the day, and persuaded a couple of them to shoot video of the cart on the more difficult terrain.

The red-and-white-striped markers of the GR10 were not as prominent as the scallop shells had been, and it was handy to have the GPS. The views were stunning: eagles soared below me and after I gave up trying to catch them on video I spent an hour just watching them.

The towns through the Pyrenees were, like the golf resort outside Bidarray, oriented towards holidaymakers rather than walkers. In Ainhoa, on a balmy evening, I sat in a street restaurant sipping Navarre rosé, which had become my drink of choice. The waiter topped up my glass without prompting, and nodded towards the interior.

'Is that your cart?'

'Yes—is it in the way?'

'No, but don't leave anything valuable in it.'

I had my wallet, passport and phone with me, but went inside and retrieved Zoe's charm and a safety pin. I had a fantasy of returning it to her with the news that I had fulfilled Monsieur Chevalier's prophecy that it would go to Santiago. I pinned it inside the breast pocket of my jacket.

When I returned to my table, my glass was empty.

Uuuuuurgh.

I wasn't sure if Sarah's message, on my phone as I came into Biriatou, still in the Pyrenees, was a reaction to a careless error in an assignment or to something more personal.

The previous evening, we had spent an hour talking about a maths problem, and she had even turned on the video at the end. She had never seen me with a beard and was suitably surprised. I was permitted to leave it on—especially if Zoe liked it: 'C'mon Dad, you are going to see her again. I really am okay with it.' But we turned off the sound and video before she messaged the *Love you Dad*.

Tonight, it was text messages again. It seemed the engineering student was keeping his options open and managing to divert any blame to his partner, who was selfishly trying to hang on to the father of her child.

She doesn't love him.

Why do you think he's staying with her?

She guilts him out. Love for his kid would have been a worthier answer.

How old's the child?

A few months. He tried to make it work.

Right. By hooking up with a seventeen-year-old.

Mum thinks I should dump him. Totally. Not see him ever again.

Julia was totally right, except in offering advice. Though maybe she needed to give Sarah a clear statement of where she stood.

I had a limited toolkit for dealing with human relations. Don't give advice unless it's asked for; assume self-interest until proven otherwise. Sarah's engineering student was getting the best of both worlds as long as Sarah and his partner let him get away with it. And Sarah had Julia's and my attention.

While I was thinking, she texted again. *What do you think?*

Depends what you want to happen.

Are you being a shrink? What do you think?

What would you like me to think?

DAD!

;-)

If I got pregnant, he'd have to choose who he really wanted.

She was pressing my buttons. Which was what she was getting out of this in the first place. If I reacted, she would get positive reinforcement for the behaviour; if not, she would push harder or find other ways to do it. If there were more effective ways than telling her father she was thinking about getting pregnant in order to test her relationship with a married man.

I left it till she continued: *Gotta go. Test tomorrow.* Then: *Science test, not pregnancy test. Haha.*

LoL here. Not. Good luck.

Love you Dad.

xxx

Hey, is Zoe the woman in the short dress? The white one. On your blog?

No. Zoe's AMERICAN. They were Brazilians. Read caption.

Good. She looked like trouble.

———————

Walking the next day, I allowed myself a little pat on the back. The boyfriend hadn't gone away but the communication lines were still open, and I had given Sarah a bit to think about without imposing my view. When we talked maths, she had her head on straight, so her angst seemed not to be interfering with her studies.

My holiday in the Pyrenees ended at the seaside. After walking through the suburbs of Hendaye, I said goodbye to France with a dozen oysters and a glass of Mâcon Blanc before catching the ferry for the short crossing to Hondarribia. I could have taken a roundabout urban route via Irun to avoid using a boat, but my new guidebook counselled otherwise. Ancient pilgrims would not have refused the offer of a boat ride, and I was happy to follow tradition.

Almost as soon as I disembarked, I realised that the Camino, no longer the Chemin, would be different in more than name. A crude yellow arrow painted on a concrete wall pointed the way, and a series of similar markers took me into town and past my first tapas bar.

I found a quaint *pensione* at a more than reasonable price. A foot race was in progress, and the streets were full of people in a festive mood cheering the finishers on. I propped in a bar and ordered a glass of fino, which they heard as vino. When it was made clear I was in the wrong region for sherry, I settled for a rosé and some *pinchos*, and began to get into the mood of Spain.

I felt good, and mildly philosophical, sitting alone with a glass of wine, a toothpick loaded with anchovies, chilli pepper and olives, and a basket of bread. Was this what it was about? Suppose Zoe's charm did deliver happiness. Would it just give me day after day of this until it palled and I sought something deeper?

It was 11 p.m. when I returned to my room, well fed and thinking it would have been cheaper to buy the whole bottle of rosé in the first place rather than order it by the glass. As I tossed my phone on the bedside table, ready to charge, I saw there was a series of messages.

The first told me everything I needed to know. It was from Julia. *Call me urgently. Sarah has disappeared.*

47
Zoe

I arrived in Biriatou beat, physically and emotionally, and nearly broke. Though there were plenty of cheap hotel options, I didn't want to hand over the reserve that I would need for the first *albergues* on the Camino until I found some massage clients. The *épicerie* owner was sympathetic when I told him I had been lost. He may have thought I had been robbed. A phone call and a short walk later, I had a bed in a barn. The owners offered me a shower and a hot chocolate, which I accepted gratefully, and a glass of liquor, which I refused. As I drifted off in Todd's sleeping bag, I reflected that at least I wasn't giving anyone bedbugs—which I probably didn't have anyway—and I wasn't cold or hungry.

The next day there was some improvement in the weather but it was something else that helped my spirits. Right in front of me was the sea. I had arrived in Hendaye. I was only a short boat ride away from Spain.

I have always loved the sea, never more than when it is at its most treacherous. I was craving a little of that to hurl some anger at. But the day was mild and the sea peaceful and, as I leaned on the wall looking out across the beach and water toward my own country, the anger drained out of me. I knew that whatever Keith had done, however misguided he might have been, he would never have deliberately hurt me or the girls.

On my side, as much as I had failed him, it had never been my intention. We had differed on so many things that I ended up being just something else to worry about. I wondered about the silences when I had insisted on paying a good wage to his immigrant workers and a fair price to his foreign suppliers. I had wanted him to be a progressive and he had wanted to be a businessman. He tried to be both, for me, and ended up succeeding at neither. I took for granted so many things: his getting dinner on days I was stressed out; his common sense, which steadied me when my teenage girls had pushed me to the edge; and, of course, the encouragement he gave for me to follow my dreams, at least as he understood them.

In the end, it wasn't the sea that took me from the dark place I'd inhabited for the past five days. It was a sign, advertising *glaces*. On vacations, Keith would buy an ice cream every day, for him and the girls, some unhealthy confection of chocolate and fat and artificial flavours. In the end, I'd given in and joined them.

I bought an ice cream from the local store, sat on the beach with my shoes and socks off, toes wiggling in the warm sand, smiling as I licked the chocolate covering that had been his favourite, and celebrated the good things we'd had.

48
Martin

I didn't call Julia. I texted Sarah.

You OK?

Yep dw. It took me half a minute to work it out: *don't worry.*

When the relief that flooded over me had receded, I was guiltily aware of something left behind: a sense of satisfaction—of *smugness*—that at least one parent knew what to do. Unfortunately, this was not the parent that Sarah was dealing with day to day. Whose fault was that? There was no way in the world that Julia would have let me have sole custody, if that was the right term for a relationship with a now demonstrably independent and wilful seventeen-year-old.

Where are you?

Safe. DW.

Text me later, OK?

Whatevs.

Tell your mum. She's worried.

You tell her.

And that was the real message, the literal bottom line. I guessed Sarah was holed up with a friend and quite safe, following a fight with Julia or the engineering student. I would have put money on the former. However angry I felt towards Julia for failing to look after our daughter, for creating the situation in which I could not be there, I could not let her hang.

I texted: *Sarah safe dw.*

The message came straight back.

DW??

Don't worry.

Fuck you.

Well, no change there. I left the phone on in case Sarah texted again.

I had a day up my sleeve before I was due to meet the Germans in San Sebastián, and decided to spend it in Hondarribia. The hotel was pleasant and there were more tapas bars to explore. It was raining, quite hard, and the forecast suggested that delaying the walk for a day would be a smart move. More importantly, it gave me an opportunity to skype Sarah, at her convenience rather than mine.

I used the time to construct a parking brake—a simple wheel lock—for the cart to prevent further runaways and to demonstrate that I was using my experience on the Camino to refine the design.

The Sarah situation aside, the scallop charm seemed still to be working. There was an email from Jonathan asking for a copy of the plans for the cart. *I obviously can't promise anything, but those video clips through the Pyrenees were bloody impressive. We're always looking for low-cost solutions in places where we're trying to hand over to the locals.*

My blog following was still growing, although the emphasis was increasingly on me rather than the cart. If anything, the implication was that I was a quixotic character doing it the hard way—not quite the impression I was aiming for.

Fantastic achievement. Tough enough with a backpack, let alone that cart.

You must be getting incredibly fit hauling that beast.

If you don't sell the design, you'll have no trouble getting a job in China as a rickshaw man.

I posted a rejoinder about how easy the cart was to

pull, but could not help thinking of Zoe bouncing along beside me on that last day together. She had definitely been doing it more easily. On the other hand, she had not been carrying a tent.

Richard from Tramayes had asked for news of Zoe, and I replied that she was on her way home. Five minutes later, Sarah popped up on Skype.

Zoe gone home?

Yes. What about you?

Are you OK about it?

Of course I am. WE WERE JUST FRIENDS.

Were?

Enough. What about you?

I'm OK.

Where?

Friends. Did you tell Mum?

Yes. But you should have.

I did. Right after I talked to you. Like you said. Bugger. But she'd got what she wanted.

How's the engineer?

Finished.

You OK?

See earlier message.

Going home?

Maybe. Coming home?

Got some walking to do first.

Have fun. Love you Dad.
xxx
Sorry about Zoe.
Sorry about the engineer.

Unlike a normal conversation, a dialogue conducted in short messages sits on the screen, begging to be reviewed. I thought I'd done well: kept the lines of communication open, not been judgmental, and shared a little in my response to the final 'sorry' statement without bothering her with my issues. Except for the one glaring, hit-me-in-the-face-why-haven't-I-seen-this-before, shameful exception.

xxx. I could fix it. I just needed to type three words.

The next morning the rain had cleared, and I set off for San Sebastián, twenty-six kilometres up some steep but smooth hills, with frequent glimpses of the sea to my right. Blog posts notwithstanding, hauling the cart uphill was still not much fun, although it was second nature now to have it behind me, and to position myself and the sticks to avoid being pulled over backwards. I wondered what Jonathan's boffins would make of it. I suspected that for light loads a fit young Afghan soldier would prefer a backpack, but perhaps there was a point at which the weight became such that the cart came into its own. I had never tested heavy loads over any distance, but my intuition was that the cart would do a good job until the hills became too steep and the cart pushed or pulled its bearer over.

After finding my way through the Pyrenees, the abundance of signposts on the Camino was almost insulting. Stone markers emblazoned with the scallop-shell symbol gave a stronger sense of permanence to the Camino than the stuck-on squares in France. They were supplemented by the crudely painted yellow arrows which I had thought were a local anomaly in Hondarribia. The French, and for that matter the English, would not have countenanced such eyesores. The clash between the arrows and the otherwise pleas-ant bucolic environment dramatically expressed the two different mindsets one might bring to the walk: contemplation of nature or a focus on getting to Santi-ago. The journey or the destination. I'd have said that my own motivation was more in line with the arrows. I still didn't like them.

It was a good day to be freed from worrying about navigation. The Sarah situation was not working out; she had sailed through the early teen years pretty well, but now, on the verge of adulthood and university, she was doing it hard. I still felt I had given her the least worst option. Better for me to be absent than for her to have to choose a side in the poisonous relationship between Julia and me.

That said, the recent contact was enabling her to play us off each other. I was getting the better deal but it was not about me. There seemed no easy solution beyond keeping the communication lines open. And getting over the problem—*my* problem—of the xxx signoff. It wasn't that I didn't love her. On the contrary, it was too painful to confront my feelings for her. It *was* about me. Sarah was bearing the brunt of my being an emotional cripple. As a shower of rain wet my glasses and made the going treacherous, I resolved to do the hard thing next time we skyped.

49
Zoe

The Spanish Camino was different right from the start. The French scallop-shell signs were largely gone, and instead the locals—perhaps many at different times—had painted yellow arrows. Small, large, paint dribbling and uneven, on roads, posts and anywhere the holder of the brush thought they could be seen. The tradition had apparently come from a priest painting arrows on trees to assist *peregrinos* to find the way through the mountains around his town. I liked them. Their bold, naïve and slightly rebellious style was a contrast to the formality of the stone guideposts.

While part of me still wanted to wallow in self-pity, I didn't have that luxury. My fitness and familiarity with Spanish made things easier, but I had to face the reality of my situation. Had I taken Monsieur Chevalier's advice and gone on the Camino Francés, I would have had plenty of new pilgrims with sore muscles that needed a massage, and access to heaps of hostels. On the Camino of the North, the hostels were less frequent and the *peregrinos* thin on the ground. There was no way my fifty euros was going to get me through more than a couple of days. Fate and I had severed ties.

Keith had thought I needed taking care of, and I guessed that if he had been watching me from somewhere this would be the moment he would have felt needed. But it was not the financial support that I missed—the house, the furniture or the imaginary bank balance. Instead I longed for the warm arms around me at night, the laugh over the morning paper and the feeling of someone sharing my life.

A week before he died, Keith had come home to find me too angry to give him even a perfunctory hello kiss.

'I can't believe they won't put a ban on fracking,' I'd said.

'I can,' said Keith. 'It's about finding a balance.'

'Between what? The planet and gas-company profits?'

'What do you want me to do?'

I hadn't answered and he didn't come to bed until after I'd fallen asleep. I yearned to go back to that moment—to follow and sit with him.

Once, he would have told me to lighten up—got me to draw a caricature of the governor, made us both laugh. I couldn't remember when I last saw Keith laugh. All because of money. Had he forgotten that I'd coped as a single mother with two girls—always found a way through? I told myself I could do it again.

I scanned my memory for the appropriate inspirational quote but those that spoke of healing felt too shallow. I recalled something the artist Clyfford Still had said, and it resonated: *How can we live and die and never know the difference?*

I got by for a few days: one hostel let me clean in exchange for a bed, and I had another night in the open under my poncho. The hills continued but I hardly noticed. Whether it was the warmer weather or more efficient walking, I was no longer constantly hungry, which was lucky. The yellow arrows got me through San Sebastián without the job of searching for scallop shells amid all the city signage. But I had no answer to my financial crisis.

Until Gernika—the Guernica of Picasso's painting. In the urban sprawl I was stunned by graffiti art covering wall after wall. I soaked it up with a mixture of admiration and jealousy. It was everything my art had never been—bold and angry, perceptive and innovative. I thought of all the art classes I had been to at college, and of the ones Keith had pushed me to do, and felt humbled that these artists had just gone and done what they needed to. My careful lines and reworking of landscapes had no room for this approach. Because I had no talent. More like, no courage. Except when I drew my cartoons.

All the way to Bilbao I let my thoughts brew.

'Anybody can draw that crap,' my father had said.

'It's disrespectful.' My mother.

'That isn't art.' Any one of my teachers at college had I been brave enough to show them, which I had not been.

'That's great, honey.' Keith.

'Can you draw one for my teacher?' Tessa.

'Can you draw one *of* my teacher?' Lauren.

Richard and Nicole putting them on the wall and their website. The Americans in St Jean Pied de Port commissioning caricatures of themselves.

Plenty of people could draw good cartoons, so what could I bring to the form that was any different? That people might pay for?

50
Martin

San Sebastián has a reputation as a great place to
visit: the centre of Basque culture, a coastal location
and more Michelin stars per head of population than any
other city in the world. Its attractions were less apparent
to a lone walker. It was bigger than any of the French
towns I had passed through and I had to negotiate the
suburbs on my way to the centre. I had some experience
of pulling my cart into a hotel in kit more suited to a
tent, but the Hotel Maria Cristina, with its grand marble
foyer, was a step up again. To be fair, I was treated as if I
was in a suit and tie, and conducted to a room in keeping
with the general opulence of the place. The Germans
had booked me for two nights and left a message that
they would meet me the next day at 3 p.m. to inspect
the cart, which I had brought to my room.

I spent some time browsing the internet, learning about the Ruta del Costa. I had no desire to spend time in a city or on crowded beaches. But it seemed I was going to have to get used to a more urban environment. The online information about the northern Camino was a touch more realistic than my guidebook, which had promised miles of deserted sand. This was Spain. Not the Costa del Sol, but the coast nevertheless, with resorts built on every available vantage point and the main highway hugging the coastline most of the way.

When I did head out to dinner, on a solo tapas-bar crawl, the accents around me were English and American. It was early and the Spanish take their evening snacks famously late, but I felt more tourist than pilgrim.

The next day I cleaned up the cart for its inspection, updated my blog, then killed time on the internet again until my meeting with the Germans. No sign of Sarah.

The Germans defied the national stereotype and knocked on my door almost two hours late. There were four of them, all male, middle-aged, in suits. They introduced themselves and apologised for their tardiness, then three watched as one physically inspected the cart. After no more than three minutes, he was finished.

'Thank you,' said one of the others in English. We

shook hands and they departed. As a younger person might have texted, *WTF?* Had they found something they didn't like and seen no point in proceeding or did they just want to see it in the metal, given that my website had provided all the details anyway? I had walked 135 kilometres from St Jean Pied de Port for this?

Apparently not. An hour later there was a text message: *Please join us for dinner at Arzak restaurant. We will meet in hotel foyer 9 p.m.*

If their choice of restaurant was an indication of the depth of their pockets, then things were looking up. A quick search informed me that I would be dining in one of the ten finest restaurants in the world. In my spare pair of walking pants. Unless I wanted to surprise them with the blue dress. I lashed out and bought a pair of slacks. My knit top would have to do.

We arrived at the restaurant by taxi, the first time I had been in a car in almost two months. It felt like cheating, even though I was making no progress on the Camino.

A quick glance at the reservation and we were greeted, seated, and furnished with Manzanilla sherry and anchovies with strawberries. No problems with the attire.

We ate brilliantly, and I was plied with liquor. I managed to strike a balance between enjoying the wine and not losing my judgment. I recalled Anders the Swede's warning—these guys had a bigger agenda than just chewing up the expense account.

We talked about the food and my walk as the theatre of the degustation menu played out. I had little doubt as to what Monsieur Chevalier would think of this gourmet version of the pilgrimage.

The arrival of coffees heralded an abrupt change in conversation. 'So, Dr Eden, we are prepared to purchase the design for your cart—outright—for seven thousand, five hundred euros. The offer stands until the cheque for the meal arrives.' The man who appeared to be the senior player smiled and made a scribbling motion to the waiter.

I had not expected game playing of this kind. Frankly, I considered it pretty childish. In any case, the offer was not what I was looking for. It was a single buyout figure rather than an investment, and I had not thought in those terms. Was it enough to make a new start? Not even close.

The waiter was coming towards the table with the cheque, and 'no' was almost on my lips when something distracted him and he turned back, giving me time to think.

There was logic behind their offer. It was a 'go home with something to show for your journey' proposition.

The walk would be paid for and I would have some handy change. And, to a certain extent, face. The image of Zoe skipping along while I dragged the cart came back to me. They were taking a risk and offering me a viable option. I could be on a train to Cluny tomorrow. Better, I could go back to England, see Sarah, think up a new venture. I could track down Zoe.

It was the last thought, pushing itself in front of the others, that decided me. I wasn't going to let myself be swayed by a holiday romance that wasn't. As the waiter placed the bill on the table, I stayed silent.

My hosts remained all smiles, and the deal was not raised again. The next morning there was an email confirming their offer, which they were happy to extend until a week before the trade fair. I replied with thanks and said I would continue to consider it. And, in the meantime, walk on.

51
Zoe

I bought some paper and pencils, propped myself outside the Guggenheim Museum in Bilbao—ignoring a building that at another time would have held my attention all day—and started drawing.

Several tourists stopped and commented. I may not have replied, though I smiled. I think. I was pretty consumed. A Spanish man sat down beside me.

'You are good,' he said, in English.

'*Gracias.*' I kept on drawing.

'You are drawing like . . . fire.'

I *was* on fire. I replied in Spanish, and he started telling me about how he always wanted to do such pictures and instead he was stuck working in his family's hotel. It didn't seem like he was going away anytime soon. I looked up. He was older than me, heavyset, with grey streaks in his thick black hair.

'Does your hotel have a business centre?' I asked.

Only weeks ago, I would have said fate had sent him. But now, if he hadn't found me, I would have found him. *Si*, the hotel had a business centre and, when I told him what I wanted it for, he was excited.

'When you are famous, you will put me in your autobiography, no?'

'Business centre' was a stretch, but they had a computer and scanner. There were several emails waiting from friends. I cut and pasted a summary of my journey with a promise that I would be home mid-May.

Longer emails from Lauren and Tessa: reading between the lines, they were both doing well but mystified about what I was up to. I could imagine Tessa saying, 'She's probably found a guru to follow,' and Lauren googling to see if there were any weird sects in Spain that might swallow me up. I assured them I was coping.

And wonderful news: my travel agent spent three paragraphs making sure I knew she had performed a miracle, and I was now booked on a flight out of Santiago de Compostela to LA via Paris and New York for the evening of May 13, *but this is neither refundable nor exchangeable. Please reply to confirm you understand this.* My visa would expire then anyway. The one thing I was sure of was my capacity to walk the mere two hundred and fifty miles that remained. But the change cost two hundred dollars that I needed to pay in the next week.

It took me three hours to scan my cartoon and write the accompanying article, and then send it off to every American newspaper and journal with a travel section whose email address I could find.

The cartoon I had chosen was of Martin (or, at least, a well-disguised version of him) with his cart, contemplating several bags of sins. Which would he pick up as his burden?

I titled the proposed series *Pilgrims' Progress.* The first part would be *Pèlerins' Progress,* set in France, and the second *Peregrinos' Progress,* in Spain. *There is a lot of interest in the Camino,* I wrote in the covering letter, *but my angle is that my articles will cover alternate, less-known routes.* I imagined myself a year ago, reading my way through the paper over a weekend and saying to Keith, 'Have you heard of the Camino? Seems like there's more than one.' I wished he could be here to see me pitching an *angle.*

I had no idea how long they would take to get back to me—or if they would reply at all. Traditional-media staff were being laid off everywhere. Before today, even if my insecurities hadn't stopped me, that would have. Now I was filled with purpose. I wasn't going to accept no for an answer.

I walked around town a while. At 6 p.m. I couldn't wait any longer, and went to check. It would be 9 a.m. on the west coast but midday on the east.

I had sent thirty-two emails. There were four replies, including one bounce: the *Tucson Travel Weekly* was probably out of business. The *New York Times* sent a formulaic response: don't call us, we'll call you. The *Indianapolis Star* said they'd pass it to their travel editor.

The fourth email was from the *San Francisco Chronicle*, sent just five minutes earlier. *We've been looking for something like this*, wrote Stephanie, the travel editor, under my cartoon. *Love the wit and your clear sense of your character. Would like more of him. But let's talk.*

'Make sure you keep the rights to the originals,' said Martin's voice behind me.

52
Martin

I'd had a week of Spanish tourist towns and seafood restaurants, and become used to it. The food was brilliant, the rooms in *pensiones* spotless and the wine in the bars consistently good.

The walking in between, though less rural, had its attractions: spectacular sea views from clifftops, occasional stretches beside the water, military ruins. The sections on the highway were not so pretty, but I put the miles away easily.

The Spanish eat their main meal mid-afternoon, which was about the time I usually arrived at my destination, but, rather than change the habits of a lifetime, I settled on eating in the evenings. The smaller, family-owned bars would cook anything at any time if you asked. Away from the big smoke of San Sebastián, there was less variety. In Basque country, most of the tapas were bread-based, and the olive, pepper and anchovy combination was ubiquitous. In the morning, I'd run on coffee for the first two or three miles, then stop for a tortilla and a freshly squeezed orange juice. If the day got warm, I'd grab an ice cream before the final stretch, a childhood indulgence that I could afford with all the exercise I was getting.

As I followed the yellow arrows along the coast, letting the days and the miles accumulate, I had three problems to deal with.

The first was the German offer. I didn't want to sell myself short. If they were willing to pay that sum now, there was no reason why they should not carry it through to the trade fair, tactics notwithstanding. The Chinese manufacturer and Jonathan's army people were still in the mix. I'd heard nothing from the French distributor since their response to my original enquiry.

The second, and most important, issue was Sarah. She had gone quiet. No response to Skype messages or texts, with one exception. *Are you OK?* drew a one-word reply: *Yup.*

And Zoe. Should I try to contact her? If so, when?

Then I walked into my hotel in Bilbao, and she was sitting in an oversized Chicago Bulls sweater at a computer with a cartoon of me on the screen.

I wasn't sure which I was more surprised by: Zoe, who should have been an ocean away, or the cartoon of me, which was (perhaps deliberately) a poor likeness. Except that she'd managed to capture something that I recognised only now that I saw it—a man with every possibility in front of him, but hesitating, not quite able to seize the day.

She interrupted my contemplation of how others— or at least one other—saw me by standing and throwing her arms around me, as she had on the night of the English Bastards. 'Oh God—I'm so sorry . . .'

I had long ago come to terms with what had happened in St Jean Pied de Port. 'I'm the one . . . Or are you apologising for the cartoon?'

'It's only your cart. It's not meant to look like you. No beard. Listen, this is so rude but I've got to reply to this email. But there's a whole lot I want to explain.'

'I'll buy you dinner.'

'You don't have to . . . shout.'

'Have you been to the Guggenheim yet? We'll go there first. In half an hour?'

I met her in the foyer. She was in walking trousers and a baggy T-shirt hanging off one shoulder and tied in a knot over her hip.

'I lost all my stuff in St Jean Pied de Port. So, forget anywhere fancy.'

'I went to one of the best restaurants in the world in what I'm wearing now, more or less. You look great.'

Outside Frank Gehry's extravaganza of random curves and interconnecting stone, glass and titanium that caught the light and made it part of the building, Zoe hesitated. 'What do you think of it?' she said.

'What do you know about modern architecture?' I didn't want to talk down to someone who'd studied art. She might have done a thesis on deconstructionist and expressionist design.

'Zip.'

I took her through some of the background to the style, with the advantage of a real building to illustrate. I didn't hurry: I had a sense that she wasn't sure about going inside. Possibly she was uncomfortable about being put on the spot and having to explain a range of art she wasn't up on.

'You love this, don't you?' she said. 'Not just the architecture—talking about it.'

'Very observant of you.'

'So why aren't you an architect?'

'I told you, back in the church in Estaing. I got a

scholarship in engineering. I was pretty grateful to get to go to uni.'

'How old were you?'

'Twenty-one. I'd been working for two years.'

'And you're going to let a decision you took back then define who you are for the rest of your life?'

'I've adapted. I teach design theory, which has strong connections with architecture—but I do it as an engineer. Did it. And now you're going to ask why I don't become an architect. I'm fifty-two.'

'I'm forty-five. I might have just got my first real job as an artist—what I've wanted to be all my life—today. What are you going to do next? I'm guessing you're not going to spend the rest of your life improving your cart design.'

'You want the truth? I haven't thought much beyond it. How long's the cartoon job for?'

'No idea. So, here we both are in the middle of our lives, starting again. Are we going to be bold or just go back to what we were?'

'There's a slightly more urgent decision we need to take.' I pointed to the museum. 'The sign says it closes at eight. It's late, but I guess we're not going to get another chance.'

53
Zoe

When I'd sat outside the Guggenheim sketching earlier in the day, I was on a mission and my mind was racing with ideas. I was too busy to think about going inside. Now, I realised it was more than that. I was a walker on a walk, not an artist on a tour of the galleries of Europe. I hadn't had this feeling at the churches in Estaing or Conques, which had seemed part of the Camino. But even as I walked through a modern city, looking in shop windows and taking advantage of its technology, I felt separate from it.

Fortunately, Martin pushed me—he didn't insist, but after his lecture on the exterior architecture I wanted to show him I knew something too. Great. Having turned me into an entrepreneur, the Camino was now making me egotistical and competitive.

For whatever reason, I got an hour's taste of amazing art. And I had the perfect companion for touring a gallery renowned for its interplay of art and architecture.

As we stood before a huge Clyfford Still canvas, with its bright colours in stalagmite formations, he made a big deal of looking at it from every angle short of standing on his head.

'Stop it,' I said. 'Go find some Old Masters if you're not interested.'

'Tell me about it.'

I had been to the Still museum in Denver, so this was not the first of his works I'd seen. I wasn't sure what Martin knew about modern art but felt he might be better able to put Rothko and Klein into perspective by seeing a Still first.

'He was considered the first of the abstract expressionists,' I explained. 'American.' Martin was taking it in, seriously now. 'Unlike the artists after him, his colour-field paintings are not regular. Paint laid on canvas—he wanted colour and texture and images to fuse.'

I found us a Rothko.

'No point in altering head position for this one,' he said.

'More challenging, agreed,' I said. *Sensual*, my Russian-born art teacher had told me; then, like Martin now, I struggled to see anything in the rectangular shapes.

'Truth is,' I told Martin, 'for years, anything I saw in Rothko was too ephemeral for me. I preferred Georgia O'Keeffe. Colour and imagery that's evocative and accessible.' As a student in St Louis I had loved her work, only to move away from it as I tried to be more sophisticated. Now, I thought of her words and she inspired me again: she had always been terrified but had never allowed her fear to stop her.

'The flowers or the vaginas?' said Martin.

'Why do men see sex everywhere?' But I doubted Keith would have known that much about O'Keeffe's work, if he knew of her at all.

'Do you really want an answer to that?'

'As it happens, I do think there was subconscious imagery happening. Makes them all the more powerful.'

'And these rectangles?' Martin looked back at the Rothko.

'Spiritual. Agony and the Ecstasy, without religious icons. Though he was religious—collected a lot of religious art for his chapel. He was . . .' I looked at the painting: *Walls of Light*, in yellow and red. 'It seems to hover, don't you think? Like we are looking at a landscape and yet . . .' The size and vibrancy of the painting in real life, compared with the reproductions I'd seen in books, allowed it to do what I guessed the artist, preoccupied with death, had intended. For me, in the moment, this picture was not a landscape but a look over the horizon into another world. Rothko had committed suicide. There, in the distance, was the world he—and Keith—now belonged to.

Martin was looking intently, not just trying hard but taking something from it.

As 8 p.m. approached, the museum staff began pushing us toward the exit.

'We could come back in the morning,' said Martin.

'We could, but I might never finish the walk. Or draw cartoons. I'm a professional artist now, remember?'

I was. For the first time in my life. A professional artist—a *cartoonist*—and writer, living on my wits, three-quarters of the way into a thousand-mile walk. And a widow. Three months earlier, I could not have imagined any of this. Now I was about to go to dinner in the company of a British adventurer with a hint of a Harrison Ford smirk, with whom I'd just spent two hours talking art and architecture at the Guggenheim in Bilbao. On—let's face it—a date.

54

Martin

I felt I'd managed to invite Zoe to dinner without giving the impression of it being a date. I was finding my way with her again, and not keen on a repeat of the events in St Jean Pied de Port.

It wasn't as if it was the first time we'd eaten together. That said, Bilbao is a serious city, the biggest on the Camino del Norte, and the restaurant was a world away from what we'd become accustomed to in rural France: modern, sharp, small tables and stools at the bar, and a glass-topped display of tapas with a focus on seafood and vegetables. It felt out of place on a walk, even a little disorienting, but San Sebastián had prepared me. Zoe's smile indicated I'd made a good choice.

We secured a table for two as the place was filling up with locals, young people having after-work drinks.

With a couple of glasses of rosé and a round of tapas on the table, I threw it over to her. 'Go.'

'You first.'

'No, you. I'm the one who's *supposed* to be walking to Santiago.'

She filled me in, from the Skype call with her daughter, to the week in the Pyrenees wilderness, to the email from the *Chronicle*. She would have spent the whole meal apologising for standing me up in St Jean Pied de Port if I hadn't dismissed it, sincerely: 'For God's sake, I thought it was an understandable thing to do even without the news.'

She didn't mention her financial situation, but I could guess. She had changed her top but not the trousers.

Her husband's—Keith's—apparent suicide was not so easily dealt with, and she was still coming to terms with it.

'I let him down,' Zoe said. 'If I had been there for him he might still be alive.'

'You think that was what it was about? How much support you offered? That was all?'

'I guess not. But I should have seen the signs.'

'Or he could have told you. It cuts both ways. *If* that's what happened. If it wasn't an accident. You don't know. You can't know.'

She took a deep breath. 'His business was in trouble. He took out an insurance policy. A big one.'

'Doesn't mean he planned to die. He had money problems? It was a way he could put some protection in place, *if* anything happened. Do something positive at a time when he was struggling to find solutions . . . And if he had stuff on his mind . . . he could have been distracted when he had the accident.'

I could see she wanted to believe it—but didn't. 'The more I think about it, the more it seems all the signs were there. I should have . . . stepped up.'

'I don't want to sound harsh, but we're responsible for ourselves. We make our own decisions.' There had been moments when I'd thought—fantasised, rather than truly contemplated—ending it, and for the worst possible reason. To get back at Julia. Who would have been rightly angry back at me. 'If you do believe it wasn't an accident, then in all the pain I guess there must be a bit of anger too.'

She drank some wine, and tried the shrimp and peppers. Then she nodded, slowly. 'You're right. I was pretty angry with the universe, pretty angry with myself . . . I was angry with my mother for a while . . . after all these years.' She stopped and I let it sit.

'Something else,' she said. 'You know I said I forgave my mother? In Conques? I've been wondering what would have happened if I'd forgiven her first back then—when she was dying. Maybe it wouldn't have meant anything to her, but I could have tried.'

'Tough thing, to forgive someone when they're in the wrong.'

She laughed. 'That's what forgiveness is. Anyway, thanks for listening . . . for understanding.'

'I wish you'd let me do that in St Jean Pied de Port. But fate seems to have brought us together again,' I said. 'Not just you deciding to walk on, but us both taking the northern route, and then today . . .'

She laughed again. 'It's been good to have someone to talk to.'

'Do you want to walk with me tomorrow?'

'Thanks, but I think I need to stay here another day, do some more cartoons . . .'

'I'll wait, if you like.'

'Thank you. But . . . I don't think it's a good idea. I liked walking with you in France, but I wasn't thinking about what I needed to think about.'

'I can keep shtum.'

'You do that most of the time anyway. It's more than that. I need to be independent, and if I was walking with you . . .' She waved her hand to indicate our surroundings. 'Five-star restaurants every night.'

'They only go up to three.'

'Whatever. I need to do it myself.'

She reached across and took my hand. 'One day, when this is all done, when I've got my shit together . . . This is just the wrong time. Maybe for you too. Maybe you need to deal with the past before you can move on.'

'It's more about accepting it than dealing with it, if that distinction makes any sense. I'm not good at that—I'm more about finding solutions. I don't know there's anything else I can do.'

She looked at me thoughtfully. 'When we get stuck, sometimes, instead of pushing at the problem, we need to look inward and question the things we believe, the stuff that might be blocking us. Is that too Californian for you?'

'Not at all. I say the same thing to my students, in pretty much the same words.'

'So, maybe think about it.'

I walked her back to the hostel and kissed her goodnight, starting with a peck on each cheek and finishing with something more intense.

'I'd ask you to come in,' she said, 'but . . .'

'We could go back to my hotel.'

She thought about it, then shook her head. 'Not a good idea.' She kissed me again. 'All right, I'm torn and will regret this as soon as you leave. I would like to spend time with you, but I need to get my head straight, feel that I'm solid in myself, in case I disappear before I've fully rediscovered who I am. I really do.'

'I'm thinking I'll try to meet the Brazilians in Oviedo,' I said. 'They arrive April 28.'

'You didn't tell me that.'

'See, we need more time to talk. They're taking three weeks off, then doing another section, the Camino Primitivo. Turn left at Villaviciosa; it's about the same length but not along the coast, which I think's a good thing. Not so much development. It's supposed to be the toughest Camino.'

'Keep talking.'

'When do you have to be in Santiago?'

'My flight's May 13.'

'That's my due date in Paris. I need to be in Santiago on the 11th to catch the train the next day. *If* we both happen to hit Oviedo on the same day *and* your head's clear . . . Call it fate.'

'I can't promise . . .'

'I'm not asking you to. Five p.m. at the tourist office in Oviedo on April 28—two weeks tomorrow. Or not.'

'No promises. Either of us.'

'I heard you. How's the money holding out?'

'Fine, now that I've got a job.'

'I mean right now? It'll be a month before you're paid. Minimum.'

'I'm fine.'

'I'll lend you five hundred.' It was my daily withdrawal limit. And about the limit of what I could spare.

'I . . . How would I pay you back? I'll only take it if I can pay you back.'

I took out the packet that held my passport, cards and cash, and she wrote down my account number. Then we went to an ATM, sorted it out and kissed goodbye for the third time. She didn't mention the scallop shell and nor did I. It would give me a reason to contact her if we didn't connect in Oviedo.

That said, I hoped she would take the Camino Primitivo, if only to keep open the option of meeting. And, paradoxically, that we wouldn't see each other on the track until then.

55
Zoe

CARTOON: An elderly Caucasian woman is walking slowly, carefully. Her bag of sins is open and empty, and her face is glowing. Ahead of her, a man of colour, some grey in his thinning hair, is waiting for her. He has a picnic prepared on a table.

STORY: Marianne, from France, is eighty-two. She and her three closest friends had dreamed of walking the Camino ever since they heard about it in elementary school. The time had never been right: too young; too busy; their families needed them. And now, they have accepted that they are too old. Except Marianne.

Marianne has been widowed ten years and has had a stroke, which has left her with a limp. Her daughter thinks she should be in a nursing home but Marianne does not think her life is over, and wishes to pay homage to the church that has seen her through difficult times. She will walk the Camino for herself and her friends. Her daughter makes her call in every second day and interrogates Marianne to check that she is not losing her mind: *Who is the French president? What is the capital of Morocco?*

Marianne left from her own home, as the pilgrims did in the ninth century, and carries a picture of her three friends with her. She holds the photo in every shot that is taken of her and posts it on Facebook for them. She can manage only five to eight miles each day. Along the way, she meets Moses, a Kenyan man of sixty, who grew up in a Catholic orphanage and, after caring for other orphans his whole life, is on a pilgrimage to thank God for his fortunes. He started in Rome and walks ten to sixteen miles a day, but stays two nights at each place, because he wishes to spend a full day seeing and making sense of everywhere he goes, visiting each church and religious monument. Every second night, he waits for Marianne. When Marianne calls her daughter, he has Google ready to help with the answers.

Neither had anyone to share their experiences and thoughts with, because other pilgrims move on. Until they found each other.

I was working harder than I had in years. I had a deal with the *Chronicle* and my contact there, Stephanie, wrote chatty emails with critiques. She didn't care much about specific routes. It was all about the people. She loved the Martin cartoon—and Martin—but I managed to convince her that an entire series about him would not do justice to the diversity of the Camino. I told her that he had his own story and was blogging it; she could mention that at the end of the article if people were interested in following him.

All right, but can we have some Americans? Not counting the group I'd met at St Jean Pied de Port, that would be Ed Walker and me.

I was keeping up the pace to ensure that I got into Santiago in time for my flight. And Oviedo. Martin's argument for taking the Camino Primitivo made sense. The coastal route might have been pretty in the ninth century, but the highway now covered the original trail, and a lot of the beach had fallen victim to property developers.

At a push, I could make Oviedo on April 28, and the thought of seeing the Brazilians filled me with warmth. Truth was, I wanted to see Martin too—a lot. I just wanted to be sure, before I did, that I was ready. I had woken one night thinking of something he had said to me: *I wished you'd stayed in St Jean Pied de Port and let me listen.* The time hadn't been right then, but now I felt as much in need of a friend as a lover.

Thanks to Martin's loan, I had solved my immediate financial issues, including paying for the ticket change. I hadn't wanted to take his money, but I figured that someone who could afford to stay at hotels and eat at three-star restaurants wouldn't miss it—and I would repay the debt as soon as the *Chronicle* came through.

I had something to do—a kind of job—and I was looking forward to meeting with the San Francisco team to see if they had further opportunities. I wondered if I should move there. I'd always preferred the Bay Area to LA, but somehow it seemed too big a decision. My friends were in LA, even if neither of my daughters were now. Maybe I should move closer to them? I felt more adrift at the prospect of moving home to the States than I did on the Camino, spending each night at a different hostel.

I was eating better. Vegetarian was not too hard once I learned to avoid the traps: *salada mixta* contained tuna; *menestra*—an otherwise wonderful vegetable stew—had *jamon*, and so did the *bocadillo vegetal*. Ham is apparently not meat in Spain. My one indulgence was a glass of rosé after my work was done for the day.

Camille emailed me to say I couldn't be happy without love: a Spanish man, perhaps? They were reputedly good lovers, though she could not offer personal experience. She seemed to have forgiven me for sending her halfway from Cluny to St Jean Pied de Port.

Walking around Castro Urdiales in the evening, I was blown away by the silhouette of the church on the harbour edge, the Madonna and Child illuminated through a large square window. I had an urge to tell Martin about it, how I saw the work of the artist without the filter of negativity toward the church. His words about Keith and his power to choose stayed in my mind, and I felt that with each step my grief diminished, or at least the self-blaming part did. And I acknowledged that the anger the crucifixes along the path had stirred had been as much about Keith as my mother.

I would never know for sure what was in Keith's head on that last ride, but I no longer felt I had been at the wheel. Though I missed Keith, when I woke up at night it was Martin I thought of. I wasn't ready for a relationship yet—but I was ready to think about one.

The stage to Laredo was harder than it should have been. The night before, there were only three others in the dormitory: all of them apparently had several zippered items of clothing that needed to be stored, retrieved and repacked in zip-lock bags at crazy hours.

Walking on the highway was always exhausting, with the fumes and noise and need to stay alert. There was a hole in the sole of one of my sneakers and the stitching was coming apart in both. It rained all day; even regular boots would have gotten soaked.

After roaming Laredo in the rain, I found a *pensione*. My routine was to start early enough to get the walking done before 1.30 p.m., when everything except the restaurants closed. After lunch and a siesta, I would work on cartoon ideas until 11 p.m. The drawings came easily; it was the stories that took time. But today, I fell asleep as soon as I arrived.

I missed lunch—even the crazy-late Spanish lunch—but the kitchen was happy to make me a tortilla and salad at 6 p.m. Trouble was, with the change to my routine I forgot to check my socks, drying on the radiator. The room was warm but the heat was coming from somewhere else. I ended up having to wear wet socks the next day.

The route from Laredo ran beside the sea all the way, and much of it was actually on the beach. I had enjoyed the coastal aspects of the walk, but I'd lived a long time in California. It wasn't as breathtaking as it might have been if I'd come from Arizona. And sand is difficult to walk on. My sneakers let it in, and my socks slipped. Five miles in I pulled off my shoes and socks and, sure enough, I had blisters. Not just one, but at least two on each little toe, and one developing on the sole of my left foot.

Monsieur Chevalier had said I would have blisters and perhaps I had become overconfident after escaping them for nine weeks. It wasn't like I'd never gotten blisters before. It happened every time I bought a new pair of sandals at home.

The cure for new sandals is to walk in them for small periods of time, days apart—not an option right now. Then there were my experiences of other people's blisters on the Camino. Tough young men hobbling at night, changing to sandals and strapping their huge leather boots to their packs, sometimes abandoning them or even the walk altogether. I had quietly felt superior, taking some pleasure in my age not being a disadvantage in this contest. Now the laugh was on me. I stopped at Nojo after only ten miles.

It was worse than I thought. There was a huge blister on my big toe too, a result of changing gait to protect the little toe. By the time I had burst them all and left threads hanging to drain them, my feet were like pincushions.

One thing I knew was that I could easily walk to Santiago in time for my plane. God must be laughing. With Martin's money, I could of course catch a bus or train to Santiago and sit it out there, working on my cartoons, waiting for the 13th.

No. Damn. Way.

The next day my feet were no better. One blister looked like it could be infected. I needed to get myself somewhere with a pharmacy and maybe a doctor. The next large town was Santander, twenty-two kilometres away. Plus a boat ride, something my fellow *peregrinos* assured me was an accepted tradition. Like it mattered. Of course it did.

My progress was slow. Painfully slow. I longed for the blister pack Nicole had given me on the second day of my Camino. I had thought I was strong—I only had to look at the new contours of my calves to remind me of the mountains I had traversed—yet here I was about to be crippled, my walk brought to an end by a few bits of red weeping skin. Anywhere else on the body wouldn't have been an issue. But my feet were critical. If they couldn't heal while I walked, I would have to catch a bus. I didn't have the time to sit and wait.

Why did that feel like a cop-out? It wasn't as if I had promised myself: Santiago or die. I wasn't doing it for anyone else. And I hadn't made a deal with the universe: walk to Santiago and I will have given back all I took from Keith.

'The Camino walks you,' Richard had said in Tramayes. 'Walking the Camino will help you find what you've lost,' Monsieur Chevalier had assured me. Would taking a bus instead of arriving on foot detract from the thousand miles I had already walked? For reasons I did not understand, the answer remained an unequivocal yes. Not walking, for me, would be cheating—peace of mind was within my grasp, and I would never get it, never feel I *deserved* it, if I didn't walk.

When I arrived at the port for the ferry across to Santander, it was late—too late for even a Spanish doctor, unless I went to the hospital. But I hit the pharmacy and bought enough antiseptic and blister Band-Aids to start my own store.

On the boat, sitting and watching the town stretched out across from me, hilltop churches and piers giving way to working docks, I started tending to the worst of the wounds. My fellow passengers were probably horrified, or more likely disgusted, but I was too beat to care. One patted my shoulder and muttered *Buen Camino*.

After settling into a hostel and finishing with my

feet, I washed my clothes and went out for a glass of rosé. I'd gotten used to the trash on the floors of Spanish bars—wrappers and stuff—a contrast to the bathrooms, which were always clean. Someone had told me the mess was to make work for the cleaners who might otherwise add to the country's unemployment problem.

'Why am I walking?' I asked myself, but no answer came. I got another glass of rosé.

'There is nothing to prove,' the devil said. It wasn't as if it would make any difference to anyone back home whether I walked one thousand miles or twelve hundred. Either amount was too hard to imagine unless you'd done it, and they'd be in awe—or think I was crazy—either way. The bartender waved the bottle in front of me and I nodded.

Santiago was no big deal. The head of St James? More like a gullible shepherd boy and a smart operator in the ninth century seeing a business opportunity—though even he couldn't have imagined it would still be paying dividends a thousand years later. And if it was the head of Christ's disciple, transported by stone boat to Spain—so what? Cute bit of history, but I could get a bus and see it too. Why did I feel so compelled? Magic or stubbornness? Or something else?

'What had I learned?' Monsieur Chevalier had asked. I had said I could walk. Now I couldn't, so maybe this was the lesson—not to be proud; not to take anything for granted, as I had with Keith. But was it also a lesson to still have faith enough in myself to be independent? It was a confused message, which may have had something to do with the third glass of rosé.

I slept badly, though the dorm was quiet. My dreams were full of my *pèlerin* cartoon characters, Monsieur Chevalier assuring me I would find what I was looking for, the Brazilians laughing and Martin waiting for me to show up in Oviedo. In the morning, I still didn't have an answer. But my feet were not as red and my socks were dry. I got up, used some of Martin's money to buy proper shoes and painted my feet with iodine. Then I did what I did every day. One day at a time.

I walked.

56
Martin

I kept walking, appreciating the mix of urban and rural. Between Portugalete and Castro Urdiales, there was a spectacular walking and cycling track, about twenty kilometres over motorways and through countryside. The best of both worlds and perfect for the cart.

That evening, I had an email from the American photographer we'd met in the Estaing church: *Thanks again for the history lesson and hope you like the photo.* I did: the surprise was that at our feet, directly in front of us, the colours of the stones formed a distinct heart—clearly a deliberate design. I hadn't noticed it at the time; Zoe the artist surely must have.

I crossed the railway bridge between Boo de Piélagos and Mogro illegally on foot, rather than taking the train as recommended by the guidebook—or the long deviation prescribed by the purists. I was a bit down, concerned that Sarah had gone quiet again, and pessimistic about whether Zoe would be in Oviedo.

I had also begun to think about what I would do after the trade fair, now just a fortnight away. In all the time I had been walking, this basic question had not been on my mental agenda. Questions of accommodation, food and finding the next signpost had kept me occupied. I had literally been living a day-to-day existence. I wondered if Maarten the Dutchman was making any progress with the same question.

There was something else I had to face. Even after ten weeks of walking with the cart, learning how to place my feet, sticks and body weight to best effect, I would rather have been carrying a backpack. The cart was remarkably manoeuvrable for a wheeled vehicle, but it could not compete with two feet. Lifting it over stiles, which tended to present themselves one after another, was an absolute pain in the neck and all parts below.

The Chinese manufacturer had sent a list of detailed questions that could only mean they were serious, but no sum was mentioned. Nothing more from the Germans or the French. Somewhere in a British Army facility, my cart's twin was being put through tests that were doubtless more strenuous than anything I had inflicted on mine.

Jonathan, the Chinese and the Germans would deliver the verdict, but there was a danger that my market would be limited to people like Maarten who could not carry a backpack at all, rather than those who had a choice.

In Mogro, I had booked a room in a family hotel a few minutes' walk from a bar. The chef would have not been out of place in San Sebastián. I was regaled with a *menu degustation* featuring foie gras, wild mushrooms, octopus and veal, which I washed down first with a glass of rosé and then, after seeing the array of wine in the rack on the wall, most of a fifteen-year-old Rioja, leaving just a glass for my host.

Remembering the night with Dead Walker, I refused a digestif of Spanish brandy, but it came anyway, gratis. I went back to my hotel room and composed a reflective blog entry about the people you meet on the Camino. Such as Zoe.

Reading it the next morning with a double espresso in my hand and a couple of aspirin in my stomach, I was only mildly embarrassed. It could have been worse.

It turned out to have been bad enough. As I packed

my phone, I saw there was a message from 3 a.m., an hour earlier in the UK. From Julia: *Call me. Urgent.*

I went to my room and rang her. It was the first conversation we had had for nine months, if you could call it a conversation. Sarah had taken an overdose: Julia's sleeping pills washed down with vodka. *Yes, my sleeping pills—what's that supposed to imply?* Sarah was okay, physically. She had had her stomach pumped and spent the night in hospital. There was a suggestion that the unpleasant remedy was more about delivering a lesson than about life and death.

Of course it was a cry for help, you fucking self-absorbed *prick.* Does she need you? Does she fucking need you? What do you fucking think? No, she doesn't want to talk to you. No, don't *ever* come back. Go and live in fucking *America.*

I texted Sarah: *I'm coming home.*

After a fortnight without communication, the response was instant: *Please don't.*

I want to see you.

I'm OK now. Won't be if I have to deal with u and Mum. And then, knowing me all too well, that I'd trust a professional over the judgment of a seventeen-year-old: *I talked to the psych this morning. She was good. I want to talk to you but not till I've worked out what I want to say. OK?*

Are you going to keep seeing her?
For a while. OK?
OK. I love you, Sarah.
xxx

I walked the twenty-one kilometres to Santillana del Mar on autopilot. Rain drizzled all day, and the path followed agricultural pipes painted with the ugly yellow arrows. All I was thinking about was how to get back to England, where I could take the Germans' offer and use the money to rent a flat in London, and get Sarah away from the woman who had left potentially lethal sleeping tablets for a troubled teenager to find.

I dumped my gear at a painfully quaint hotel and found a *sidrería*—a cider house. Despite having drunk too much the previous night, I ordered a drink. Where was Dead Walker when I needed him? What would he have said? What would Zoe say? That I should look within? Christ.

But as I watched the bartenders doing irritating tricks with the cider for the tourists, I became conscious of how much my anger was clouding everything. Zoe was right. There were things I hadn't dealt with.

57

Zoe

My blisters were getting better and there were no new ones. The Camino gave me more seascapes and paths of every kind, including some coast-hugging freeways, with startling blue water on one side and huge trucks bearing down on the other—which was too often the side I had to walk on. At home, I would have sent angry letters to city hall. But here I was in the hands of St James. Or in my own unsteady and uncertain ones. I watched the roads carefully. Fate may have been occasionally causing a casualty, but I was not going to be one of them.

In Santillana del Mar, the cobblestone streets were as old as the Inquisition torture machines in the museum, but the town was in other ways modern, bustling with tourists, and I was grateful that I did not feel the presence of past souls whose blood had soaked the earth I was now walking on. I sketched a laughing waiter as he splashed still cider into my glass from a great height to make bubbles.

Loving the cartoons, Stephanie wrote. *The old lady made me cry; you captured something saintly in her. Hope her daughter doesn't read it! Did you find religion on the Camino?*

I didn't answer her query: too complicated. I let my cartoons say it for me. 'Marianne', who I'd met at a hostel in Moissac, *had* radiated something quite magical.

There was also an email from the American photographer—with the photo he'd taken on the steps of the church in Estaing the day of the rainstorm. I sat in the *cybercafé* staring at it, not wanting to leave it behind. It wasn't just that Martin and I looked totally like a couple. It was my expression. I couldn't remember the last time I had seen myself looking so happy.

As I came out of Ribadesella, there were no trucks on a deserted trail, and only a white fence between me and the sea. After a short detour away from the coast, the Camino took its final section by the beach, before heading inland along roads and paths surrounded by overhanging trees and dense foliage.

The following day, I got myself a little lost on what I thought was a short cut. In late morning, I found myself in mist, surrounded by dew-covered spider webs stretching over acres of bushes. I sat for maybe an hour, just taking it in.

When I parted from Martin in Bilbao I had known I needed more time alone. I had begun to realise how much I'd adapted to Keith's needs and preferences. Just small stuff: what time we went to bed, which side I slept on, not cooking cauliflower. Allowances and adaptions anyone in a long-term relationship has to make, accumulating over time. But I wasn't in a relationship anymore. I wanted to know what of myself needed to be reclaimed.

Maybe because I was consciously thinking about it, I felt the layers I had built up—the part of me that I'd developed to relate to Keith—falling away. A day before Oviedo, I took stock and felt I was near enough. I knew who I was again. Martin would be at the tourist office at 5 p.m. So would I.

The final day into Oviedo was a long one, or at least I would once have thought it long—twenty miles or more. I barely noticed it. I didn't have any illusions that my affair to remember would be anything other than a vacation romance, but it would be a kick start for midlife confidence.

The stage was typical of the Spanish walk in the worst way: long sections of road with no sidewalk and construction works that made it difficult to avoid the traffic. But then the path led into the old city and the twenty-first century was left behind: narrow lanes dwarfed by stone walls, courtyards opening onto churches, cafés where the weather now permitted a sprawl of outdoor seating. I was early, and I figured Martin would have organised a hotel, as he had in St Jean Pied de Port. I bought a coffee and did a sketch of the beggar who had accosted me on the outskirts.

The tourist office was hard to find—I had under-estimated the size of the town or overestimated my navigational skills. Maybe I was unconsciously wanting Martin to get there first.

He didn't. It was Paola who was waiting for me. I had almost forgotten that the reason for choosing this date was the Brazilians' arrival for their next stage.

We hugged each other, but before I could ask about her three-week break, where her daughter was and whether the others had arrived, she gave me a half-smile and drew back. I'd delivered plenty of bad news in my life and I knew the look. It flashed through my mind that thinking of *An Affair to Remember* had jinxed Martin. He'd been in an accident. He'd been killed by one of the trucks. Paola must have seen my expression.

'He is sorry,' she said, 'but he cannot make it. He asked me to give you this.'

She handed me a package. I opened it with shaking hands, thinking that at least he wasn't dead.

It was the blue dress from the boutique in St Jean Pied de Port, my scallop-shell charm and a note.

Dear Zoe

You were right: the Camino has things to teach us and we need solitude to reflect on its lessons. Thank you for the charm. It has brought me this far, and I hope it finds you again and accompanies you safely to Santiago and home. You won't need it, of course: your resourcefulness is truly astonishing. Thank you for your help with Sarah. We're not there yet, but you've helped me to look at it differently. Or at least realise that I need to.

I hope you find the peace you are looking for.

Buen Camino

Martin

58

Martin

I stopped at a hotel a few kilometres out of Oviedo, mentally exhausted from talking to Paola, who had intercepted me as I crossed the main square.

Zoe had been right: we needed to resolve our present problems before beginning anything new. I'd tried. I'd walked for a week and two hundred kilometres, speaking to no one except to organise food and accommodation. By any reasonable measure, I'd given myself time out to think—about Sarah's need for parental guidance, the freedom she needed to make her own mistakes, and the complicating factor that was Julia's and my relationship. This was why people walked. And the result? Nothing. Just despair and anger, some of the latter directed at the self-indulgent waste of time that was the Camino.

As for Zoe: if two months of walking had not been sufficient to forgive herself for Keith's death, it was going to be a hard nut to crack. She didn't have answers to my problems, nor I to hers. In the event she had turned up at 5 p.m., it would surely only have been to tell me that. Or to reunite with the Brazilians. We might still catch up in the final fortnight. One for the universe to decide.

I came down to dinner to find a group of five middle-aged men at a table being addressed—or possibly blessed—by a sixth, a tall bespectacled chap. At the conclusion of his speech he beckoned me over from the other end of the room, where I'd seated myself.

His name was Felipe: the men were old friends, now scattered over Spain, who walked two weeks of the Camino every year as a sort of male-bonding exercise. One of their number was rostered to drive the van that ferried their gear or anyone carrying an injury. There was much drinking and consumption of good food in addition to the walking and talking. All bar Felipe were married, but it struck me that if I found myself in a hostel with them and the Brazilians I could say goodbye to sleep.

After dinner one of them came over and we chatted for a while. Marco was an Italian-born haematologist with excellent English. He was a little guy who looked like he'd had his nose broken at some stage, perhaps by a jealous husband. He had paid the price for a wandering eye—three marriages, with kids from two of them and another from an extramarital dalliance—but was philosophical about it and optimistic that his current wife would see him through to old age.

I was not in the habit of sharing much with other men, even Jonathan, but Marco had been frank about himself, and it was in the spirit of the evening. I told him about my divorce, about Sarah and then, after a digestif, a bit about the situation with Zoe. He had little to offer about the first two, beyond putting them behind me, but pressed me for details on the opportunity, as he saw it, with Zoe. His conclusion was that she was probably looking for someone to take her mind off her problems—and a bit of well-timed persuasion would get her across the line. But I'd never see her again. If that was what I wanted, fine. If not, I should wait until she returned to America and could think about a possible relationship in the context of her family, rather than as part of a transition. That much seemed like good advice.

59
Zoe

CARTOON: A man with a cart walks down the road, throwing up dust clouds behind. His bag of sins is half full and tied up. He is looking back: his expression shows a determination to make the best of what is ahead, mixed with regret for what he is leaving behind. In the foreground, a woman drinks a glass of wine—there are other pilgrims around her but she is oblivious, in her own space.

STORY: The Camino expands and contracts like a concertina; people move at their own pace, but with rest days and injuries they turn up again in a café or bar, at the *gîte* or in the bakery. There are hugs exchanged, drinks bought, stories shared. Each time you know that you may see them tomorrow—or never again.

Buggy Man has come on a long journey, and his eyes

have opened to the world around him, but moving forward on the Camino is the same as moving on in life: it can mean leaving things—and people—behind.

He is a resolute walker, but he now needs strength of a different kind—life's disappointments have hardened his heart and he must allow it to crack.

The Camino whispers its magic, and around the next bend are more reunions and new friends—and maybe the answer he seeks.

I could have been angry at Martin, but it was my pride that was hurt, and that was not his fault. The blue dress made me all the sadder, reawakening my guilt at leaving him back in St Jean Pied de Port. I was disappointed that I wouldn't be walking with him for the next two weeks, and that we would not arrive in Santiago together. I didn't know why it should matter, but it did. As I was powerless to make it happen, I vowed not to think about it. At least I was back with my old friends the Brazilians, who had reunited after travelling separately for three weeks.

Paola had taken me to her hostel, where I spent a while in the shower, pulling myself together. When I came out there was a young woman on the bunk bed, plugged into her phone.

'Tina,' Paola said, nodding in her direction. 'My

daughter. She flew alone from Brazil.' The girl gave me a brief smile. She was a younger, slimmer version of her mother, with large blue eyes made bigger by the black makeup caked around them. Margarida arrived next, with an extra bag.

'Good shopping in Spain,' she said. 'And Italy. Have you seen Bernhard?'

I hadn't seen him since France and had thought he was taking the Camino Francés.

'He is coming to join me—all of us,' said Margarida. She showed me a series of messages on her phone.

He arrived in time for dinner, along with Renata and Fabiana. There was a path from León on the Camino Francés to Oviedo—one hundred kilometres on the Camino del San Salvador. He brought plenty of stories from the most famous pilgrim trail. One couple had skipped the flat section to take a plane to the Grand Prix; a Korean guy navigated by choosing a walker each day and following two paces behind, stopping when they stopped and refusing to pass; a priest had performed an impromptu marriage ceremony for two pilgrims to allow them to consummate their relationship without guilt.

'Irish, Australians and Kiwis—New Zealanders,' he said. Looking at me, he added, 'And Americans.'

Bernhard had met Todd, whose discarded possessions had saved me in the Pyrenees.

'Todd has rocks in his head. He follows the shortest route on the map. Because of this, he is always on the highway, which is bad for the feet.' Tina was hanging off every word and Bernhard was playing to it.

His summary of the Camino Francés was: 'Too many walkers, too much commerce.' I figured he meant: too much competition, not enough handouts.

He added, 'And flat. Flat and boring. Perfect for Buggy Man.'

'Where is Martin?' asked Renata.

Paola answered for me. 'He came through this morning. He is moving on.'

Fabiana was subdued. She had spent the time out at a religious retreat and seemed to have recovered some of her piety. She'd have a tough time keeping a hold of it with Margarida around.

So began the last leg of my Camino: two weeks and a bit more than a hundred and twenty miles. What had once seemed impossible to contemplate now seemed not worth worrying about. The coastal section of the walk had been lonely and, as if to mirror my emotional turmoil, the beauty of the ocean and the countryside had been slammed up hard against concrete and progress.

Now I was on the Primitivo, the most ancient Camino, where at times my feet would tread on the original stones of a path pilgrims had taken for a thousand years. I started feeling both humble and strong, in the company of good people. Even Bernhard.

The next day he slept in and Renata left early. Fabiana was deep in conversation with Paola, which left me with Tina and Margarida.

'Have you done any other walks?' I asked Tina.

'No. I'm doing this thing only for my mother.'

'Why do you think she wants you to walk the Camino?'

'My father died on it.'

That was a conversation stopper. Margarida was the one to break the silence. 'I think for her, it is a walk about love.'

Tina didn't look like she wanted to think about her parents being in love.

Margarida persisted. 'It is a very romantic story.'

If you like romances with unhappy endings. I wondered about Paola's need to walk and re-walk.

By the end of the day, I was walking alone and headed for the *albergue* in Grado. The Brazilians had a hotel, and I had arranged to meet them for massages and dinner. We were joined there by another walking group completing their first day, six Spanish men in their forties and fifties. Two spoke good English—the tall, serious Felipe, and Marco, who had those dark good looks and bedroom eyes that give Latino men their reputation.

The next day, I met Marco on the trail.

'Why this Camino and not the traditional one?' I asked him in Spanish.

'The Camino Francés? Too many Americans.' He grinned. 'And we have walked the Camino Francés already. Over three years.'

'I think you can blame Hollywood for the American take-over,' I said. 'Apparently there's a movie.'

Marco laughed. 'I have seen this movie. It makes a big mistake.'

He didn't elaborate until that evening, when he and his friends insisted on buying drinks for the Brazilians and me.

'Look,' said Marco. 'Watch this and tell me if it seems like it is true.'

We gathered around his phone screen to watch a scene from *The Way*, somewhere in the middle of the movie. I recognised Martin Sheen from *Apocalypse Now*: he was having his pack stolen by a Roma boy and giving chase. I was about to call out the racism and the fact that I'd never felt at risk of losing anything to anyone, beyond human error in St Jean Pied de Port. But

Paola got in first, laughing. 'He is running. *Running*. Who can run after a day walking the Camino?'

The following morning, I walked for a while with Marco before he stopped at a bar to wait for his companions. I figured he'd show up in the evening, but for now I enjoyed the contrast: I was no longer lonely in my own company.

The hills to Pola de Allande never let up, yet the countryside was beautiful, reminiscent of France in parts, and the weather was warmer. I wanted to take in every scene and experience, so that I could recreate it in my mind later. The urge to paint was stronger than it had been in years. The landscape was full of vibrant colours and I could imagine putting them on paper—I pictured the brushstrokes and longed for my paints. But I was also dreaming up cartoons of the Spanish Six.

I was still working hard at night—not just drawing but doing massages for the Brazilians again. As soon as the Spanish Six learned that I did massages, Marco lined up. Of the five men walking he seemed to be the fittest, and I had a sense that it was more about an excuse to chat than sore feet. Perhaps more than chat.

In Pola de Allande, after looking at me a little too intently during his foot massage, he positioned himself next to me at dinner. I thought of Camille's comments on Spanish lovers. Margarida winked at me several times.

'Good man,' she whispered in my ear at one stage. 'Very cute butt.'

This was the sort of conversation my daughters had. I couldn't help but smile—and he did have a cute butt.

That night I had an email from Stephanie at the *Chronicle*. She loved Buggy Man. I hadn't intended to draw Martin again, nor include myself in a cartoon. Not that Stephanie knew.

You manage to put so much into your pictures, she said. *Will the concertina bring them back together?*

I was certain the answer was no. If Martin and I met again, it would have to be because one of us had a change of heart and chased the other, and we had gotten past that. Martin had made his intentions clear enough with the return of the scallop shell. I had his bank-account details: as soon as the *Chronicle* paid me I would return his money. And that would be the end.

60
Martin

Coming into Castroverde, just five solid days from my destination and no further advanced on resolving the situation with Sarah, I had an extraordinary encounter. Walking out of town in the opposite direction was a man pulling a cart, albeit a more primitive one than mine. It looked to be the same model as the one that Maarten had carried into Cluny one life-changing morning, nine months earlier. As we approached each other, I realised it was the model Maarten had pulled *out* of Cluny, with its improved wheels. He was still pulling it.

It was only a minute before we reached each other. He recognised me and we threw our arms around each other, British and Dutch reserve notwithstanding. He had lost weight, but the trolley had survived. He confirmed that our repair had held. The ENSAM team back in Cluny would be chuffed: I took a bunch of photos for them and my blog.

Since I had last seen him, Maarten had reached Santiago via the Camino Francés (three months), then made a return trip on the Camino del Norte, stopping at the French border because of the cold weather (a bit over three months), followed by a return trip to Lisbon on the Camino Portugués (three months).

'Bloody hell—when are you going home?'

'When I am too old to walk. Then I go straight to the care home. I sold my house and now I can stay in the *pensiones* some-times and eat well. And no communication with my relatives or the Dutch government.'

He had not seen Zoe: I presumed she was still behind me.

I persuaded Maarten to return the half-kilometre to town and stay with me. It was like running into an old friend and we had stories of the road to share. The invitation turned out to be one of the poorer decisions of my life.

At the hostel, he examined my cart and took it for a test run. 'If you manufacture it, perhaps I will be your first customer,' he said. 'It is definitely superior.'

'Not really.' The German accent was unmistakable. Bernhard had appeared, apparently from the hostel behind us. Paola had warned me we might see him again. Whatever the Camino had taught him, it was not humility. 'I see you have made a parking brake, as I suggested,' he added.

'Nice to see you,' I said. 'Maarten, Bernhard. Bernhard, Maarten. Despite neither being an engineer nor having pulled a cart all over Europe, Bernhard knows more about carts than either of us.'

And nothing about sarcasm. Margarida and Renata had joined us. I'd have been happy to let it go, but Bernhard wouldn't. 'Two wheels provides superior balance. The Dutch cart is stable but the English cart wobbles when he walks.' He demonstrated a wobbly English walk. 'Buggy Man disagrees.'

'That's right.'

'Then we should do a scientific experiment. I will race you.'

'Jesus—you don't know what science is.'

Margarida was hot-footing it towards the hostel. I had no doubt she would return with her companions. Or how it would play out after that.

'If you want,' I said.

Margarida returned not only with the Brazilians, but the Spanish Men's Club. All it needed was Zoe, but she was apparently a few kilometres back in O Cávado.

I guessed Bernhard would have the edge in a sprint,

but I was a former marathon runner. Longer would suit me. Regardless of the relative merits of the carts, I had one huge advantage—familiarity. If I couldn't beat Bernhard with a cart I'd pulled behind me six or more hours a day for almost three months, I might as well give the game away. And I really wanted to put the little shit in his place.

Marco, the smooth haematologist, appointed himself course steward and judge. The Camino ran right past the hostel, and we walked back about half a kilometre. The return route gave us a climb followed by a downhill run. It was wide enough for both carts all the way—a good thing, as I didn't fancy playing chicken into a chicane.

Marco allowed me to remove a bag to equalise the weights. I had my sticks; Bernhard needed one hand to hold the golf-trolley handle. He had taken his shirt off, and I followed suit.

With the Brazilians, Maarten, the Spanish Men's Club and a few other pilgrims in clumps along the track, Marco blew a whistle and we were off. It only took me a few paces to see what the problem was going to be: I'd never *run* with the cart, and the longer strides and higher kicks had my heels touching the bag, threatening to trip me up. I had to limit my extension. The sticks helped up the hill, but not as much as at the usual pace.

Bernhard was right beside me. I didn't know if he was holding something in reserve or was flat out, as I was, muscles and joints protesting at being called on again after a day's walking. Marco, unencumbered, was jogging on my side.

Approaching the crest of the hill, I was panting hard, but so was Bernhard and I sensed he was only just keeping up. If I could open a gap as we went over, it would turn into a longer, discouraging lead when I hit the downhill run first. I gave it a big effort and pulled ahead. And then, just as my cart's wheel must have been passing Bernhard, I felt it lock up. I knew immediately what had happened—Bernhard had flipped the parking brake. I was at a standstill as he went past.

My response was driven more by instinct than anger—a desire to stop him from getting clear. I pushed my stick into the spokes of his left wheel, letting go as the torque grabbed my wrist and turned my whole body around. Bernhard spun, tripped and tried to hang on, and he and Maarten's trolley went over into the ditch beside the path. I stopped and waited. Bernhard was screaming but only at me. Marco raised his hand—race over—and went to check on Bernhard.

He was followed by Margarida and Tina—Paola's daughter—who reached him together, dropped down to attend to him, then stopped and looked at each other. Their expressions said it all: *I thought he was my boyfriend.*

Bernhard was okay, but once he had righted himself Marco added insult to his injured pride by declaring me the winner. Bernhard had been cunning enough to sabotage my cart while Marco was blindsided, but he had reckoned without the video umpire. Renata had been filming the race, and had been placed perfectly to catch the action.

I stood where I was as Maarten's trolley was righted. It was undamaged, though my stick had taken some punishment. Then I waited until all but Renata had headed back.

'What happened to Torben?' I asked.

'He continued on the Camino Francés. We are not in communication.' She laughed. 'I told you, I'm not good at relationships. Sex, yes, I am very good at. Relationships, not so much.'

'One–nil to you. I'm not doing too well at either.'

We returned slowly: as my body had twisted with the force of my stick in Bernhard's wheel, I'd felt my knee go.

61
Zoe

Renata was at an outside café in Castroverde when I walked in after making an early start. An empty plate was all that remained of her tortilla and she was digging into a slice of Santiago cake, a Galician specialty, moist, lightly citrus-flavoured and probably flourless.

'Big night,' she said.

For the Brazilians, that was saying something. I had purposely avoided the party the previous evening. But meeting new people and telling the same stories had its downside too. I had gotten over how amazed people were at how far I had walked.

'Oh.' I saw her expression and remembered the tension around Bernhard. 'Man trouble?'

Renata nodded. 'Martin and Bernhard.'

I put my coffee down. 'A fight?'

Renata shook her head. 'They had a cart race.'

My vision of Gregory Peck and Charlton Heston duking it out at midnight in *The Big Country* was replaced by the latter in *Ben Hur*.

'Centaur versus golfer,' she added. 'Martin won. I have video, if you want to see.'

'It's okay, thanks. But it's good that they dealt with all that negative energy.' I was a little ashamed, remembering my behaviour with the blueberry beer. Martin and Bernhard had found a way to resolve their hostility in a civilised way, without harm to anyone.

'Maybe,' said Renata, 'but I am not sure how Martin will be this morning.'

Exhausted—*stuffed*—from the race, or from celebrating afterward? I didn't pursue it.

'But there is more,' said Renata. 'Bernhard's secret is revealed. Two lovers. Two Brazilian lovers.'

'Margarida and . . . Fabiana?'

She laughed. 'Not me and Paola? But you are still wrong. Margarida and Tina. Paola may murder all of them. Tina is young: she will deal with it. Margarida . . .' She shrugged.

'Was he . . .'

'He was bedding both of them. All men like young girls, but Bernhard, he also likes older women. Although I think I would be too much for him. Unfortunately.'

I replayed all the times he had 'slept with' women in France. I may only have escaped his attentions the night we shared a *gîte* because he had a better option. But . . .

'In a dormitory?'

'They attempted it in the bunk above me—back in France. Fortunately I was able to capture Bernhard's foot on the ladder. He was carrying his sleeping mask—and I would have liked to know what he was planning. But I don't wish to be crushed to death.'

'So how do you know that they actually . . .'

'If people want to have sex, they find a way. In the dorm, they start quietly, then they don't care. Not Tina, obviously. Her mother is there. But the laundry is empty at night; maybe they did it on the washing machine. Or . . .'

'Okay, okay, I believe you.'

'Now,' said Renata, 'I walk on alone. I am over this soap opera.'

She ordered another coffee and I took the opportunity to move on first.

Tina caught up with me—carrying nothing but a bottle of water, almost jogging.

'No one is talking to me.'

'Ah. Bernhard?'

'Right. But the problem is Margarida. She needs to get over herself.'

'What about you?'

'I am on vacation. Unfortunately, with my mother.'

Bernhard was the next to catch me. Up until today it had been rare for anyone to pass me; this was not going to be an average day.

'Have you seen Tina?'

'Why?'

'I need to talk to her.'

'She's way ahead,' I said.

He strode off. I was half-expecting Martin to show up next, but I should have known it would be Margarida.

'Have you seen Bernhard? You heard?'

'I heard.'

After we had walked a little way I asked, 'Margarida, why are you doing this pilgrimage?'

She looked like a deer in the headlights. 'I think it might be good, to think. Where my life goes, yes?'

'Great idea,' I said. 'There's still time to do it.'

This time, I was the one who strode ahead.

By Lugo I had put the whole Bernhard–Brazilian mess out of my mind. The beauty of walking alone on the

Camino, when you are fit, is that you feel one with nature: time is suspended and everything else fades away. The wind was fresh, the panorama of heather-clad mountains topped with wind turbines awe-inspiring, and I was determined to enjoy every minute of these last days.

The town itself was imposing. High on a hill surrounded by Roman walls, it conjured up pictures not just of pilgrims but El Cid and his army. Or maybe I'd just got stuck on Charlton Heston—which was a bit awkward, given his role in the NRA.

I was brought back to reality by a shout from Marco, who was sitting in the bar in the old town and insisted I join him for a drink. 'Tonight,' he said to me, 'I'm asking you to have dinner with me. I'm hoping the answer will be yes.'

This was not Martin, nor the peace I had been looking for. I thought of the awkward evening with Henri in Pommiers. But I didn't feel I would be taking advantage of Marco. He was divorced—I guessed for some years—and I had the sense that he was enjoying life, and would take the flow of wins and setbacks. His almost childlike enthusiasm would have bugged me long-term, but there was no chance of that happening.

'Sure,' I said.

Before dinner, Marco loaned me his computer. I had emailed the girls several times recently but we hadn't skyped since St Jean Pied de Port. It was Lauren's birthday, and Tessa had flown in to celebrate with her. I texted them to let them know I would call and checked my emails; Albie told me the realtor had found a possible buyer for the house.

Lauren was delighted—or at least relieved—to hear from me.

'I have my ticket booked on the last flight from Santiago on May 13, so I'm going to be home on the 14th.'

'Santiago?' said Tessa.

'You're in *Chile*?' said Lauren.

I realised I had never told them about my walk, only that I was travelling in France and Spain. They and the walk were so much a part of my life, it was hard to understand how I could have separated the two. They were quiet long enough for me to explain.

'What? How far did you say, Mom?'

'What do you mean, you *walked*?'

'I thought you hated religion.'

Most of this was going to have to wait. I gave them the abbreviated version.

'Can you stop over in New York on the way home? I'm missing you,' said Lauren.

Lauren, missing me? I could see she was trying to hold something back, but she couldn't contain herself. 'I didn't want to tell you before, with Keith and everything. But you're going to be a grandma. I'm due in July.'

62

Martin

Eighteen miles into the London Marathon, I had known I was in trouble.

I kept going, conscious that I was exacerbating the damage to my knee. By the twenty-mile mark I was walking, hoping only to finish. Two miles from the end I pulled out, finally acknowledging that pressing on against the pain would put me in surgery.

I had left it too late and got the worst of both worlds: a knee reconstruction, with several months of rehabilitation, and no finisher medal.

Now, in Spain, less than a week's walk from Santiago, after nineteen hundred kilometres—almost twelve hundred miles of pulling the cart up and down hills, through fields, along paths and tracks and highways, through snow and mud and sand, heaving it over stiles and rocks and fences—it seemed that history was in danger of repeating itself.

In my room, I rested the knee for an hour, covered it with a wet cloth, then stretched it out and tried some weight. Not so bad. In marathon training, my other knee had given me problems but been manageable. I still had a day up my sleeve. I'd see how it felt in the morning.

It felt fair in the morning. I made an early start and decided to try for Lugo, my original destination, taking it carefully.

Taking it carefully was not so easy. The terrain remained hilly. Uphill was not too bad, but on the downhill stretches I had to plant my sticks and right leg to take the weight, then drop the injured left leg into place.

I took every opportunity for a break. Renata caught up with me as I cooled my leg in a stream and offered me more sympathy than I deserved.

'Of course you accepted his challenge.'

'You're being remarkably understanding. Most women would be telling me what an idiot I was.'

'I'm not most women. I'm in a better position to understand men. As you may have guessed.'

She looked at me, smiling, and I looked at her strong jaw and thought: fair enough.

'Sorry—I hadn't guessed. I hope that's a good thing. Was it long ago?'

'Not so long. It's one reason why I'm walking. With people who are meeting me for the first time.'

'You seem to be doing pretty well.'

'That's my intention.'

We continued for a while in silence before I had to take another break and she walked on.

By the time I reached the hostel, my knee was giving me a fair bit of grief and I decided that I would rest up for a day. I had a private room on the first floor, with a view. The hostels in Spain had moved with the times—and an older, more well-heeled clientele—and many offered double rooms as well as the usual dormitories.

The owner found me some ice and a filled roll, and I propped in my room, calculating time and distances. If I took the next day off, I would be on wood—no margin—at least, if my plan was to take the train to Paris. But a plane could get me there late on the same day and was probably cheaper than the train, anyway. Into Santiago on the 13th and a late flight out. That was Zoe's departure date. I might see her at the airport.

I fired up the computer to make the booking and found a short email from Sarah—she was doing okay, getting on with Julia, and would be ready to talk to me when I returned to the UK, which she was guessing was at least a fortnight away. I read it as the least painful way of buying herself two weeks without me bothering her. I'd posted nothing about Zoe on my blog since the overdose.

There was bad news from Jonathan.

Basically, as history would suggest, the rucksack remains the best low-cost option for carrying light loads in the mountains. For bigger loads: donkeys, horses and mules. The cart performed better than any wheeled option we've seen before, but at the end of the day feet beat wheels. Sorry it couldn't be better news, but I thought you should know before the trade fair.

The Germans and the Chinese might well reach a similar conclusion, even without a prototype to test. The German buyout option was starting to look like the best deal I could get.

It was after 10 p.m. when the sound of laughter prompted me to look out the open window. Below me, a couple was walking towards the hostel. I assumed they were not pilgrims, unless the woman was Margarida. She was wearing a short dress and high heels, and had the best pins I had seen for a while.

As she stepped into the light, the first thing that hit me was the colour of the dress. The man holding Zoe's hand, and about to kiss her, was Marco.

63
Zoe

Dinner had been a bigger deal than I'd expected. 'We are cooking here,' said Paola before I left the hostel. 'You can tell us about it when you return.' The tension in the hostel was an even better argument for eating with Marco than the food or company. Margarida had gone to the dorm. Tina was plugged into her phone in the shared space and didn't look up. Bernhard had the sense to stay elsewhere.

Fabiana was getting ready to go out. 'Margarida needs to go to a bar,' she said. She was wearing a black dress and looked good, though I wanted to tell her to add a bright scarf. But it was she who gave me the dress advice. 'Do you not have something to wear?'

I did look . . . like a walker. Fabiana followed me

into the dorm, where Margarida was huddled under a blanket, and I pulled the blue dress Martin had left for me out of my pack.

'How about this? I can't imagine it will fit.'

Fabiana smiled. 'You are not seeing in the mirror.'

I took off the walking gear that had been my uniform and wiggled into Martin's gift. Fabiana borrowed a pair of heels from Margarida. They fit, and when I looked in the mirror I was shocked. For eleven weeks, I had worn walking pants and sweaters every night.

I barely recognised myself, a slim woman whose skin had a healthy glow and whose calves were shaped in a way they had never been: not exactly what a model would want, but *toned*. The blue of the dress accentuated my eyes. Martin had been right. It suited me, at least physically, though looking at this person I wasn't sure who she was. I didn't look like anyone's grandmother.

I felt sorry it wasn't Martin who was taking me out in it. I could have talked to him about how shaken Lauren's news had left me. I was pleased for her: being a mother was obviously what she wanted. But she was still so young, and having children early had stopped me following my dreams. Or had it? My new self-awareness wasn't going to accept that story. I'd had children partly to escape my fear of failing as an artist.

I didn't want to think about whether it had anything to do with what had happened with Camille.

'Oh wow!' said Fabiana. Margarida sat up in her bunk and added, 'Very sexy, gringa.'

Okay. Being a grandmother didn't mean I had to take up knitting.

Paola did my hair, and by the time I went out I had the full Cinderella makeover. It took Marco a moment to recognise me.

'*Eres muy hermosa*,' he said, kissing my cheek. Very beautiful.

He was a sophisticated companion, trim and witty, his slightly crooked nose fitting his character. It helped that he was Spanish, comfortable with the language and the menu, though he was the kind of guy who would be comfortable anywhere.

And the food was good: Marco ordered a parade of vegetarian dishes for both of us. We talked about the grown-up children he didn't see as much as he would like: 'I do too much work.' I knew he was a physician; I heard more about the work he did in his clinic and as a volunteer in Haiti.

'So, you have a wonderful balance—important work, but you can kick your heels up on vacation,' I said.

He frowned and I reworded it. 'You are enjoying life.'

'Most certainly,' said Marco. 'I am still young and healthy; I walk the Caminos each year; I travel often. I have many friends.'

'Do you get lonely?' I asked, thinking more of me than I was of him, wondering what my future would look like when the walk was over.

'Yes,' said Marco, suddenly serious. 'But—I am forever searching for the right woman.'

He accompanied me back to my hostel, not far from his own *pensione*. Walking in heels after so much hiking was not easy. Then he took my hand.

It felt awkward. When I closed my eyes for the kiss, awkward became more like plain wrong. I dealt with the immediate problem by a turn of the cheek; it is the European way, after all. But the *I'm expecting more* look needed a clearer response.

I was now quite sure I didn't want a kiss goodnight—or anything more. Our energies weren't aligned, but it wasn't just that. I felt I'd be betraying—not Keith, but Martin.

While I was trying to decide between *I really like you but* and *I promised Paola a massage*, he took my face in his hands. I had one foot in the flower bed when the door of the *albergue* flew open.

Paola ran over to me, ignoring Marco. 'Can you stay with Tina? I must go to the hospital.'

'Hospital?' Marco and I asked at the same time.

'Fabiana. Margarida and she are poisoned. I must see the situation and let her family know. Your friend Felipe is with them.'

'What sort of poison?' asked Marco the physician.

Paola hesitated. 'Alcohol.'

'I will drive you to the hospital.'

Paola wasn't going to waste any time. I waved Marco off, unsure what I would have said had we not been interrupted, but not sorry we had been, circumstances aside.

Tina, hair in pigtails and dressed in Minnie Mouse pyjamas, wouldn't have been able to convince anyone she was old enough to drink—not even in Spain, where you only had to be sixteen. Now, I figured, I was going to get the tears and rant.

'Do you think it was my fault?' she said.

'Were you there? Did you drink the drinks?' I was channelling Martin.

'I don't think so.' Brazilian accent, but valley-girl eye roll.

'Fabiana and Margarida have their own problems, nothing to do with you or Bernhard.'

'Bernhard. He is so, like, not important.'

Then: 'Why don't you and Martin tell each other how you feel? About each other?'

I was still trying to work out what she'd been told and by whom when Paola returned. Tina disappeared without saying goodnight. I looked at her mother and shrugged. 'She's okay. How are Fabiana and Margarida?'

I made Paola herbal tea while she brought me up to date. Fabiana and Margarida had been drinking with the locals. Both had become ill, but Fabiana had passed out. An ambulance had been called. She was being kept overnight for observation.

'Margarida stays with her.'

I caught something in Paola's voice. 'You made her?'

Paola shook her head. 'No, I think finally something shakes sense into this girl. It is time she grows up.'

'And Felipe?'

'Felipe will go back in the morning. He is a good man, understands Fabiana.'

'She had problems in love? A married man?'

Paola looked surprised. 'She told you this?'

I shook my head. 'Not exactly, but it wasn't hard to guess.'

'Did I give myself away also?'

'You?'

'You know my story? Like you, I lost my husband.'

Paola had first walked the Camino twelve years

earlier. The traditional Camino Francés, five hundred miles from St Jean Pied de Port.

'Then, I carried my pack,' said Paola. 'My husband and I were making a true pilgrimage. He was a man of God who had left the priesthood to marry me. But he knew there would be a price to pay. We both knew it.'

Tina was standing in the doorway. The friction between them about Tina's behaviour seemed to dissolve. She came and sat by her mother, snuggling into the maternal hold in a position instinctive to them both.

'He got cancer, and finally there was no more that the doctors could do.'

'Papa had always wanted to walk the Camino,' said Tina. She would have been four or five. I wondered how much she remembered and how much was family storytelling.

'It was a hard six weeks,' said Paola. 'We had to go very slow at times. Sometimes, I carried his pack. He died in Melide. Two days before Santiago.'

I felt my own grief stirred by her story.

'There was much to be organised. But later I returned with his ashes. I left some in Melide, the rest in São Paulo.' Paola smiled. 'So now you see we are both torn between the Camino and Brazil, he and I.'

Paola had decided to bring the Camino to other peo-

ple. She'd written two books in Portuguese, so everyone in Brazil knew her story, and now she ran tours. I
guessed that at home she was a bit of a legend.

'Each year I come with another group, and each year
I stop in Melide. I go no further.'

'You've *never* walked into Santiago?'

Paola shook her head. 'The last two days are simple
to navigate—the group walks without me. I think they
enjoy it.'

I thought of Martin returning my scallop shell, how
I hadn't wanted it back. I realised I needed to finish
the Camino, without it—to show I believed in myself,
rather than luck or chance. Monsieur Chevalier had
said it was destined to go to Santiago. I knew now who
to give it to.

64
Martin

I took a day off in Lugo, resting my knee and forcing myself not to dwell on Zoe hooking up with Marco. It was probably a positive for her: a step towards moving on without the risk of a relationship. Marco would surely be returning to his wife and family after the holiday fling was over. I wondered if Zoe knew he was married. I didn't want her to get hurt, but it was no longer my place to intervene, nor to judge. Still, I could have done without watching it from my box. And helping out by giving her something to wear.

In the evening, I ventured downstairs. The swelling was down a bit, but there was not as much improvement as I'd hoped for. I was sitting at the table in the courtyard, watching the track for arriving pilgrims, when Tina appeared.

'Still here?' I called.

'Evidently.' She walked over. Not happy.

'Why?'

'Fabiana got sick.'

'Is it serious?'

She shrugged her shoulders. 'I'm not supposed to talk about it but . . . you can guess.'

'Too much partying?'

'Drinking shots. She's not used to it. She goes to Mass, then she gets smashed. She choked on her vomit—totally gross.' She rolled her eyes, then looked at my leg, elevated on the chair on the opposite side of the table. 'Bernhard hurt your leg?'

'*I* hurt my leg. I didn't have to race him. Or play his games. If there's something you learn as you get older, it's that most of your problems are of your own making. Like Fabiana's.'

She managed a laugh at that, and I pushed a little further. 'Let me guess: she was drinking with Margarida.'

'Right.' Long pause. 'You saw. After the race.'

'What about you? Are you okay?'

'Totally.' Where had I heard that before? *DW.*

'Have you had dinner?'

'Not yet.'

I pulled a twenty-euro note from my phone wallet.

'I can't walk. You want to get some tortillas—or burgers and chips or something?'

Tina was back in twenty minutes with a square box, grinning. Pizza. And cola.

'I need some advice,' I said.

'From me?' She laughed. 'It's about Zoe, right?'

'Wrong. I've got a daughter about your age. Her mother and I split up about a year ago, and she's finding it difficult.'

'Tell me about it.'

With the Brazilian accent, I wasn't sure for a moment whether she was asking me to elaborate or just showing empathy. I settled on the latter: she seemed to have a good grasp of English—or American—vernacular. I told her about it anyway as we ate the pizza.

'So, what do you think she'd want me to do? What would she say to me if she could?'

Tina sipped Coke from the can. 'Don't believe her if she says she's not in love with . . . What's his name?'

'Don't know.'

'You should ask. Anyway, she *is* in love with him—obviously, or she wouldn't be doing these things you think are stupid. Everyone falls in love with the wrong people, but you don't want to have to defend them to your parents, because they'll just tell you why they're wrong for you . . . which you know already. So, you tell them you're not in love.'

'Like with Bernhard.'

'Do you know how crap it is travelling with your mother watching you all the time? And one of her . . . clients . . . who's old enough to be his—Bernhard's— mother . . . almost kills someone by doing stuff that *I* wouldn't do and *I'm* the one . . .'

'I haven't had the experience, but I think crap is probably the right word.'

'I wish I had a father like you.'

'Why?'

'Because you care so much about your daughter. I thought you were going to ask me about Zoe, but you asked about Sarah. Like she was the most important person in your life.' And suddenly, out of nowhere, Tina was crying.

I put a hand on her shoulder, then both hands, awkwardly as we were both sitting, but she leant her head on my arm and sobbed. Eventually, she pulled back.

'I'm sorry.'

'It's okay. You should have seen me a year or so ago. Your dad's not around?'

'He died when I was five. And you know what he spent the last month of his life doing? Walking the fucking Camino with my mother. While I was with my aunt and my cousins, waiting for him to come back. I knew there was something wrong, but nobody told me I would never see him again.' Pause. 'That was not a problem I made for myself.'

'Point taken. You felt like he put your mother first?'

'Don't tell her I told you this. She was only doing what he wanted. I think this walk is supposed to make up, like she's finally bringing me along. She thinks she's doing something for me, but it's the other way around. You know what I mean?'

'I do. I wish I could say something to help. But as you know, I can't even work out what to do for my own daughter.'

'You care about her. You're putting her first. Number one. If she knows that . . .'

'Maybe your mum's trying to put you first too.'

It was the best I could manage.

I sat by myself for a while as the sun set, feeling oddly calm, and not because a teenager had given me a vote of confidence. Rather, she had reduced all the turmoil to a simple question: what did I have to do to put Sarah first?

The equally simple answer—the one I had been

avoiding for the last week, or year—was: resolve the conflict with Julia. The only way that was going to happen was if I said, 'All is forgiven.'

It was galling. The one thing I had held onto through the separation and divorce saga had been my sense of righteousness. It had been Julia who had cheated. I had denied myself time with my daughter so she would not have to suffer our mutual hatred. I had given Julia all my money.

Zoe had forgiven her mother. It wasn't quite the same. Infidelity is not just about morality—it's personal. But, unlike Zoe's mother, Julia had said sorry. She had made a mistake. She had wanted us to repair the marriage. And I had been too consumed with righteous anger to listen.

Back in my room, I composed the email. I was not going to delay it like the 'I love you' to Sarah, but I couldn't do it verbally. Sarah and I were as one there.

Dear Julia

We need to do something about the situation with Sarah, and I think that means putting our relationship on a more civil and co-operative basis. Let me be the one to start. I forgive you for the affair. I apologise for not doing so long ago. Though I know

it's too late to try, as you offered, to rebuild our
marriage, I'm willing to do what we can now in
Sarah's interests.
With love
Martin

The 'with love' came spontaneously—and
unexpectedly—and was the only part I considered
deleting. But it was, of course, true. Or I would never
have been so angry.

I was prepared for a protracted back-and-forth and
much consumption of crow before we reached an understanding that would benefit Sarah. Julia was hardly
going to respond with a male engineer's matter-of-fact
agreement.

Wrong, as usual. By the time I'd showered and
washed my clothes, there was a reply on my screen.
Thank Christ, or whoever you've met. After that it was
all about Sarah. And just to ensure I had not a shred of
moral superiority left to cling to:

I gather you know that Sarah hopes to study medi-
cine, which will keep her at university well beyond
21. I assume that was the reason for the cheque you
sent me. It provided both of us with some reassur-

ance that you still had some interest in her during the period that you were out of contact. I assure you it has been put aside for her.

I was sure that neither Julia nor I would be able to refrain indefinitely from sniping, and I wondered what was behind 'whoever you've met'. But the break-through had been made. I replied, thanking her for being so gracious and asking the obvious: *What do you want me to do?*

The reply was instant. *I don't need you to forgive me. I just need you to put your anger with me aside so we can do what's right for Sarah. If you can do that, I can work with you.*

I could do that.

65
Zoe

In the last weeks of my Camino I had felt the spirit of every walker past and present buoying me toward Santiago, so I wondered why in the hell I was feeling lonely on my evening in Melide. I had joined the Camino Francés and the *pulpo* bar was full of pilgrims from that route catching up and sharing the excitement of the end being only two days away. But none of my friends from the Camino Primitivo was among them. I had taken an extra day in the hope that the Brazilians might catch up, but there was no sign of them.

I had a strange feeling of emptiness. I couldn't help thinking of Paola's husband, who had died here without finishing. What was the point? If I'd stayed in LA and seen a therapist, I'd have worked through the same stuff. Without blisters. I wondered where Martin was.

'Nearly there,' someone said behind me, and it was only when she added, 'and soon we can decide if we have wasted our time,' that I realised who it was.

'Renata!'

She flopped down on the wooden bench opposite me. There was a roundness to her shoulders that hadn't been there before.

'Where are the others?' I asked.

'Still behind. A day or two. I need to finish this thing.'

'So why did you start it?' Of the Brazilians, she was the one I knew least about.

Renata picked at the bread left over from my dinner. 'To contemplate. That's what it's supposed to be about, isn't it?'

'About anything in particular?'

'Life.'

Well, that narrowed it down. I guess I hadn't shared much either. Renata laughed. 'You first. You've had more time on the Camino. You started . . . where?'

I was about to say Cluny, but realised I was wrong by a day. 'Los Angeles. That's where I walked out the door and left everything—I mean everything—behind. That's what we're supposed to do, isn't it?'

'You left your possessions behind. Do you miss any-thing?'

I shook my head. To be honest, in the moment I didn't even miss the girls, though I was looking forward to seeing them again. And . . .

'You know, my husband died,' I said. 'Only four months ago.' Four months. The time had stretched without me noticing. 'I'm desperately sorry it happened, and I wish I'd been able to do something to prevent it . . . but . . . I'm not missing him.'

'Martin?'

'You mean, has he taken his place? Back in France, I think I might have let him, but it would have been a mistake. I needed to work out who I was again.'

'And have you?'

'Not really.'

'Paola told me that you've discovered you're a cartoonist.'

'I was thinking about something deeper than that. Maybe I've lived too long in California.'

'I think so. You find a new career, you learn that you have strengths you never thought you had, maybe you've fallen in love—and you say you haven't found anything important.'

I could hear Monsieur Chevalier saying, 'The Camino has given you all this, not to mention forgiving your mother, grieving your husband and forgiving yourself. And you are asking for more?' But I was.

'I'm still missing something.'

'What does it feel like? The thing you are missing? The gap, the hole?'

'Just a feeling . . . some part of me I've lost.'

'Okay. Tell me a story. I like stories. Tell me your most important story.'

The choice came without thinking. I told her about Camille and our drive from St Louis to San Francisco, two thousand miles each way, about detouring via Fergus Falls to see my folks on the way home and the fight that had erupted.

My father was away, and my mother must have sensed something. When she said grace, she inserted a long reference to unborn children and Camille fled the table.

'Murderer,' she'd said. Camille and I left without eating.

Even now, I could feel my skin prickle with the shame, for my mother and for what I'd exposed Camille to.

'So she was my reason for coming to France,' I said.

'A long journey to create the problem and now a long one to heal it.'

'Too late. My mother died before we could reconcile.'

'It happens.' The server put a wooden board of sliced *pulpo* sprinkled with paprika in front of her.

'I could have done something.' I thought of the anger

that I had tried to deal with through meditation after Lauren's birth. My mother had sent a card. *Congratulations on your baby.* Nothing else. I'd been insulted. But I could have seen it as an olive branch. A start. If I'd chosen to.

Now, more than twenty years after her death, I told Renata what I should have done. 'I could have sent her an invitation, asked her to visit. Sucked it up and told her I wanted and needed her.' I could have shown up on her doorstep with my baby. I thought of Lauren telling me she missed me.

'Regret,' said Renata with her mouth full, 'is a waste of energy. I have offended so many people that I have no one left who speaks to me. I am estranged from my family. Recently, my relationship broke up. It was only three years but I have been single since then. I had a big disagreement with the church a long time ago.'

'Over?'

'Politics. But everything is political. I am good with big causes, not so much with individuals. So, I walk seven hundred miles to change myself. By being alone.' She laughed.

'Does not play well with others.'

'Sorry?'

'It's a thing teachers say at school. About kids who are . . . independent. A joke when we use it for adults.'

'That is me. I do not play well with others for long. But I am comfortable with myself. For me, this is more important than anything else. But tell me, how did you feel? In your story?'

'I told you. Terrible. My mother disowned me and then . . .'

'You must have guessed that would happen. I mean, you took your friend to your mother's home after the abortion. I'm asking how you felt when you were driving this old car across America.'

'Camille was so scared . . .'

'I'm asking about *you*. You were young, you were on a road trip, you were helping a friend, rebelling—testing your mother—putting important things at risk. This was maybe the most courageous thing you have done. The best thing. The story that defines you. That's why you chose it to tell me.'

'But it had . . . consequences.'

'Of course. Always big things have consequences. Pain, and things lost maybe forever. But this is why you are here, is it not? You came to France to find Camille. But you are afraid to do . . . to *be* what you were then. I think that for you is the hole.'

66
Martin

Before setting out from Lugo, I had an early break-fast and waited for Paola. As I'd hoped, she came down alone, in keeping with her role as tour captain.

'I gather you've a sick crew member,' I said and she nodded.

'Fabiana was ill. This is expected sometimes with travel and was not serious. We will still have time to finish. We are hoping to move again tomorrow. Renata has gone ahead—with my permission.'

'Well, I'm off this morning, so I just wanted to say *Buen Camino* in case we don't meet again. Maybe in Santiago.'

'Sadly, we will not meet in Santiago. Tina and I go only as far as Melide. The tourist agent will meet the others at the end and we will see them in Madrid.' She must have known an explanation was needed, and added, 'My husband died in Melide without reaching Santiago. I stop there, in his memory, on every walk.'

'Except this walk is different, isn't it?'

'Why do you say that?'

'You have your daughter with you. So, this time it is about the future rather than the past. If you want it to be.'

Monsieur Chevalier did not have a monopoly on the heavy-handed dispensation of wisdom.

I walked to Melide in two uneven days. On the first, the terrain was flat and I pushed past San Román de Retorta, my original goal, for another four and a half hours and fourteen kilometres, keeping myself going with the thought that every kilometre down was one less to do the next day. My muscles had benefited from the day off—my knee not as much.

When I arrived in As Seixas, I got a more substantial boost—a long email from Sarah. It was mainly a list of tests and results, but the content didn't really matter. What mattered was that she had written a letter, or at least the modern equivalent, to her father. The medium was the message. My relief at reading it eclipsed any feelings about my knee, the viability of the cart, and Zoe.

On the second day, it took me twelve hours, starting just after dawn, to walk fourteen kilometres. I was taking double the recommended dose of the anti-inflammatories I had bought in Lugo, but my knee was blown up like a football.

Coming into Melide, I stopped at the first hotel I saw. In front of me, at the reception desk, a slim woman of perhaps forty was checking in and asking, in a German accent, for her backpack, which had been transported.

Her younger companion didn't need to open his mouth for me to know where he came from. It was Bernhard. I watched it play out: one room, her credit card. Nice work if you can get it.

Bernhard saw me as he turned. 'You have injured your leg?'

'How did you work that out?'

'I saw you walking. Just a minute ago.'

'Yeah, well, I did.'

'I told you, the cart is not good for knees.'

I walked—or at least limped—away, into the bar, rather than make a fuss by putting my fist into his face. I rested my knee on a chair and fired up my computer. There was an email from the Germans. The other Germans.

We thank you again for the opportunity to make an offer for your invention. As agreed, that offer has now expired. We are also aware that a Swedish company is progressing with an almost identical design in association with a Chinese manufacturer. We look forward to seeing your future inventions.

It was over. I didn't need to guess who the Chinese manufacturer might be, and I had little doubt about who was behind the Swedish initiative. I was not in any position to launch legal action. The practicalities of suing a Swedish—or Chinese—company for a design that had not been patented and that was worth, on a buyout basis, only seven and a half thousand euros meant the project was effectively dead. I would not even achieve my worst-case scenario.

My own fault. I had over-valued my design and refused what was in retrospect a generous offer. And, two days short of Santiago, with an injured knee, I had no reason to finish the Camino. I posted a blog entry to the effect that, though the cart had held up well, my knee had not, and I was finishing my journey. I cancelled my flight to Paris from Santiago: no need, no rush.

I went downstairs and spent half an hour reading postcards that had been stuck to the inside surface of the glass door and adjacent wall. Every one of them recorded a journey in progress, from the minimum hundred kilometres to someone who had walked from Norway. What they had in common was that they all expected to reach Santiago in two days' time or thereabouts, collect their certificate and celebrate a personal achievement. I went to my room, took a business card from my pack and added it to the display. It was smaller than the postcards, but it was marking a more important milestone. The end.

Then I went to the hotel's restaurant, and got good and drunk.

In the morning, there was no doubt I had made the right decision to stop, German rejection or not. My left knee looked as bad as the right one had the day after I pulled out of the marathon. I would be lucky to avoid another operation, and luck had not been running my way.

The streets of Melide were full of pilgrims. Now, more than ever, I did not want their company. But I had a hangover and nothing to do. After lingering over breakfast, I went on a slow walk to the pharmacy, taking both of my sticks to keep the weight off my knee.

I bought paracetamol and more bandages, then found

a restaurant and had an early-afternoon Spanish dinner with a couple of glasses of rosé, and, in keeping with Spanish custom, crashed in my room. I was spiralling into a funk. A miserable two days short. The whole purpose of the walk blown, along with my knee. A pointless exercise. No money, house, partner. Zoe would be arriving in Santiago about now, without me.

The last hurt more than I expected. I must have had a subconscious fantasy of us meeting up and arriving together.

67

Zoe

CARTOON: A young man is sitting cross-legged on the edge of the road looking at his iPad, the soles of his shoes hanging half off. He is focused—so much so that he appears unaware of the truck coming down the busy highway and threatening to wipe him out. On the hill behind him a traditional pilgrim with cloak, staff and scallop shell is surrounded by birds and flowers.

STORY: Who makes the rules? There is an unwritten hierarchy among walkers. Real pilgrims do it cheaply, regardless of what they can afford and the impact their stinginess has on the host countries. They stay in dormitories, carry their own backpacks, stop when they're tired and rely on luck to find a bed. At the next level are the walkers who stay in *pensiones* or the increasing number of private rooms at the hostels, often booking ahead, but still walking all the way and carrying their own backpacks. Then there are those who have their packs transported—eight euros (about eight dollars) a day is the going rate. Below that: those who take the occasional bus for a tough or boring stretch, or when they're tired or hurting. And finally, the tourists, doing occasional stages with a daypack to get a feel for it, or even driving between the Camino towns and villages.

Chris, a twenty-six-year-old from Iowa, argues that the ancient pilgrims would have taken the fastest route between their lodgings in the abbeys and monasteries. Often he finds himself on the busy roads the Camino avoids, but which probably follow more closely the route taken in the Middle Ages. He is usually first to the hostel. But the Camino teaches the pilgrim to respect his own limits, and unless he learns this lesson his feet and knees will ensure that it is by the roads—on a bus—that he arrives in Santiago.

Alongside the rules of walking are those that the pilgrims bring with them, and which they have to adapt—more or less—to life on the road, in another culture: what and when they will eat, who they mix with, what they share of themselves.

Chris walks to prove himself, but the original pilgrims walked to find God, seek forgiveness or give thanks. Now, to earn their *compostela*—the certificate that recognises completion of the pilgrimage—pilgrims are expected to walk for a spiritual purpose, but that term remains undefined, for there is no one way to achieve enlightenment, atone for sins or recover from grief.

There is only one formal, unbreakable rule: if they want their *compostela*, they must complete the last sixty miles (one hundred kilometres) on foot, or the last one hundred twenty miles (two hundred kilometres) on a bike.

I would need to cut some words before sending it to Stephanie, but I smiled, thinking of Todd, whose first lesson on the Camino had saved me in the Pyrenees.

The final day, from A Rúa into Santiago de Compostela, was thirteen miles. My Camino was almost over and, while part of me would be sorry, another part felt the pull of reality for the first time in many weeks. Monsieur Chevalier had made three predictions about the pilgrimage. Four, if you counted me finding what I had lost. It seemed that one wasn't going to happen. The first had come to pass: I had gotten blisters. He said the Camino would change me, and it had, in many ways. But would I cry when I saw the cathedral? I had cried in Conques for my mother and in the Pyrenees for Keith. What did I have left to cry for?

I walked with Marco and Felipe: given the number of pilgrims celebrating the last day, solitude wasn't possible. Felipe rarely spoke anyway, and was even more withdrawn than usual. He had spent a lot of time with Fabiana, and might have hoped to walk in with her. I would have liked to be with Renata, so we could have commiserated together, but I hadn't seen her since Melide.

The other Brazilians were two days behind, resolving their problems. I had assured them I would send photos. I hoped they would make it in time to say goodbye before I caught my plane. I would have two nights in Santiago to recover before heading home and maybe see the swinging of the *botafumeiro* in the cathedral.

It was, I gathered, a bit of a crapshoot as to whether they swung the big silver urn, the largest censer in the world. The local clergy pushed back on the tourists' demands to have burning charcoal and incense waved over them by the rope-pulling monks—once a daily event, because the pilgrims hadn't washed. I now had no doubt I would get there, but I would leave one thing to fate. I told Marco that if the *botafumeiro* swung on the day of my arrival, I would move to San Francisco to start my new life.

The route took us through small villages with bars and welcoming signs as well as vending machines, incongruous among the rural cottages. Every bar had stamps—*sellos*—for my *credencial*. In the last sixty miles, the official requirement was to have two stamps a day instead of one: a half-hearted attempt to frustrate the taxi riders.

We stopped at a roadside ice-cream stand on the outskirts of Santiago to wait for the remaining Spanish men to catch up. While Marco bought a drink and Felipe stared ahead, I watched the steady stream of pilgrims making the final descent. If I cried, it would not be for the joy of enlightenment that Monsieur Chevalier had anticipated. Somehow, I had managed to walk over twelve hundred miles and still not find what I had been looking for.

My thoughts were interrupted by someone calling my name.

I looked up and saw it was the person I least wanted to walk into Santiago with: Bernhard. No, that was too unaccepting. On the trail, familiarity counted for a lot. He'd been with me almost as long as Martin had.

He was walking with a woman of about forty. He introduced her as Andrea, another German.

'We have nearly done it, you and me,' he grinned.

'I guess so,' I said. 'I hear you and Martin had a race.'

'We did. I won.'

'That's not what I heard.'

He opened his hands and smiled. 'I am here. He is not.'

'What's that supposed to mean?'

'He is still in Melide. Stopped.'

Marco and Felipe had joined us, and Bernhard's grin disappeared.

'Finished. Done. The Buggy Man walks no more,' said Bernhard pointing to his knee.

I could not believe it. Martin was not going to let anything get in his way. He had planned to arrive today, at the latest, to catch his train to Paris. It occurred to me that my decision to arrive two days before my flight might have had something to do with that.

'Just tell me what happened.'

Bernhard smiled again and took out his phone. A minute later he thrust it in front of me. Martin's blog. His knee had given out and he was unable to continue. Felipe took the phone from me.

I had started this walk with Martin, however unintentionally. Among many paths, we had always taken the same one. Like it or not, our Caminos were entwined.

I could see Santiago. The universe had looked after me—a ticket home, despite everything. If I walked on, I would reach the town and make my plane. I thought of the warm familiarity of LA, crisp white sheets on the bed, laid-back Californian accents and unsweetened cereal. A life ahead with children, grand-children and a new job. After the *Pilgrims' Progress* series, maybe I would find another buyer for my cartoons, ease into being a grandma and not live with either of my children. Maybe there would be another man in my life one day.

If I went back to Melide, I would be spitting in the face of my good fortune. If I didn't make my flight, I would have no way home and no visa. I hadn't paid Martin back. I didn't know when the *Chronicle* would pay me, and it wouldn't be enough for a flight home when they did. If I missed the birth of her child, Lauren would never forgive me. I wouldn't forgive myself.

But I wanted Martin to stop sabotaging himself—he had done it with his marriage, his relationship with his daughter and now with this.

The universe wasn't going to go back for him.

The three remaining Spanish men had caught up.

'Can you call your driver?' I said to Marco.

'She wants him to drive Buggy Man to Santiago!' Bernhard was laughing.

'Can you help?' I asked Marco. 'Some painkillers or something?'

'He won't walk,' said Bernhard. 'He's given up. He's—'

Then Felipe caught Bernhard's eye, stopping him mid-sentence. I saw just a glimpse of what did it: something compelling in Felipe's expression. I had not thought of him as a big man, just tall, but I saw now that he was. It was more than that: a quiet, self-contained certainty. Bernhard got the full force. 'Come with me,' said Felipe. Bernhard followed him and they disappeared behind the ice-cream van.

A few minutes later, the men's own van pulled up. There was some animated discussion in rapid Spanish, some shaking of heads, then nodding as they looked toward where Felipe and Bernhard had disappeared.

'We are all going back,' said Marco, throwing my pack into the van. The Spanish Six piled in, along with, to my amazement, a subdued Bernhard. Andrea had gone on ahead. I sat in front as we drove back to Melide.

Bernhard pointed out the hotel, but did not come in with us. As he began to walk away, Felipe stopped him and offered his hand. It took Bernhard a few moments before he shook it. Each of the Spanish Six followed and, lastly, Bernhard shook mine. 'I apologise,' he said. 'I hope you are able to get him to Santiago.'

I watched him walk back into the town, before I asked Felipe: 'What did you say to him?'

'He is walking the Camino because he wants to become a man. It's not so easy. Even harder today for a young person. We know some things about this.'

'So, tell me what you said to him.'

'No.' He smiled, just for a moment, then led us into the hotel.

I was suddenly nervous. I hadn't seen Martin since Bilbao, and our last communication had been the return of the scallop shell. How would he feel about me coming back? Flanked by the Spanish Six, I looked like I'd brought a team of reinforcements that wouldn't take no for an answer. I certainly didn't intend to.

He was in the hotel bar.

I was going to need the reinforcements.

68
Martin

There was no point wallowing in misery. I dragged myself downstairs with my computer and ordered a coffee. I took the opportunity to check my blog, and was overwhelmed. There were dozens of messages of support, condolences and advice. I'd acquired a swag of new followers, because Zoe's cartoon in the American newspaper had included my URL. They had no interest in the cart, only in Buggy Man's wellbeing. In fact, nobody referred to the commercial impact of the cart not reaching Santiago; it was all about me.

There were three personal emails. Jonathan, not knowing about the German–Chinese debacle, said that two days should make no difference to a hard-headed commercial decision: Melide was as good as Santiago, so long as the cart had not broken. Sarah had sent me a long email of general reassurance and 'proud of you, Dad' sentiments. And Julia had written:

I realise this was supposedly about proving your cart, which you have obviously done whether you finish or not. Pardon my cynicism, but I think there might have been more to it than that. Well, if you set out to find some answers, you seem to have done so, and that is a good thing for us all.

I hope the knee recovers without the need for you to spend weeks being waited on by someone. ;-)

I was letting all this settle in when I felt a hand on my shoulder. I turned to see Zoe. And behind her, the Spanish Men's Club.

The last thing I wanted was to share my defeat with them. And the second-last was to be cajoled into walking again.

Zoe must have seen it. She took a different tack. 'Marco has to see your knee. And then we're going to get something to eat. I know a good *pulpo* restaurant.' It was easier not to argue.

Marco and I went to a bench in the foyer and I pulled up my walking trousers. It took him about one minute to diagnose a torn cartilage and only a few seconds to tell me not to walk.

I looked at Zoe waiting at the other side of the bar and reconsidered. She'd come this far—I guessed she must have come back—to try to get me to Santiago. 'I just need some better anti-inflamms and painkillers,' I said to Marco.

'You need rest and probably an operation. I guarantee you'll need one if you walk on it.'

'Just give me some morphine or codeine or whatever you can prescribe.'

'I can't do that. It will only mask the pain. It would be . . . irresponsible.'

I let him sit on that word for a while, then pointed towards Zoe, sitting with his mates.

'Does she know you're married?'

He spent a few moments looking not at Zoe, but at Felipe, then spread his hands like the Italian he was and shrugged.

'I will find you something. You are a man: make your decisions and take the consequences.'

The good *pulpo* restaurant was a walkers' haunt. Zoe wanted to find a way for me to complete the Camino, and avoided questions about her own deadline. I recalled she had two days—which would have been exactly enough if I could have managed my normal daily distance.

'I won't make it.'

Zoe put down her fork. 'Get this clear. I will not let you sabotage this. You're going to Santiago, even if I have to carry you.'

After we had shared a bottle of rosé and a huge wooden platter of octopus of similar colour, I was inclined to be persuaded. The knee was probably screwed anyway, and if I could pull a final fifty-six kilometres out of it, I could have a tick on my bucket list and two days walking with Zoe.

'By the way, you were right about me and my daughter,' I said. 'And my ex.'

'Right about what?'

'Forgiving her.'

'I didn't tell you to do that. I'm not exactly a shining example.'

'Well, what you said helped, even if it's not what you think you said. I patched it up with Julia. Forgave her for screwing my boss.' I had to add the last bit. Just to confirm that my anger hadn't been totally unreasonable. Only selfish. It got a suitably shocked and sympathetic reaction.

But she did seem a lot more centred. The bubbliness after Ostabat looked, on reflection, a bit forced.

'How are you feeling about things back in the States?' I asked.

'Ready to tackle life again. And my daughter's having a baby.'

'First?'

'Uh-huh. Don't say it.'

Even pumped with painkillers, and with Zoe insisting on carrying some of the gear I didn't leave behind at the hotel, the next morning was brutal. We started just after dawn, and the terrain was reasonably flat: we were out of the mountains. But I knew I was destroying what was left of the cartilage in my left knee. All because I couldn't bring myself to tell Zoe that there was no point, that the cart project was dead.

Less than a kilometre out, I had to stop. I unhitched the cart and swallowed a few more of the pills I'd got from Marco, figuring that I was big enough to handle a bit extra for a couple of days. Zoe peeled me a mandarin. She had brought fruit, nuts and chocolate.

As I pushed myself to my feet to continue, an awkward manoeuvre with a stiff leg, Zoe grabbed the cart and danced off with it. I was hardly going to chase her, and, after a few token protests, I gave up and let her pull.

'Hey, this is pretty easy,' she said.

'That was the idea. Wait till we get to a hill.'

'You can have it back then.'

She had left me the sticks, and I leant on them. I managed about a kilometre, very slowly, with breaks.

'Give me a minute to see if I can bend my leg,' I said. I took hold of my ankle and slowly folded the knee. 'There's a bandage in the outside pocket of the little bag.'

Zoe found the bandage and strapped up the leg. I needed crutches and, after some experimentation, shortened the sticks so I could put my palms over them, straight-armed.

'Five hundred metres,' I said.

'Let's see you do a hundred first.'

Zoe's estimate was closer to the mark. It took twenty-three hundred-step sections and two fifty-step sections to get us to the door of the *albergue* in Boente, the next village. We had travelled a grand total of five kilometres. In the bar, Zoe undid the bandage, immediately relieving a considerable amount of pain. I collapsed on a chair, fished my passport out and gave it to her. She returned, smiling.

'I got us a room on the first floor.'

'I hope you mean ground floor.'

'What I said. There was nobody in it last night, so we can have it when we want.' She turned away, no doubt self-conscious about the 'us' and 'we'.

The pain of the knee was receding now that the

stress was off, but I knew that no quantity of painkillers or jollying from Zoe would get me through another day.

'I'm stopping here,' I said. 'Sorry.'

'You couldn't do it on crutches?'

I shook my head.

Zoe paused. 'Okay then, we take a cab to Santiago tomorrow. One ride in—what—ninety days?'

That was the problem. I had come this far without cheating. As had Zoe. The official rule for this last section was our rule too.

'You can make it if you keep going today,' I said. 'I'll get a cab in the morning and beat you there.'

'We're going to finish together.'

'With the cart in the boot.' As I spoke, I realised the problem, and the stupidity of it all. The bloody cart. After Zoe had indicated that she was prepared to sacrifice her own Camino. For what? She walked away to the bar to give me time to answer that question.

By the time she returned with two coffees, I had reached the conclusion that my relationship with Zoe might just be more important than my relationship with a worthless cart.

We sat in the bar, finishing our drinks and comparing notes on the Brazilians, delaying the short walk to our shared room. We had plenty of time on our hands.

'The cart was pretty easy to pull,' she said.

'That was the idea. But I've thrown away half my stuff.'

'Would it take your weight?'

'What do you mean?'

'If you could sit on it, I could pull you.'

'Forget it.'

'I'm asking.'

'No. Putting aside the fact that you're not going to pull me to Santiago, if I sat on it, it would collapse inwards. It's designed for the side struts to take the weight.'

'Couldn't you modify it?'

'I can't see the point. First of all, I'd be too heavy for you to pull—'

'I'm stronger than you think.'

'Not strong enough to pull seventy-five kilograms. Not uphill.'

'I'd take small steps. Like I did on the hills in France, when I wasn't as fit as I am now. Anyway, it's flat into Santiago.'

'How do you know?'

'It's in the guidebook,' she said.

'Anyway, a, I couldn't modify it, not without a welding torch and steel tubing, which I'm guessing are a bit thin on the ground in downtown Boente; b, it might not be possible anyway; and c, I can't see the difference between me sitting in a cart or sitting in a taxi. Except you half-killing yourself.'

I was sounding peeved. I *was* peeved, getting this close to Santiago, and with her now making inane suggestions rather than just letting it go.

She gave it back to me in spades. 'So much for the great engineer. "It might not be possible." And if you can't tell the difference between riding in a taxi and sharing the load with your partner, accepting help and actually finishing something you started rather than sabotaging yourself again . . . Do I have to go and get a real drink so you can process that?'

'Probably. I'm pretty slow. I suppose I hadn't been thinking of you as my partner.'

'*Walking* partner. Don't get ahead of yourself. I'm going to get more coffee. You can decide whether you're going to tell me what kind of tubing you need or pay for another room for me.'

Since she put it like that, I had little choice. She was right, of course, this woman who I had criticised for refusing my offers of meals and accommodation. But I needed the time she spent in the bar to push aside, barely, the ignominy of riding in my cart, pulled by—yes, it did make a difference—a woman. I thought the Camino had taught me all the lessons it had in store for me, but it had saved a hard one for the end.

She came back with coffee for herself—and a scotch for me. It was 10 a.m.

'Three-quarter-inch. So, eighteen millimetres, minimum. And I'll need about six metres to be safe. It won't be expensive. Maybe in Melide. We'll get a taxi there in the morning.'

'Not if you want to catch your plane.' She gave me the room key. 'When I come back, you better have a design that works. So I'm not wasting my time. She took a sketchpad and pencils from her pack, put them on the table, then walked towards the door.

'Stop,' I said. 'You need to know something. The investors pulled out. I'm not going to the trade fair. There's no plane to catch. Really, not even any reason to go to Santiago.'

Zoe looked at me for a while with what I guessed was frustration at my final attempt to sabotage myself.

'Right. No reason.'

'We'll need a welding kit,' I said.

'I figured.'

I didn't fancy her chances.

In the room, I started on the redesign. I had to make do with the components of the existing cart, plus what

I'd ordered from Zoe, assuming she managed to find steel tubing and a welder. I wished I had asked her to get a pack of assorted bolts, duct tape and, as the design developed on the page, hinges. And tools. Obviously, tools. I'd have to find some locally.

The logical place to put my weight was over the wheel. I could bunch myself into a seating position, but would still need to increase the length of the cart. Given I had to do that anyway, I decided to spread the weight with a longer extension that would enable my leg to stretch out.

A configuration in which I lay flat with my bum over the wheel and my head and shoulders trailing behind would not be workable—my head would be an unprotected protuberance, crashing into trees and walls as we rounded corners. But it would be better on straight stretches. I designed a simple extension that could swing up to provide a seat back or down to form a bed, in the manner of a reclining car seat. Hence the hinges. I'd have to fashion something from the tubing.

I put the plans on the desk, soaked in the bath for half an hour, took a couple of painkillers and fell asleep.

69

Zoe

A welding torch and steel tubing. Right. I hoped what he'd written would make sense to a Spaniard.

Without even thinking of alternate transportation, I turned around and walked back to Melide. I took my pack, automatically. Swung it up on one shoulder, nudged it with my elbow, put the other arm in. It was so much a part of me now that I forgot it was on my back until a mile or two had passed, along with many pilgrims walking in the opposite direction.

About a mile from Melide, I saw Bernhard walking toward me, looking hungover—and surprised, I guess because I was walking the wrong way.

He was friendly—more than that, *contrite*. Felipe must have gotten to him big time.

I explained where I had come from and why.

'You can't pull Martin in the cart.'

'Because I'm a woman? I've walked—'

'Because you are maybe fifty kilograms and Martin is eighty. And the cart is designed for weight at the sides . . .'

'I know that. He's redesigning it.'

I showed him the list.

'Can you explain what he is trying to make? Exactly?'

'I don't have time.'

'Tell me while we are walking.'

He followed me back to Melide.

It was Bernhard who found the auto-repair business after unsuccessful attempts at a bicycle shop and an appliance store.

I tried to explain in Spanish what we were after.

Bernhard, who had been casing the workshop, picked up a piece of metal. 'Ask him if he has something like this but longer.'

Over the next thirty minutes, I established that I had no future as an interpreter and that I never wanted to see the inside of a workshop ever again. It was like being lost in a Walmart where every employee sent you back to aisle ten, even though you'd looked for the item there a hundred times already. In the end, everyone, including the owner's wife, bought in. Tubes arrived and were rejected or accepted for no apparent reason, as was an assortment of metal, wire, bolts and things that apparently had no name in Spanish or English. When we were done, there was a box of junk that they were prepared to sell me.

Now, the welder.

They had one but did not want to loan it out. I suggested that the operator come with me and I would pay for his time.

No. They were busy, it was too close to lunch, maybe they could come later. Like next week. Maybe I could bring the cart to them. *If* I did that, how much would it cost for four hours, then? Okay, I'll pay that and take it in a taxi and bring it back. I'll leave my passport. Please?

'Enough,' said the owner's wife. 'Your husband is experienced with the *soldador*? He will not damage it?'

I nodded and she delivered a bit of body language to her own husband.

Bernhard had waited for his moment. 'Tools,' he said. 'Hacksaw, screwdrivers . . .'

Señora understood and nodded again.

Bernhard said to me, quietly, 'This will not be easy. Tell him good luck. Now, I am walking.'

He was out the door before I realised there was no way I could afford all this stuff.

I thought of my words to Martin, how I had yelled at him that he wasn't a lesser person if he asked for help. It was coming back to bite me.

I could ask Martin for the money. If I wanted to walk back to Boente. After all this time, I didn't have his cell number. It didn't seem to be something that belonged on the Camino and of course I didn't have a cell of my own.

I could call Lauren, but my children needed to see me as independent. And how to explain Martin, the cart . . . and that I was going to miss my plane?

From my passport folder, I retrieved the piece of paper that had travelled with me from Cluny, then waited outside, watching the pilgrim parade. On my first attempt, I found a middle-aged American couple who were prepared—delighted—to let me use their cell. 'I'm Marcie and this is Ken and we're both from Delaware and every day on the Camino we try to do one good thing for someone. Karma. So *we're* thanking *you* for helping us get it done right at the beginning of the day.'

The phone seemed to ring forever.

'Zoe?'

'Camille. I need help. I . . . there's . . . I need to get

someone to Santiago. I met him. He's from Cluny—Martin? I mentioned him in the email? Anyway, he's got to get to Santiago. For his daughter. If he gives up it'll be just another failure and he'll . . . He has to get his buggy—'

'Stop, stop.' Camille was laughing. 'You're in love. And you are asking for advice? From me? If so, you will need to speak slower.'

'No, I'm asking for money.'

'How much?'

I told her.

'They accept *carte bancaire*?'

I ducked back inside and, with me as interpreter, Camille gave them her credit-card details.

'I can't thank you enough. I'll pay you back . . .'

'You are not paying me back. This is a gift.' There was an edge in Camille's voice that said: *do not argue with me.*

'Thank you.'

'It is me who is thanking you. At last. Finally, you let me thank you.' My God, she was crying. I was, too. It had never occurred to me to blame her for me being estranged from my mother—but she had blamed herself. And over twenty-five years of invitations to visit her in France and then my walking out on her in Cluny, I had never let her pay me back.

'This buggy,' she said, 'it is not a cart, with one big wheel?'

'*Oui*,' I replied, and Camille started laughing. 'My God, you're in love with the crazy Englishman from the ENSAM. Of course! After Jim, I was going to ask him to dinner next. But I think he is too serious. Am I right?'

'Partly,' I said. 'I'll email you when I get to Santiago, but I'm using someone's phone . . .'

Ken and Marcie wouldn't take any money from me.

When I returned to Boente in a taxi with the welding apparatus and the box of parts that looked like stuff you'd put out for the junk collection, Martin was not around. His cart was sitting in the covered driveway and I left the pile there. The *albergue* owner gave me the room key. Martin was out cold on the bed. He didn't look good, but he was breathing steadily. Alcohol and painkillers, I guessed. Plus the exhaustion of dealing with the pain. On the desk was a sketch of what seemed to be modifications to the cart. I decided to let him sleep and took the sketch to the bar to see if it had any connection with the stuff Bernhard had identified.

I didn't have to: Bernhard was there to do it himself.

'What are you doing here?' I said.

'Walking the Camino.'

Bernhard pulled the plan from my hands. He frowned, grunted and finally nodded.

'Where is he?'

'Asleep.'

'We start without him. But first we fix the design.'

'I don't think so.'

'The design has . . . problems.' I could see him struggling to quell his arrogance. 'He did not know what materials were available.'

Bernhard spent an hour and a half sitting in front of the cart and the hardware, sketching on the drawing paper I brought him.

Then he got to work. He seemed to know how to use a welder, and he worked quickly, in safety glasses, motioning to me to pass items and to hold things steady. The *albergue* owner came running out, accusing us of wanting to set fire to the building.

Bernhard looked at him sternly. 'You will stop a dying man getting to Santiago for absolution?'

The owner stuck around and started handing Bernhard the tools.

We worked all afternoon, with no sign of Martin. When we were done, the cart looked like a stretcher on wheels.

'Here,' said Bernhard, pointing to steel tubes extending from the back. 'I made handles. For once, the single wheel is an advantage. Space on the sides.'

'Will it work?'

'Of course it will work,' said the man who had told me it wouldn't. 'But the extra handles are for a reason. You will not be able to pull this alone.' He threw the welder in the box and went to the bar for a beer.

The *albergue* owner offered to send the welder back to Melide. Saving a man's soul probably rated higher at the Pearly Gates than walking to Santiago. Maybe even saving an atheist Brit with a sore knee.

70
Martin

I woke and it took me a while to register that it was 6 p.m. and not 6 a.m. And where I was and why. And that my knee was still stuffed. And that Zoe was lying on the bed next to me.

She must have seen me stir. She jumped up, and the look on her face told me that my plan had not worked out.

'No joy?' I said.

'No, I mean yes, but it might not be what you want.'

Half of me had been hoping she wouldn't find the tubing or the welder. It was going to take me hours, using unfamiliar kit, with no guarantee of success. The mechanics of doing the work was going to play hell with my knee.

Zoe led me to the carport. It took me five minutes to get there, using my sticks as crutches.

Christ. The job had been done—or at least *a* job had been done. The result resembled my design only in the most basic sense; the welder had decided, as tradesmen do, to do it his own way. I silently cursed Zoe for not waking me, and myself for not giving her clearer instructions.

Shit, shit, shit.

Zoe was standing, watching me, obviously hoping for a positive reaction. I couldn't manufacture one. I managed, 'Give me a few minutes to look at it.'

'Would you like a beer?' she said.

I didn't think my stomach could handle one. 'Just water,' I said.

Calm. I was as much upset at the vandalising of my cart as anything. And that would have happened even if the welder had followed the design.

I had a look at the welding first. Professional job. At least rural-repair-shop professional. That, I could have expected. But the design?

One way to test it. I gingerly lowered myself onto the stretcher. The straps held. The structure held. I shook myself a bit. Still okay. I bounced, simulating the pounding it would take on the road. I was still bouncing, mentally as well, when Zoe returned with the drinks.

'Strong enough?'

'Cart is. Don't know about you.'

71
Zoe

Over dinner, we didn't talk about the cart or about walking. Instead we talked about what the Camino had taught us.

'I've learned to accept help,' Martin said. 'Regardless of what happens tomorrow . . . thank you.'

'Let's have a toast.' On my way to the bar, I made a detour to his room—our room—and pulled out the blue dress.

It wasn't something that any of the past versions of Zoe Witt would have worn and I was not sure that a future one would either, but there had been no doubt about Marco's reaction to it and it had made me feel good about myself.

Though I might not have been worldly in the way Camille was, I had two wonderful children and a lifetime of experience with men I had loved as much as I could. If my sex life had died away in recent years through familiarity, middle age and what I now understood was Keith's being in a bad place, it did not negate the years before. My body had shown it was capable of walking twelve hundred miles, and a marathon distance—carrying a backpack up and down hills—in a single day. Over the next two days it would pull Martin to Santiago and I was proud of it, blemishes and all. Right now, it was giving me a very clear message, and I listened.

When I walked into the bar, Martin looked so blown away that I nearly lost my confidence. But the bartender's grin and low whistle did the job of taking me back to being in my twenties again for a moment. I stood in front of Martin, trying to play it cool.

'It really isn't hostel gear,' I said.

'Marco like it too, did he?'

I felt like a pin had burst the balloon of my self-confidence: *you idiot, what were you thinking, you're going to be a grandmother.*

I stopped myself. I knew this man now. I'd seen his reaction when I walked in. He was jealous. But more than that, he was doing what he always did. Sabotaging himself.

I knew how to deal with that, with him. Just like I'd

dealt with Keith going to bed before me and not eating cauliflower. Tonight could be the first step in changing myself to suit Martin.

Instead, I said, 'Actually, yes, Marco did. He liked it a lot.'

And after I said it, I realised that being true to myself worked the other way too. And that wasn't so easy.

I thought of what I had said to Renata, about how my anger had built a wall between my mother and me, when all along I had the option of offering an olive branch.

'Marco's a nice guy,' I said. 'We had a lovely dinner. To be honest, it felt wrong wearing the blue dress, but I didn't think I was ever going to see you again, and . . .'

'You look great in it.'

'It was—is—a symbol of a new beginning,' I said. 'One you were a part of.'

'Were?'

He couldn't help himself. Nor could I. 'The walk's supposed to change you. I'm happy you've forgiven your ex-wife, that's very big of you, but you're still sitting in judgment on women. You weren't planning to see me again; what the hell should it matter to you if Marco—'

'Hey, hey, I hear you. Let me get a word in. I'm sorry, I just reacted—'

I realised I was standing. 'He kissed me goodnight,' I said.

'Seriously, I'm sorry. You're right—it's none of my business.'

'I'm trying to tell you that when he kissed me, all I could think of was you.'

Martin stood awkwardly, pulled me to him and kissed me. Whatever it might mean beyond today, in the moment it felt right. Synchrony.

The bartender brought us over two glasses of something strong—he looked relieved.

We downed them quickly, and we walked, slowly, to our room, where I slipped into the bathroom, heart racing for all my supposed maturity. I didn't have a negligee, and I stopped and stared at my flushed face in the mirror. Did I dare? I thought about it as I prepared in the bathroom. I had never been a femme fatale and I was hardly that now. But still . . .

I tried several different poses in front of the mirror. I might have been proud of my body but I wasn't crazy. Having your arms above your head does wonders for gravity, and, as I wasn't wearing a thing, in front of a man who had never seen me naked except through a frosted screen in a hotel room weeks earlier, I thought first impressions were important.

My impressions of him weren't my first. Well, not

from the waist up, which was all that was showing. He looked great. Slimmer and fitter than Keith had been when he died, and with all the desire Keith had when we first got together.

I stood in the doorway, trying to look nonchalant.

'It's a queen bed and no cartoons on the curtains,' I observed, but he wasn't listening.

'You're going to have to come over to me,' he said.

I slipped under the sheets next to him and silenced him with a kiss. Making love never quite works the first time, and I was concerned not to hurt his knee, but the connection was there in the way he cared about how I was dealing with it, in the concern for what I wanted. For me, his physical response was gratifying, and for the first time I felt I saw the vulnerability behind his mask. We fell asleep with our arms wrapped around each other.

72
Martin

When I woke in the morning, Zoe was not there, and for a moment I thought she might have done a runner again, but she appeared with coffees—black and no sugar for me—and I thought: she knows how I take my coffee. Bet she wouldn't have known what to get for Marco. By way of further assurance that she wasn't regretting the previous night, she kissed me, and then we got to work on the business of getting to Santiago. I was in no hurry, still basking in the afterglow. With drink and painkillers on top of the injured knee, I hadn't been at my best, but Zoe didn't seem to notice.

We dumped everything we no longer needed, right down to Zoe's bedroll, and set out to finish what I had started eighty-seven days earlier, and Zoe eighty-nine: to walk to Santiago. I'd have been happy to stay another night or three in our shared room but, by my calculations, Zoe was already going to miss her flight by a day, even if we reached Santiago in the two days that it would normally take.

I tried the knee in the faint hope that it might have recovered enough for walking, but a jolt of pain made it clear that we would be staying with Plan A.

We were on the road at 5.30 a.m., in the pre-dawn light. I wanted to allow as much time for breaks as possible. Our goal was the same as the previous day: A Rúa. If we made it, we would have to repeat the distance tomorrow to make Santiago. Zoe was brimming with energy. She was going to need it.

It was quiet on the track so early in the morning. We'd left it till this close to the end to experience the sun rising as we walked.

I soon established that the flat position on the cart was more comfortable for my knee than sitting upright, though it made me feel helpless. We compromised on about thirty degrees of elevation. The home-made hinge worked.

The first stretch of road was wide enough that my head was not at any risk of being swung into anything.

In any event, the rear handles offered protection. I was beginning to feel some admiration for the welder from Melide.

Zoe moved along at an impressive clip until the road sloped upwards, then her pace fell off. The suspension was doing brilliantly, and even over stones the shock absorbers did a better job of insulating my knee from jarring than I would have expected. That much was unchanged from the original cart.

'Take a break,' I called.

'I'm okay. I've walked as far as you have, remember? More than you now. And still walking.'

Not for much longer, she wouldn't be. The problem wasn't the cart's design; it was the simple physics of the slope and my weight.

The road tilted down for fifty metres or so and Zoe picked up; then we rounded a turn and faced a real hill. She couldn't possibly haul me up it. I could tell she knew it too.

And at the bottom of the hill, sitting under a tree, watching our fools' errand end—again—was the insufferable Bernhard, drinking from his thermos.

'Do you want some help?' he said.

We needed the help. Even with Zoe on the front handles and Bernhard pushing from behind, it was hard going. They pulled and pushed for an hour, taking breaks every fifteen minutes.

At the second break, Zoe said to Bernhard, 'Tell him.'

'You can tell him if you want.'

Zoe gave me the story of the cart's redesign and construction. I was lost for words.

An hour later, we hit another big hill and I could see Zoe was exhausted. She was almost in tears. She pulled her pack off and threw it to the side of the road. More symbolic than practical.

'Enough,' I said. 'You've given it your best shot.' Then she did cry.

Bernhard stood looking awkward. He couldn't do this by himself either.

'Fuck. I stop asking the universe for help, and take responsibility myself, and this happens. I'm not stopping.' Zoe took the handle again.

At that point, the universe answered.

A group of four walkers—two men and two women—caught up with us. They were Spanish, mid-twenties.

'Where are you come from?' asked one of the women.

'Cluny,' said Zoe, leader of the expedition. 'In France. Two thousand kilometres. Bernhard has come from Stuttgart.'

According to my GPS, prior to becoming a pas-

senger, I had walked two thousand and twelve kilometres. 'Cart tested over two thousand kilometres of
the Camino' would have been a more than adequate
headline, had anyone been interested anymore. Perhaps it would boost the sales of the Swedish–Chinese
knock-off.

The woman looked gobsmacked. 'Like this?'

Zoe laughed. 'Only since this morning.'

Without further consultation, the two men took a
rear handle each and began pushing.

73

Zoe

In the end I believed not just in fate, with all its capriciousness, but in the special power of the Camino. It reminded me that sometimes there are things we cannot do alone. Martin had needed to learn to accept help, and not just from me. And, as it turned out, not just from Bernhard. I had hoped I might get Martin to Santiago in three or four days, and worry later about immigration, deportation and not having a ticket or any money to buy one. But the universe had its own plans.

The path became everything that the scallop shell had promised when I held it in my hand in an antique store in Cluny a lifetime ago: not just a new beginning, but the love that the birth of the goddess Venus heralded. A universal love. We had forgotten that this was a pilgrims' path, that many were doing this for spiritual and religious reasons, and that all of us were united in a common goal. It seemed that at each moment I was ready to give up, someone—man or woman, young or old, from Irish to Koreans to Hungarians—stepped up and helped get Martin to Santiago. At each point where we stopped for our *sello*, the man or woman looked at us all and stamped everyone's *credencial*—including Martin's.

'You have walked two thousand kilometres. We will not argue now.'

'People do this in wheelchairs.'

'If he is working less, then you are working more. Is the same.'

I was hugged, encouraged and sung to. I felt like I was floating. Maybe God wasn't with me—but I felt Keith was, giving me his blessing and wishing me well with whatever life sent me.

'How far do you go today?' asked an elderly woman as we stopped for orange juice and another stamp at the side of the track. Thanks to the early start, we had covered twelve miles. We would make A Rúa easily.

I looked at Martin and he looked at me. But it was Bernhard who said what we were both thinking.

'Santiago. We are going all the way.'

Even as Bernhard said 'Santiago', and there was again the possibility of me making my flight, I wondered whether there would be enough walkers to help us later in the afternoon, when most pilgrims would be done for the day. But as we came into A Rúa, thirteen miles out from the finish, we saw a sight that belonged to the Middle Ages. Six pilgrims, dressed in what looked like sackcloth robes, all with hoods, single wooden sticks and the distinctive pilgrim hat, were approaching, shuffling out of an *albergue* or its café to join the parade.

The two volunteer haulers who had taken the baton about half an hour earlier stopped so we all could get a look. About fifty feet from us, the six pilgrims pulled up their robes to hide their faces and, as they drew alongside, their heads were down, sombre in their religious duty.

Then, as one, they ripped their head coverings back. 'Marteen! Zoe!'

It was Margarida. Her companions were the other Brazil-ians—all of them—and Monsieur Chevalier.

'Paola!' She had taken my scallop shell past Melide. Or was it the other way around?

She smiled. 'Do you think I would leave my daughter on the Camino with this man?' She glared at Bernhard.

Monsieur Chevalier smiled at Paola.

'And Renata? I thought you were ahead?'

Renata nodded. 'This is true. But they sent me a message . . .' She shrugged. 'Perhaps we are learning to play together.'

Bernhard had been in contact with the Spanish Six, and they, in turn, with the Brazilians. The men had held off finishing, waiting in A Rúa so we could all do the final leg together—and, now, help pull the cart. They emerged from the bar, without robes. Embraces all around except for Martin, on the cart, and Bernhard, who stood to the side until Felipe shook his hand and then hugged him. Fabiana told me that she and Margarida had rented the costumes in Melide.

As we started up again, three of the Spanish men took handles, and Renata was about to take the other when Monsieur Chevalier waved her aside and took it himself. As bearers changed on our march to the outskirts of Santiago, Monsieur Chevalier never gave up his place. Tina danced around us, shooting video on her phone, obviously delighted that the ordeal was almost over.

'You know Monsieur Chevalier well?' I said to Paola as we were moving again.

'We met when I gave a talk in St Jean Pied de Port,' said Paola. 'But when we saw each other in Melide . . . we decided to walk together.' She shrugged her shoulders and looked at him. I looked at the scallop shell around her neck and smiled.

'Why didn't you just take a taxi?' asked Tina.

'It's not in the spirit of the walk, is it?' I said.

'We cheat on many things in life,' said Fabiana. 'But some things matter more than others.'

It was a long haul to the ice-cream vendor where I had met Bernhard two days earlier. This time we continued down the hill until we reached the bridge and the sign.

Santiago.

I looked at Martin and there was a silent agreement. We wanted to do this together. The Brazilians smiled and kissed and hugged us before racing ahead. Tina had linked arms with her mother.

There was maybe a mile to go, through the outskirts and then the narrow tourist-filled streets of the old town, where I became conscious of being part of twelve hundred years of history. I pulled slowly and we hardly spoke. In those last thirty minutes, scenes from the whole walk were flashing before me and I was so lost in thought I barely noticed Martin's weight or the pilgrims around us. The edge of the cathedral was to the left as the final descent appeared ahead: stairs. Martin pulled himself out of the cart, taking his sticks.

'I want to walk in. With you.'

'We're leaving the buggy?'

'I don't need it anymore.'

'Without you in it, I can do it easily.'

'No. Leave it. It doesn't matter.'

We turned to the shout of 'Zoe!'

The Brazilians were running up the street waving the cardboard tubes that held their *compostelas*. I felt I already had mine: the battered *credencial* with almost a hundred stamps.

'She deserved hers,' said Fabiana, hugging Margarida. 'She saved me.'

'No, I nearly killed her,' said Margarida gravely. 'But this scared me more than her, I think.'

'And me also,' said Felipe. He was holding Fabiana's hand.

Tina hugged me tightly. 'I passed on the *compostela*. Because of the taxis. Next time, for sure.'

Monsieur Chevalier looked at Paola in adoration. What better person for her to share the walk with in the future? She might even corrupt him a little.

'Are you going to Mass?'

'I'll see you all there,' I said.

That would be later. Martin and I were not done yet.

We walked the last fifty yards together, him leaning heavily on me. As we got closer we heard music. A quartet with a violin case open for donations serenaded us under the archway that thousands, maybe millions of pilgrims before us had walked beneath. I emptied my pockets of coins. Classical music—it was the same as I had heard in the fog so many weeks and miles ago. The 'Toreador March' might have been more appropriate but this was more magical—'L'amour est un oiseau rebelle', I now recalled: love is like a wild bird. It evoked the triumph of spirit, as my body, mind and soul soared to its refrains.

For a moment, we stood side by side, looking at the magnificent façade of the Santiago cathedral. We had done it. Despite everything—despite all the obstacles that perhaps fate, or more likely we ourselves, had put in the way—we had made it. Together.

My legs had started to shake, and I thought I would join other pilgrims who were laying on the cobblestones against their packs, when Martin grabbed my arm. 'Over there. I know that guy.'

'How many painkillers have you taken? It's Bern-hard.'

'No, the older guy.' Bernhard was being congratu-lated: hugged to death by a woman while the older guy stood by. They had to be his parents. 'He's a professor of engineering. Dietmar Hahn. He's German.'

'No shit.'

'All right, of course he's German, but he's famous as the most arrogant prick in engineering academia.'

'Is he good at it?'

'At being a prick? Brilliant. In his field? Best in the world. But no one wants to work with him. Imagine being his son. Christ. To know all is to forgive all.'

Martin waved, there was a quick discussion at their end and they came over. Dietmar knew Martin by reputation, though they hadn't met, and he didn't seem any more arrogant than half the Americans I knew as they got into a technical conversation about the cart. In fact, he seemed very respectful of Martin. Not so much Bernhard.

'My son was two days late—not a good look for a future engineer.'

Martin was right back at him. 'He used the time to redesign my cart. And rebuild it. I wouldn't be here if he hadn't.'

Bernhard's father nodded slowly. 'You think he'll make a competent engineer?'

Martin looked at Bernhard and then at Dietmar. 'I've walked for three months with Bernhard. He'll succeed at whatever he sets his mind to.'

We spent just a few minutes sitting silent—though there was noise all around us—taking in the cathedral. Then, there was Mass and the rush to get my plane as soon as the monks pulled on the ropes for the last time. The church might look down at indulging tourists, but it was not above taking a donation from Marco to ensure we would see the *botafumeiro* at the end of the Mass. As it swung through the air above us while several hundred pilgrims watched in awe, I felt I was once again pulling the bell cord in Conques, where I had begun the change that Monsieur Chevalier had promised: forgiving my mother, understanding what had happened with Keith, rediscovering what I had left behind. But the bell had been to say goodbye to Martin.

On the public computer at the airport, there was a message from Lauren. Good news: the house had sold for more than expected and Albie had been able to release fifteen thousand dollars into my account. I logged on, keyed in Martin's account details and transferred what I owed him. I labelled the transaction *Camino karma.*

On the flight home, cocooned in a middle seat, I reflected on the many good reasons I shouldn't have walked the Camino.

I had never walked more than ten miles in a day. On the Camino, I had walked more than that every day for three months. It was 2,038 kilometres, according to Martin's GPS—and I had re-walked the final two days, so I could add another fifty. More than twelve hundred miles, on the toughest variant.

I had never been into physical challenges. When my friends in their forties had discovered an interest in marathons, I had stuck to art. Even marathons made more sense than three months of frostbite, blisters and sleeping outside in the rain.

It was a Catholic pilgrimage and I had been angry at the church.

My husband had just died and I was broke.

I lived five thousand miles away from where the walk traversed Europe, starting in France, where I didn't speak the language, and ending in Spain, where I knew no one.

There were many reasons not to walk the Camino. But I walked it anyway. One day at a time.

It was fate that sent me but its lesson was to rely less on fate than I ever had.

I learned that it is important to know not only what to hold on to and what to let go of, but what to go back for.

Monsieur Chevalier was right. I got blisters. The Camino changed me. Peace? I knew there were challenges ahead. But now I knew I could manage them.

I had found what I had lost—the belief in myself and the integrity to take risks for something that was important. When I stood before the cathedral in Santiago, I was humbled by both my own stupidity and the evidence before me of how great humankind could be, and I experienced a sense of belonging that I had never experienced before.

And I cried.

Epilogue
Martin

The universe smiled on us, at least where it mattered and where I had not made its task impossible by my own bloody-mindedness. My cartilage did not miraculously grow back, and I endured a second knee operation. Jonathan put me up while I recuperated. One afternoon, Julia and I met over coffee and managed not to bite each other's heads off when one of us slipped back into bad habits. Sarah's exam results would allow her to study medicine and she was considering her options. The engineering student was no longer on the scene, and she seemed to be on a more even keel emotionally. Whether or not that had anything to do with the improved relations between her parents, we had a better safety net in place for future crises.

Julia knew about Zoe, thanks to Tina, who had posted footage of my ride on YouTube and added a link as a comment on my blog, complete with a teenage girl's observations on the romance of it all. Julia's only reaction was that she did not want me moving to America and abandoning Sarah again.

Jonathan also saw Tina's video. As a luggage cart, my invention was not much chop. But as a stretcher for use in mountainous areas by soldiers and civilians without access to helicopters, it was a different proposition. Carrying a conventional stretcher along mountain trails was a tough task for four men. Two, three or four—or an animal—could pull the modified cart in far more comfort and security for all. The British Army was not going to wait for a Chinese imitation and wanted to be seen to pay well for local ingenuity.

By the time I was off crutches, I had a more than satisfactory offer for the design and a contract as a consultant for its ongoing refinement. And Bernhard had a nice cheque for his contribution.

I applied for a job in the Department of Built Environment at my old university. My expertise in design theory was transferable to architecture and the Camino had rekindled my interest. I wanted to be close to Sarah, at least for a while. The university offered me a start in the new academic year.

I wrote a short note of thanks to Zoe for repaying the loan. What I wanted to say was: *Come and spend your life with me.* But, of course, I didn't. The Camino had not changed me that much.

Epilogue
Zoe

My flight from Santiago went via New York. I stopped there to see Lauren—and found that she did need me. If I had doubts about being a grandmother, hers about being a mother were greater. I had never seen her so anxious. But by the time I left, she was back to being the girl who had told me on the first day of school to not kiss her because she wasn't a baby. I returned six weeks later when their son, Lucas Emmanuel, was born, content in the knowledge I had been able to give her what I hadn't been offered by—or asked of—my mother.

I watched my daughter glow as she fell in love with her child, and I knew she would be fine; after another week, she was happy to let me go. She refused to give up the battle with the insurance company. I wished her the best with it and told her that she, Tessa and their future children could share anything that came from it. I believed that, knowing everything, it was what Keith would have wanted.

Home had been a different hostel every night for three months and I no longer had a house or belongings or ties. Thanks to the *botafumeiro*'s swing, I flew to San Francisco instead of LA, rented a studio and slept on the floor for weeks. I missed the snoring, the rustling in the night and the morning tortilla more than a bed.

I continued to work on my cartoons. The *Chronicle* directed me into political satire and I found my talent for capturing personality was even more useful in this arena. My *Pilgrims' Progress* series, including some cartoons that had not been published, was given its own showing at my friend Corrina's gallery, a block from where I had set myself up. I'd taken Martin's advice to keep ownership of the originals.

I was nervous about the opening, not just because I wanted people to like the cartoons, not just because my heart and soul was in every one, but because I wanted to sell them. I wanted Keith, through the children he had helped me raise, to see me independent and to be proud. I couldn't do anything about the irony that this made his sacrifice all the more pointless.

I wanted my lessons of the Camino shining on the

walls of the people they spoke to. Richard and Nicole couldn't come to the opening but they told me that my sketch of them was on display at Tramayes, and they bought the cartoon of Marianne and Moses from the catalogue for their home in Sydney.

I had invited Martin, writing and rewriting his invitation, wanting the wording to be right. I thought that there might be another man one day, that I had learned from what went wrong with Keith. At least I wasn't going to hold back out of fear of rejection or thinking I couldn't manage alone. That much had changed. I liked how Martin had stood up to me—Manny had never tried and Keith had retreated—and how he had been prepared to change. And his strength of purpose. I had learned to get and even like his British humour, and I could have paid him back with a little American optimism. But he didn't reply.

The gallery was full for the event and a bunch of friends had come from all over the country. I watched people grab glasses of wine and resisted the urge to stand behind them as they viewed my pictures. Ten minutes in, Corrina told me I had my first sale of the night. 'Both of the Buggy Man ones.'

I looked up and there he was: no beard, but definitely a walker and not a hunter.

'Couldn't have my picture on some stranger's wall,' he said.

I wanted to fling my arms around him, but he was radiating that British reserve.

'I've flown all the way to bloody San Francisco,' he said.

'I know . . .'

'Do I get a hug for that?'

So I flung my arms around him, and his kiss took me back to the other side of the Atlantic.

'Listen,' he said, 'I sold the cart design to the British Army . . .'

'Wow.'

'And I've persuaded them I should test the new prototype in the Alps—on the trail to Rome.'

'Italy? From where?'

'Cluny, again. The Assisi Way. As in, St Francis of Assisi. I've got a few months before my new job starts. The surgeon tells me my knee's up to it. I was wondering if you'd like to come with me.'

'That's what you came to ask me?'

'More or less. I quite enjoyed walking with you, but things kept getting in the way. Thought we could give it another go.'

Martin must have been thinking about it for a while, but right now it felt like he was the one being spontaneous and I was the one needing time to plan. My heart said yes, but . . .

'I . . . don't know. I'm doing a lot of things here. Can I think about it? It'd be good to go to Cluny again. Visit Camille. She and her husband have broken up.'

I was still thinking about it later in the evening when Tessa arrived. She liked Martin. And she brought a gift to wish me luck. She'd seen it in the market and was sure I would like it.

It was a small enamel charm—a dove. A wild bird? A sign of peace. But more than that: the dove is the symbol of the Assisi walk.

Authors' Note

We first walked the Chemin/Camino from Cluny to Santiago de Compostela, on the route described in this book—specifically Martin's, with the Célé variant—from February to May 2011 (eighty-seven days, 2,038 kilometres).

From March to June 2016, we walked from Cluny to St Jean Pied de Port (Zoe's route) and then on to Santiago via the Camino Francés (seventy-nine days, and this time, like Zoe, we didn't carry a GPS, so our best guess is nineteen hundred kilometres).

This novel was inspired by our walks and the people we met along The Way—but it is not intended to take the place of the excellent guidebooks available. While we have endeavoured to be accurate about route, timing and most locations, we have taken occasional liberties with accommodation and restaurants, which, in any case, change from year to year. The walkers are fictional, as are the hoteliers, *gîte* staff and *hôtes*, and their behaviour in the story is of no relevance to the reception you can expect in a particular place. The exception is a nod to our hosts at L'Oustal in Corn, who won our vote for best *chambre d'hôte* meal on our 2011 pilgrimage.

On our first Camino, the bells at the Abbey Church of Sainte Foy did ring us out of Conques, but they did not seem to be operating in 2016.

Acknowledgments

We drafted this book in 2012, a year after walking the Camino for the first time, and returned to it after our second Camino, in 2016. The people we met on both journeys inspired many of the stories and characters. A young Belgian man, Matthias, was the only other walker we encountered on the Chemin de Cluny, and it was he who encouraged us to collaborate on a mature-age love story.

Our editor, David Winter, has been our wise and tireless guide on the road to publication.

Along the way, our early readers provided valuable feedback at all levels, from 'Maybe you should write it as one book rather than two' to 'You missed the accent in San Sebastián': Jon Backhouse, Danny Blay, Lahna Bradley, Jean and Greg Buist, Tania Chandler, Angela

Collie (the first person inspired by this story to walk the Camino), Robert Eames, Amy Jasper, Cathie and David Lange, Rod Miller, Helen O'Connell, Rebecca Peniston-Bird, Midge Raymond, Robert and Michèle Sachs, Debbie and Graeme Shanks, Daniel Simsion, Dennis Simsion, Dominique Simsion, Sue and Chris Waddell, Geri and Pete Walsh, Fran Willcox, and Janifer Willis.

Ana Drach and Cori Redstone equipped us with background information for our Brazilian and American characters.

Thanks are once again due to the team at Text Publishing, who have supported us in the production and marketing of the book—in particular Michael Heyward, W.H. Chong, Jane Finemore, Kirsty Wilson, Shalini Kunahlan, Kate Sloggett, Anne Beilby and Khadija Caffoor.

Cordelia Borchardt of Fischer Publishing (Germany) and Jennifer Lambert of HarperCollins Canada also provided valuable editorial input.

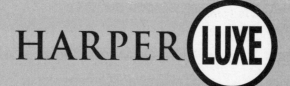

THE NEW LUXURY IN READING

We hope you enjoyed reading
our new, comfortable print size and found it
an experience you would like to repeat.

Well – you're in luck!

HarperLuxe offers the finest in fiction and
nonfiction books in this same larger print size and
paperback format. Light and easy to read, HarperLuxe
paperbacks are for book lovers who want to see
what they are reading without the strain.

For a full listing of titles and
new releases to come, please visit our website:
www.HarperLuxe.com